PENGUIN BOOKS

THE HIRELING

Leslie Poles Hartley was born in 1895 and educated at Harrow and Balliol College, Oxford. Since 1924, when he published his first book, his work attracted the attention of literary critics in Britain, though he published relatively infrequently. His first major success was a novel entitled *The Shrimp and the Anemone* (1944). His novel *Eustace and Hilda* in 1947 won the James Tait Black Memorial Prize, the first of many important literary awards to come his way. *The Go-Between* (also available in Penguins) was awarded the Heinemann Foundation Prize of the Royal Society of Literature in 1954. He was awarded the C.B.E. in the New Year Honours in 1955. L. P. Hartley died in 1972.

THE HIRELING

L. P. HARTLEY

Trop de perversité règne au siècle où nous sommes,
Et je veux me tirer du commerce des hommes.

MOLIÈRE

PENGUIN BOOKS
in association with Hamish Hamilton

Penguin Books Ltd, Harmondsworth, Middlesex, England
Penguin Books Australia Ltd, Ringwood, Victoria, Australia

—

First published by Hamish Hamilton 1957
Published in Penguin Books 1964
Reprinted 1973 (twice)

—

—

Made and printed in Great Britain
by Hazell Watson & Viney Ltd
Aylesbury, Bucks
Set in Linotype Georgian

To Roderick Meiklejohn

Chapter 1

THE car-hire driver was tall and dark and handsome; he looked the regular soldier he had been when the war broke out. He had had other occupations, for as he would say of himself in expansive moments, 'I've had a very chequered career,' but it was the Army that had left its mark on his appearance. That it was a striking appearance no one could doubt, least of all himself: but of this his bearing gave no hint whatever. He did not seem to take a pride in it; he guarded it as if it was a piece of public property. He looked smart, expensive, and unapproachable. Most people's figures have the hazy outline of something seen dimly through short-sighted eyes. His figure looked as if it had been shaved. Aiming at correctness, he somehow achieved style; if the material was plebeian, it had a patrician cut. With an impassive face he opened the car door for his customers; with an impassive face he took their orders when these were not already known to him; with an impassive face he held the door open for his customers to alight. To those who noticed him as a man and not merely as a driver, he was a little formidable, and he meant to be. His manners, which were as faultless as his looks, might have been specially designed to protect his impersonality. When he spoke, which he seldom did except when spoken to, he had the air of unbending. Pompous or supercilious he was not; he did not seem to be taking himself seriously; but somewhere about him, perhaps in his eyes which were steadier than a peaceful occasion warranted, there was a hint of menace. 'Keep off!' they seemed to say, 'Keep off!'

This was the face he turned to the world and the face he saw in the glass when, at whatever hour of the day or night it might be, he put on his business personality. But it was not the face his Maker saw, who had taken some trouble to design it. Behind his face the skull showed, the bony structure, narrow, delicate, and strong. Between his cheek-bones and his temples a hollow was scooped out. His eyes were deep-set but so wide apart that when he turned his head their convex line encroached upon the concave, like the old moon in the new moon's arms. They were the colour of gun-metal and looked as hard, and the pale gold gleam of gun-metal was in them. His black eyebrows were highly arched and one was slightly tufted; across his forehead, repeating the line of his eyebrows, was graven a deep wrinkle like a bow. His nose was straight and on the long side; below it a thin dark moustache hung like an inverted chevron. Strong vertical planes upheld these drooping crescents; they stretched from his cheekbones to his short, cleft chin, which, roughly triangular in outline, rose to a rounded plateau, divided from his mouth by a deep, downward-curving dent. On the top his black hair, threaded with grey, was thick and wavy; at the back it grew so close to his head that it might have been gummed on. His skin was not particularly dark but the modelling of his face was so clear-cut that even in a direct light it was full of shadows. In repose his expression was sad and brooding; when he laughed, which was seldom, he showed the whites above his eyeballs. Full face he looked older than his years, so much experience had left its imprint on his features, but in profile and from the back, which was the way his customers usually saw him, he looked younger. He did not look quite like an Englishman; he might have had a trace of Pictish blood.

Nature meant his face to be expressive but he did not; for an expression is a give-away and he did not want to give anything away. Personal prestige counted a lot with him; he would take offence in a moment, and often when it was not intended. In his salad days he had been known to get drunk and pick a quarrel. Not to like a man's face was excuse enough for baiting him, and if blows followed, the driver, who had boxed for his battalion and been the anchorman in many a tug-of-war, could give a good account of himself. Not that he was a bully; in such moods he was ready to fight everybody, and ready, too, to drink with them afterwards; indeed at the conclusion of a scrap he felt more at peace with the world than at any other time. His courage wasn't perfect, however. He was town-bred; and if, when he was courting, he had to cross a field with cattle in it, his flow of conversation would dry up until the danger passed.

On the parade ground and in the barrack room, if occasion warranted, he had a blistering tongue; but among his compeers and when no trouble was afoot he practised the art of understatement, understatement that was not so much deliberately ironical as an unconscious expression of the fact that he had seen too many examples of the unusual to be impressed by it.

'Nothing that could happen would surprise me,' he would say.

As for his philosophy he was, as he himself admitted, a cynic. Without having had any illusions to speak of, he managed to be disillusioned. Sometimes in the privacy of his bathroom he would sing to himself, and one of his songs ran (to the tune of 'Auld Lang Syne'):

> 'I do believe, I do believe,
> That bugs are bigger than fleas,
> For on the wall they play football
> And I'm the referee.'

That, perhaps, was the extent of his belief. But he didn't boast about it, for boasting was against his code and he was quick to make fun of it in others. 'Beating eggs with a big stick,' he called it, and it brought into his voice the lazy teasing note which was the signal, for those who knew him, to look out. 'Won't you say that again,' he would say; 'I'd like to hear it.' But being a cynic, with a cynic's realism, he held himself well in hand, and few, if any, of his customers would have guessed what was being damped down behind that handsome poker-face. For he studied their personalities and did everything he could to please them, short of gushing; for gushing, he maintained, they didn't like. He would say 'my lord' and 'my lady' and even 'sir' or 'madam' in such a way that these titles conferred peculiar distinction. He was rigorously punctual, which was more than could be said for all his colleagues in the car-hire business; and if circumstances made him late or if, as sometimes happened, he couldn't do the job himself and had to send another man in his place, he would ring the customer up and apologize – or even write, much as he disliked writing letters. This solicitude, contrasting sharply with his impersonal manner, made a good impression, and his customers recommended him to their friends as a particularly civil, reliable, and obliging man.

For this he thanked them, but he had not a great deal to thank them for. In the nature of things they treated him with less consideration than he treated them. Many a time they kept him waiting till the small hours, at a night-club or a dance, without the offer of a sandwich or a cup of tea; many a time they cancelled a good job at the last moment, without apology or the promise of redress; sometimes they forgot about him altogether. They took his patience under their thoughtlessness for granted; they didn't seem aware that he had feelings to hurt or interests to injure, and some of them talked together as freely in his presence as if he wasn't there. He had long ceased to mind this and trained himself to turn a deaf ear to their prattle; but when he overheard it, it sometimes struck him as extremely silly. Some of his customers knew each other, but didn't know they were employing the same man to drive them. The chiel amang us! Had he been given to gossiping with his customers about each other, which from policy and inclination he was not, he could have caused a load of mischief by repeating these unconsidered trifles. It was often his lot to pick up his customers after they had been lunching or dining with their friends. From the doorway came the babble of effusive thanks, but afterwards, in the car, their criticism of the food, the company, and the hostess, told another tale.

No wonder that his customers were 'they' to him, beings of an alien if not hostile race, idle, capricious, prone to change their minds and destinations, wanting him to drive against the traffic in one-way streets. But in congenial society, commenting on their shortcomings, he did not let himself sound angry or personally involved in his own disgust; he sounded as if the only sane man left was making indulgent fun of a mad world.

In spite of this the driver was a staunch Conservative and voted for the very people he made fun of, not only because they were his bread and butter but because with all their faults they represented something that he himself was striving to attain.

Two classes of customers escaped his censure. In one were some of the officers who had served with him in the war, and who employed him to do their driving for them (as he put it). With them he felt at home; talking to them he did not have to adapt himself or assume a protective personality. If he did not always use their words he spoke their language – the language of a shared experience. Narrow as the field of their relationship might be he understood it. He would lean back in his seat and let the stiffness out of his broad shoulders while his customer and he fought their battles over again.

The other class also was a small one, but much more unlikely, for it consisted of a few old ladies who had somehow – he himself could not have told how – won the driver's esteem. Old ladies were not as a rule popular with car-hire men. They needed helping in and out; their manners, dating from an earlier day, could be as stiff and awkward as their movements; they were apt to make their wants known in clear, confident, emphatic voices which invited a disobliging answer. Most drivers had no patience with them, but this driver had; though he would not have owned up to it, they could rely on him for every courtesy. 'She was a nice old lady,' he would sometimes wonderingly remark. From him this commendation meant a lot, for 'nice' was not a word that he used lightly – in fact he seldom used it except in connexion with these old ladies.

But there were not many of them and for women as a whole the driver had no use whatever. He had lived with more than one but he regarded them as a disagreeable necessity. Women were cruel, he said; surprisingly that was his main charge against them. How had they contrived to be cruel to a man who seemed such an unpromising subject for cruelty – to be, in fact, cruelty-proof, not cruelty-prone? If there was going to be any cruelty, it should have come from him. But no; women are cruel, he said; they like to make one suffer.

As often as not, when he thought of women, his memory went back to his mother's shoes. She had two dozen pairs of them. She spent money in other ways as well, but the shoes were the extravagance his father always picked on. Why must she have so many? Why shouldn't she have them? she would ask tearfully of her eldest son; and he, who was given a lot of responsibility but little else, couldn't see why she shouldn't, and cried too. She was sweet as honey to him when his father was angry with her. But not, or very often not, at other times. By turns she petted him and scolded him, he never knew which to expect, but he knew that it didn't depend on his behaviour, it depended on her mood. She always got her way over the shoes; if one pair was thrown away, two pairs were added. What did it matter, the boy wondered; what was it all about? Growing older he saw; the family was short of money, almost on the rocks; he and the others had only one pair of shoes each, but his mother's were still there in two long rows. He grew to hate the sight of them, and when she came to him crying it was his father with whom he sympathized, not her. But how could he stand up to her when his father couldn't? Her purposeful, enveloping, insidious character was too much for them both.

Inured to the climate of hostility, but tired of being a buffer, the boy ran away from home and joined the Army.

The Army seemed a paradise of non-combatants, and the band in which he played a cave of harmony. News reached him from home, tentacles stretching out; but the sight of his mother's handwriting made him tremble and feel sick; not till her letters ceased did he cease to be afraid. For many years afterwards he tried to keep his eyes off women's shoes and when he saw them, emblems of unabashed femininity, his skin prickled.

The Army appealed to almost every quality in him, his pugnacity, his cynical acceptance of futility so long as it was clothed in the proper forms of discipline, his sixth sense for the strength and weakness of his comrades (he could tell almost at a glance how much a man would be worth in a tight place), his enjoyment of ramps and rackets, his feeling for the whole living organism round him, its conventions, traditions, enmities and friendships. In the Army, he felt, a man was rated at his true value, he had nothing but himself to make him count. Recognition of his own value, by himself and others, was of paramount importance to the car-hire driver.

In the Army he enjoyed that two-fold recognition, and with each stripe he put up it increased. He believed he got it by standing up for himself: it was something he had 'won' out of the Army. But it wasn't, or only in part. He really got out of the Army the reward for what he had put into it, his courage, his patience, his conscientiousness, his loyalty – himself. On this his sense of his own worth depended. But he would not have admitted that it was so; he did not even acknowledge it in his thoughts. He would not have called duty by its name, he would have found a dozen belittling expressions for it, some with obscene prefixes, but he acted up to it and lived by it. The recruits he had to lick into shape would not have called it duty either; they would have called it, as they called him, by many other names. For though he knew his job too well to be a martinet of the old school, he did not spare their feelings or bring them their early-morning tea. On the contrary, he stuck his elbows out and clothed himself with all the awe at his command – in a position that already carried with it more visible, immediate authority than almost any other in the land. He had to be infallible; he had to say the word that stung. But he could also say the word that soothed. The men appreciated this, and later, in civilian life, more than one who had had cause to hate him came up and offered him a drink.

Recruits could, must, be licked into shape, but not so customers. Customers had to be kept sweet; only in the physical sense were they a charge to him. Only by playing up to them could he hope to make them better customers. He did it but it went against the grain, and doing it he lost the sense of value that came from reciprocal obligations. For him these obligations didn't exist in the civilian world; there it was every man for himself and devil take the hindmost. The delicate adjustments, the imponderable restraints that in the Army regulated the dealings of one man with another, didn't operate. The Army wasn't really a microcosm, it was a world to itself, male, collective, and hierarchical; to some it seemed a tyrant, but to the driver its service was perfect freedom.

The Army was his only love but in the end he quarrelled with it, thinking not without cause that it had let him down. Like any lovers' quarrel it was very bitter: 'It doesn't pay to be patriotic,' he said. Yet leaving the Army cost him more than he thought he had it in him to suffer; it was a day of emptiness and darkness, a day of desolation. With no job to go to and no one to help him find a job, he tried one thing after another, and found it wanting; wanting not in money (which was the reason he gave himself for throwing it up) but in something which he had received, together with a much smaller wage than the one he was now earning, at a deal table between two salutes – something that clothed his spirit against the coldness of the outside world.

After a time he joined the Fire Service. But he did not like the Fire Service. It was never a living entity to him, as the Army had been. And he had come down in the world and must start on the lowest rung of the ladder. The ladders of the Fire Service he was prepared to scale, but he couldn't take its other promotions seriously. Its easy-going discipline – 'Come, boys, let's get together and polish up the brass' – disgusted him, it seemed like play-acting; and he resented as childish having to slide down a pole from the rest-room to the fire-engine. He wanted to fight men, not fire, fire was too abstract an antagonist; and some of the jobs he was called out to do, such as rescuing frightened cats from trees, or separating fighting swans, struck him as waste of time.

To kill time and earn some extra shillings he did odd jobs for a car-hire firm. Driving, he made some useful contacts. Customers remembered him and sometimes when they ordered a car they asked for him by name, a piece of favouritism that the firm's regular drivers did not relish. One day a customer said, 'Why don't you start in business on your own? I could put you in touch with half a dozen people.' He didn't, when the time came; but it was this promise, fertilizing an idea already in the driver's mind, that made him take the plunge.

He bought a car on the hire-purchase system, and kept it as smart and well-groomed as he kept himself. He did not spare himself; he worked, as he expressed it, all the hours God sent. Sleepless nights made sleepy days, sometimes he could hardly keep himself awake. He lost his healthy colour and hollows deepened in his cheeks; the two suits that had served him for ten years hung loosely on him. With all his evident physical strength he looked a subject for a duodenal ulcer. And in spite of his efforts, five months after starting on his own, with no capital except the war gratuity he had sunk in his car, he was only just making both ends meet. For nearly three more years he must go on paying a crippling monthly instalment before he owned the car – by which time it would be worthless, having done a hundred thousand miles.

In Civvy Street he had no sense of union with his fellows, a sort of hostile apartness chilled his thoughts of them, his very wish to work estranged him from them. No one, he felt, had ever been any help to him, least of all the women in his life. His hand was not against every man's, it couldn't afford to be; but it was always ready to give or take a blow. A man of the Ulysses type, a sheer man, but with no Penelope waiting for him.

His thirty-five years on earth had left the driver with but one desire: to work the clock round. He scarcely thought of himself as a man, he thought of himself as 'Leadbitter's Garages Ltd, Cars for All Occasions'. As for his Christian name, he never heard it used and had almost forgotten it.

Chapter 2

NEXT to his car, the telephone was the most important thing in Leadbitter's life, and perhaps his greatest friend; of all the sounds he heard, mechanical or human, its summons was the one he welcomed most. He sat in his furnished bed-sitting-room with his ear glued to it, and he sometimes lay awake at night, hoping to hear it ring. However tired he might be, and often he was very tired, his face relaxed when he took off the receiver and his voice, announcing his number, glowed with warmth. Even when it woke him up at night, or in the cat-naps that he snatched by day, he felt no animosity towards it, and he would smile into it, to the voice which spoke to him, smiles that the owner of the voice seldom if ever saw. If the voice was one he recognized he was pleased, if it was strange to him he was still more pleased, for it meant another customer.

One morning when he was shaving, a ritual he performed meticulously, sometimes twice a day, for to be better shaved than other men was part of his defence against the world as well as a commercial asset, the telephone bell rang. Almost the only time that he resented being rung up was when he was shaving. It was a moment of deep relaxation; it brought him in touch with an aspect of himself that rightly he prized highly, his physical appearance. He was something of a narcissist; he liked to watch the muscles of his arm swelling under the light pressure of the razor on his cheek and know that after several years of sedentary life he was still as good as ever. If the ritual was disturbed and he had to begin again, it was never quite the same – to say nothing of the waste of time. So his voice was a shade less cordial than usual when he took up the receiver and announced his number: 'Hopewell 4126'.

'This is Lady Franklin's butler speaking,' he was told. 'Her ladyship wishes to know if you can take her ladyship to Canterbury on Thursday, February 10th. Her ladyship would be starting at 10.30 in the morning and would be returning in the late afternoon.'

What a lot of ladyships, Leadbitter thought. He glanced at his engagement list which he kept in a large, florid silver photograph frame beside the telephone. It had once enshrined the picture of the woman with whom he had lived longest, and was almost the only memento of his past life that he allowed himself.

'Yes, I can do that. Where shall I pick her up?'

'Pick her ladyship up?' The butler sounded shocked. 'Will you call for her at her residence, 39 South Halkin Street.'

'Right,' said the driver, scribbling on his pad. It was really an unnecessary precaution; he had a phenomenal memory for names, addresses, dates, and destinations and seldom needed telling twice.

'You won't be late, will you? You car-hire drivers are sometimes late,' the butler said. 'You try to fit in too many jobs. You won't be late, will you?'

'Not on your life!' said Leadbitter and put down the receiver. You wouldn't be alive, he thought, if I could get at you. It took him several minutes of communion with his own face to recover from the insult.

Punctually on the appointed day but not a minute too soon, for he did not believe in sacrificing time he was not paid for, Leadbitter drew up at the door of Lady Franklin's house. It was a good house, he could tell that by the gloss on the front door, by the state of the paint and brickwork, and by an indefinable but unmistakable air of wealth derived from the forms and shadows of objects within, that came through the net curtains: he was seldom wrong about those things. But he had been out most of the night, he had already done a job that morning, and before he had time to take in further impressions he fell asleep. When, ten minutes later, the butler opened the front door for Lady Franklin, they saw the driver with his chin propped on the rim of the wheel and his peaked cap, a little awry, overhanging it.

'Good heavens!' said Lady Franklin. 'Is he dead?'

'More likely drunk, my lady,' said the butler, eyeing Leadbitter with disfavour.

'Surely not at this time of day?' said Lady Franklin. 'Besides, someone, I can't think who, spoke of him most highly.'

'I will go and investigate, my lady,' said the butler, and with cautious tread, as though about to arrest a criminal, he descended the steps on to the pavement. Edging round the bonnet of the car, he peered in through the window.

'He appears to be asleep, my lady.'

By now Lady Franklin too was on the pavement, looking at Leadbitter through the opposite window of the car.

'Asleep?' she said, wonderingly. 'Yes, I believe you're right – he is asleep, poor fellow. What can we do about it, Simmonds?'

'Well, wake him up, my lady.'

'Oh no, I shouldn't like to do that, it would be too unkind. We must let him have his sleep out. I can wait.'

'Indeed, you can't, my lady,' said the butler, 'if you're going to be in Canterbury for luncheon. It's already a little late,' he added with a shade of reproach. 'I think you ought to start. But it's not a very good beginning, is it? – I mean, he might drop off while he is driving, and then where would you be? But I suppose I'd better rouse him,' and before Lady Franklin had time to protest, he put his hand through the open window and touched Leadbitter, none too gently, on the shoulder.

Slowly Leadbitter raised his head, an expression of ineffable weariness and disgust crossed his features, as if the return to consciousness was too much to be borne; this was succeeded by a look of fury, as if every quality he had always disliked in butlers was concentrated in this one. But hardly had Simmonds recoiled before the threat in his eyes than they changed; the look he kept for customers damped down their fierceness, he pulled his cap straight, jumped out of the car, and said:

'I'm sorry, my lady, I just lost myself for a moment.'

He held the door open for her to get in.

She looked up into his face, a small woman in her late twenties. Under her fur coat, which in her hurry she had left unfastened, she was plainly dessed in dark blue with touches of white, which picked up the colours of her candid, innocent, over-large blue eyes. Her manner had an eager, fluttering sweetness, into which, as though she felt she ought to, she sometimes injected a faint accent of authority, like a private person who has, all unexpectedly, succeeded to a throne.

'You lost yourself?' she said. 'How I envy you! But it was a shame to wake you, wasn't it?'

She seemed to expect him to answer, but he didn't; he stood holding the car door in his hand, looking down at her as though to say, 'However long you keep me waiting I shan't get impatient.' But she, following her own train of thought, said suddenly:

'I'd rather go in front with you, if I may.'

Leadbitter's face registered nothing, but a shadow crossed the butler's as Lady Franklin took the seat beside the driver.

'I shall be back about tea-time, Simmonds, I expect,' she said. 'There's no one coming for dinner.'

'Any orders for tomorrow, my lady?'

Lady Franklin made an effort to recollect herself.

'I shall be alone as usual.'

The butler stood respectfully on the kerbstone, his eyes fixed on the retreating car.

'Well, I'll be damned!' he said.

Chapter 3

LEADBITTER had been surprised when Lady Franklin elected to sit beside him. Some of his male customers took this liberty when they were alone, but women hardly ever. He thought it was a little forward of her, and as an individual she sank in his esteem to a point below the already lowly position occupied by women as a class. Though he would not have admitted it to himself, he was very tired, and to have been caught napping had irritated him and hurt his pride. A new customer, and titled, too, at that. He despised the whole race of butlers and this one had twice insulted him, first on the telephone and then by shoving him. He's lucky not to have his eye in a sling, he thought. As for Lady Franklin, she had annoyed him too with her glib professions of pity, meaningless from a woman who probably spent twelve hours out of the twenty-four in bed. Now he would have to talk to her. He was ready and able to do this, for conversation was part of his stock in trade; some customers expected it of him, just as others expected silence; and as far as he could he humoured them, for business came first. This morning he felt less than usual in the mood to talk; but at any rate it was for her, not him, to start the ball rolling.

Presently she said:

'What a comfortable car this is. I was told you had a very nice car. What make is it?'

She obviously knows nothing about cars, thought Leadbitter, she'll be asking if they have pups every season. But he told her.

'Oh yes, we had one of that kind once, and a very good car it was. It's laid up in the country now. I don't go there much, they think it's better for me to stay in London. My husband was very fond of motoring.'

Was? Had Lady Franklin's husband been a lord or a sir, Leadbitter wondered idly. Perhaps he had shed her or she him: at any rate they were no longer together.

'It's a very nice occupation for those who can afford it,' he said. 'You go places, you see things.'

'Yes. It takes your mind off, doesn't it? Do you enjoy driving, yourself?'

'Well, it's my job, my lady. I don't think much about it.'

'I was told you were a very good driver, and you are. It's like poetry, the way you start and stop without a jolt, the poetry of motion.'

In spite of himself Leadbitter was pleased by this, but he answered non-committally, almost brushing the compliment aside:

'I try to drive same as I would an ambulance – so that if there was a tumbler filled with water in the boot it wouldn't spill. It's all a question of getting used to it. Lady drivers ...' he stopped.

'Yes?' said Lady Franklin.

'Well, they don't get used to it in quite the same way.'

'I never learned to drive,' said Lady Franklin. 'My husband tried to teach me, but I should never have been any good at it. He was a very good driver himself – almost as good as you are. We used to take our chauffeur about with us as a passenger – rather a bore for him, I'm afraid.'

'Oh, I expect he got used to it, my lady.'

Lady Franklin smiled sadly.

'You seem to think that one can get used to anything, but can one? It's now two years since my husband died, but I haven't got used to it. It's still the same as it was on the first day. You see I wasn't with him – not with him when he died.'

I expect he got used to it, Leadbitter thought, but he

didn't let his tongue slip up this time, and said as feelingly as he could:

'That was bad luck, my lady.'

'Yes, wasn't it? At least, I keep telling myself it was bad luck, but it wasn't really. You see I'd been to a party. I needn't have gone. Do you mind me telling you all this?'

'Of course not,' said Leadbitter. What else could he say?

'The doctor said it was quite safe to go,' Lady Franklin went on. 'My husband was fifteen years older than I was; we'd only been married a few years. He suffered from his heart: he'd had two or three attacks.'

'Nasty thing, a dicky heart,' said Leadbitter.

'Yes, but between-times he seemed quite well, and he seemed specially well that day.'

She bit her lip and couldn't go on.

'Would you like me to turn on the wireless?' Leadbitter asked.

'No, I don't think so, thank you. Not just now, perhaps a little later. I've listened to the wireless such a lot! You see after he died, I had a breakdown.'

'I'm sorry to hear that, my lady. Nasty thing, a breakdown.'

'Oh well. You see I couldn't help thinking about it, thinking if only I'd been there, instead of at that stupid cocktail party. I couldn't bear the thought of him dying alone. He hated being alone at any time. If I could just have been with him, to hold his hand and say, well ... something ... anything. If he'd had just a short illness, some kind of preparation, for both of us, if there had been some last word between us, or only just a look –'

Here she herself gave Leadbitter a look so full of unhappiness that he felt quite uncomfortable, though irritation that she should talk to him so intimately was still his dominant feeling. He didn't want her confidence, but he said with all the sympathy he could muster:

'Most unfortunate for you both, my lady.'

'Yes, wasn't it? Not for him, perhaps – everybody tells me, not for him. It was a blessed way to die, they say, you could not have wanted him to suffer. And of course I couldn't. But the suddenness, the shock! Has anyone you were fond of ever died suddenly?'

As a soldier Leadbitter had seen so many instances of sudden death that he had quite lost count of them. Neither to the idea nor to the fact could he respond emotionally. But he made the imaginative effort of remembering what he had felt like the first time. The young, raw Leadbitter had been sick, yes, physically sick. Wondering at this lost self, which seemed to have no connexion with the man he had become, he said:

'It can give you a nasty turn, I do know that.'

The moment he had said this Lady Franklin looked happier.

'Yes, indeed,' she said, 'a nasty turn – how right you are. But for myself I don't think I should mind – do you think you would? – sudden death, I mean.'

'Not particularly, no, not particularly. Any time really – perhaps not just now.'

Lady Franklin smiled.

'No, not just now. Perhaps we should always find ourselves saying, "not just now". And someone might be sorry about us – about you, I'm sure they would.'

Leadbitter said nothing.

'But it isn't only that,' continued Lady Franklin. 'I could have got over that – the shock and so on. But you see it broke off something, in the way a tune is sometimes broken off. It was the tune of our lives, I suppose. We were singing it and listening to it at the same time: I'm sure you will understand that. But the meaning hadn't revealed itself – it couldn't, unless we each told the other what we thought it meant. He *had* told me something. He knew how ill he was but I didn't: he had asked the doctor not to tell me. It must have made it worse for him, not being able to tell me. I knew he had to be careful, of course: but I saw years of happiness ahead. I minded many other things at the time: but what I still mind most is the curtain coming down so suddenly, leaving it all unfinished and meaningless. If there had just been a closing phrase, however painful – well, I could have borne it better. A word could have been enough, the one word "darling" recognizing what we had been to each other, summing it all up! If only I could have suffered in his presence, instead of when he was gone! We had done everything together, but we never suffered together – except during his attacks, and he had always got better! I never met him on the plane of our deepest feelings, not in the shadow of eternity. Or have I put it too dramatically?'

'Not at all, my lady,' Leadbitter answered. Truth to tell, he had not taken in all that Lady Franklin had been saying. He had withdrawn his attention and listened with half an ear, as he sometimes listened to the wireless. But the wireless made more sense: if only she would let him turn it on!

Her last words lingered in his mind. The shadow of eternity! Rich people, who could afford to cultivate their emotions, talked like that. To him the shadow of eternity, in her context, meant the disposal, according to the regulations, of an inconvenient body which, from one moment to another, had ceased to be of interest to anyone – as his would be, if a few more of these lady-drivers drove the way they did.

But now Lady Franklin was leading off again.

'I still don't know what I should have said to him,' she said. 'I ought to, oughtn't I? I've had two years to think about it in! And I *want* to say it as much as ever I did. I know the shape and the colour of the words, and I know what I should have felt like, *if* I'd said them: it's something I shall never feel now. If I could believe that he could hear, I could find them and say them now, I think. I don't believe the dead can hear, do you?'

'I expect it's better for them not to, in many cases,' Leadbitter said.

Lady Franklin laughed and said: 'No doubt you're right.' Then her face saddened again. 'But speaking seriously,' she said, 'and I hope you don't mind – it's that undelivered message that torments me. He didn't know what I felt for him! He died without knowing! He couldn't have known, for I was very gay in those days. I can't remember what I *was* like, I seem to be a different person now, but I know I didn't comment upon life, I lived. And I was younger, much younger than he was. You see I was half-persuaded into the marriage – I was very young, and they all thought it would be a good match for me. I didn't really want to at the time; I was half frightened of the money.' (Odd thing to be frightened of, thought Leadbitter. I bet she counted every penny of it.) 'If someone said, as I'm sure they have, that I married him for his money, it wouldn't be true; but if they said, as I'm sure they have, that I married him without being in love with him, it would be true in a way; but I did come to love him afterwards. Not perhaps as you love someone who isn't ill and hasn't to be taken care of – but I did love him, and people tell me I was a good wife to him, and that he *must* have known what I felt for him. But I don't think he did. He only knew – if he knew anything at the last, while he was dying – that I had gone to a cocktail party. I went to many cocktail parties – he didn't care about them. Is there anything in life that matters – really matters – except that somebody you love should know you love them?'

Lady Franklin seemed to expect an answer. Leadbitter, whom nobody loved and who assuredly loved nobody, was at a loss.

'If it's a question of telling people what you think of them,' he said, and began to feel on firmer ground, 'if it's a question of telling people what you think of them,' he repeated grimly, 'I admit there's some satisfaction in that.'

Lady Franklin smiled.

'Oh yes, there is. But as you know, that wasn't what I meant. I think, wouldn't you agree? that one's hostility to people can be taken for granted' (Leadbitter violently disagreed but didn't say so), 'but not one's love. In spite of Blake' – she saw that Blake's name didn't register, and with a little flutter of her hands dismissed him – 'Blake thought the opposite – I think that love should always be told. I didn't tell mine.'

Would he have believed her if she had? thought Leadbitter. Would he have been taken in by all this guff? But you couldn't say that to a customer.

'Actions speak louder than words, they say, my lady,' he remarked.

Lady Franklin shook her head.

'Sometimes they do, generally they do, but not always. If I wanted to say what a beautiful driver you are, the best I have ever known, how could I say it by an action? I could only tell you.'

Leadbitter saw the force of this, and rather unwillingly swallowed the compliment.

'If there's ever anything you want to tell anyone,' said Lady Franklin, earnestly, but more to herself than to him, 'tell them. Don't wait till it's too late or it may spoil your life, as it has mine.'

Her underlip came forward, trembling, and a look of sadness, shroudedness, inaccessibility to outside impressions, closed her face like a shutter.

Leadbitter could think of nothing that he wanted to tell anyone, certainly nothing that they would want to hear. Tell them off, yes; in that sense of telling, there were a few things he could have said to Lady Franklin herself. Such as: 'If you changed places with a working woman, my lady, you wouldn't be trying to send messages to a dead husband, you'd be nagging a live one.' His mind still muddled by sleepiness, he forgot that a working woman might also be a widow. And: 'He may be thanking his stars he's out of reach of your tongue.'

These imagined retorts gave him some satisfaction: but all he said was, 'Would you like the wireless on now, my lady?'

'I don't think so, thank you,' said Lady Franklin, 'we're nearly there. Let's have it on the way back.' Afraid that she had sounded snubbing, she added, 'I'll tell you why I'm going to Canterbury.' All at once she felt she had been talking down to the driver, as if she was older than he was, though really she was a good deal younger, both in years and in experience. It's the difference in our social positions, she thought, that makes me use this artificial tone – that, and the effort to be more articulate than I am normally, or have grown to be. It's so long since I talked to anyone that my tongue can't find its way about. How difficult all communication is!

'I'm going to Canterbury,' she repeated more chattily, 'because my husband was fond of all old buildings and especially cathedrals. People used to say he should have been a monk, and I knew what they meant and it made me angry. He didn't have to have a profession but he would have been an architect if his health hadn't broken down. He had to give up so many things! One by one his interests were taken from him, his active interests, I mean, even travelling, which had been his great delight. We did a tour of the French cathedrals once, or some of them and saw most of the English cathedrals several times. He explained to me about them and wanted me to share his interest, but I couldn't quite.'

'I don't suppose many young ladies could,' said Leadbitter. 'They go more on dancing and night-clubs, and cocktail parties,' he added unguardedly.

'I'm afraid I did,' said Lady Franklin reddening. 'And in a sort of way I was jealous of his outside interests. I wanted to share them with him and yet I didn't want to. I felt I had to keep my end up with his family, for one thing, which was so much more important in the social world than mine was. I didn't want to be crushed by them, if you see what I mean. I was a little ... well ... on the defensive.'

'In my experience,' said Leadbitter, 'a family is no more use than a sick headache. I never had much truck with mine.'

'I had to,' Lady Franklin said. 'It wasn't that they weren't kind to me, they were, they almost stifled me with kindness. But they were so anxious I should be one of themselves. They had their own pattern of life and expected me to fit in. They had a special way of talking – a sort of family language – that I never could quite catch. And they saw things from their own point of view, and as if there couldn't be two opinions. I was a little defiant, I know, even with Philip, because I could hear their voices in his. So I stood up to him sometimes. He was very gentle with me – but they all were – and never tried to force his interests on me. I wish he had. I wanted to share them, I really wanted to, but there was always this little demon of defiance that made me feel that if I did, completely, I should somehow be giving in.'

'And so you would have been, my lady,' Leadbitter said warmly. In his mind's eye he saw the embattled Franklins, a hostile force, lining a distant hill. 'People like that, they always take advantage. They wouldn't have let you call your soul your own.'

'Oh, I don't know,' said Lady Franklin, wretchedly. 'I know that I can't call it my own now. . . . They fussed about him too much, I thought. How wrong I was – and when he died, well, they couldn't quite forgive me. Do you wonder? I don't see a great deal of them now, by mutual arrangement.'

'That's something to be thankful for, my lady,' said Leadbitter, noting that Lady Franklin had very few allies.

'Yes I suppose it is. But I sometimes wish that I had someone nearer to me than solicitors and trustees, and that the silence round me wasn't so respectful – though I'm to blame for that. I was an only child. My father died soon after I was married, and my mother . . . my mother . . .'

Leadbitter had all the working man's delicacy about pry-ing into other people's affairs. Nosyness. ... But he ventured to prompt Lady Franklin.

'Yes, my lady?'

'I never see her now.'

Again the veiled look, the out-thrust lip, the air of inner withdrawal. Lady Franklin jerked herself out of it and said:

'So that was how I had the idea of this – this pilgrimage to Canterbury – not as a penance, oh no, but feeling that he would have liked it, and that in thought, at any rate, I could share with him what I didn't share – not fully – while he was alive.'

Chapter 4

FROM afar the ash-grey towers dominated the city, within they were lost to view. Leadbitter missed the narrow turning that led to the Cathedral; he drove on through the town and had to come back. The mistake annoyed him, and just as he was about to park the car another trivial incident annoyed him too. A middle-aged man posted himself in their path and beckoned Leadbitter on. 'You'll get out easier afterwards if you come forward a bit now,' he said, his face beaming with good will. Leadbitter said nothing nor did he advance. Lady Franklin saw the smile fade from the man's face and a look of nervous embarrassment succeed it. Glancing at Leadbitter she saw what had scared the stranger. That steady stare would have intimidated many people.

She said pacifically:

'I think he only meant to be helpful.'

'Let's hope so, my lady,' Leadbitter replied. 'But some people are rather officious.'

The smile with which he had said this reminded Lady Franklin of the rhyme about the lady and the tiger. For a moment she felt physically uneasy, a sensation she hadn't had for years: it had been everybody's business to keep her safe. As he was holding the door open for her to get out, she said:

'Would you like to look at the Cathedral?'

'No thank you, my lady,' he answered promptly. 'I've seen it before.'

'Very well,' she said, glancing at her little jewelled wristwatch. 'I'll be back at half past one.'

What an odd man she thought, moving towards the ornate porch, upholstered with a double tier of statues. Not very responsive, was he? A curious choice for my experiment. But I think I feel better for talking to him. Poor fellow, he couldn't get away from me: how bored he must have been. Otherness, otherness, that's what the man told me. A friend is no good, find somebody unlike yourself: a waiter, a porter, a taxi-driver. Button-hole him, victimize him, be an Ancient Mariner; pour your story into his ear, don't let him get away. Make him listen to every word, and see how he takes it. If he thinks you are a fool, so much the better. If he calls you a fool, better still. This man, whose name I've forgotten, couldn't have called me a fool; it would have been more than his place was worth. I'm not sure he wouldn't have liked to, though. Rather a shame to torment him: I've never been a deliberate bore before.

But that's only half of it. Going back I must ask him *his* story. Establish his identity as a person, absolutely apart from me. Functioning quite independently of me. What an insult! thought Lady Franklin, humorously. He actually dares to have a life of his own! He is no part of my dream, any more than I am part of his. Get it into your head, my dear, that he's a separate entity and that none of your woes, or joys (if I had any), could ever make him bat an eyelid.

I must remember to ask him his name. Or would that hurt his feelings? Oh dear, I ought to know it. How good-looking he is: with a twist of rope round his neck he would be the Dying Gladiator. I had to ask him to come with me into the Cathedral, it was part of the cure: but I'm glad he didn't. What would Philip have thought? Yet I musn't be alone: never be alone, the man said, if you can help it. Marry! Marry! If only he knew how little I wanted to – how much happier I am with my unhappiness – alone, alone in this beautiful place, with a few sightseers like myself, whom I need never speak to, whom it would be wrong to speak to, irreverent, irreligious, disturbing the peace of this vast building. She looked appreciatively at the triple tier of arches springing with incredible lightness towards the intricate crisscross of the vaulted roof. 'Here if anywhere my true contentment lies. Here I could say . . . I could say . . . what I didn't say before he died.'

She sat down in a chair, one of the many lashed together, and tried to say it: 'Philip, Philip, I have always loved you!' How little the words meant of all she meant them to mean; they were self-bound, they reached no further than her pleading whisper carried. Tears started to her eyes. But the charm, which might have been effectual could she have believed in it, failed to work.

Left to himself, Leadbitter turned on the wireless. A woman's voice! The civilian world was a dull place, a tired three-piece orchestra, waiting for the word 'fun'. Moodily he got out, locked the car and went to buy himself a coffee. On the way he passed a pub, and after a few moments' hesitation pushed the door open. Few working men drink spirits in the middle of the day and Leadbitter was no exception, he couldn't afford to and besides he didn't want to smell of alcohol: he had his customers, and the police, to think of. But he felt very tired and the job with Lady Franklin would bring in several pounds, so he decided to take the risk. He chose whisky, a drink he didn't often indulge in, for it made him feel 'antagonistic', as he put it. One double Scotch sufficed to set the hostility working in him, and looking round he spied a small fat man whose inoffensive expression irritated him. He stared at him until the man showed signs first of uneasiness, then of confusion, and at last, looking every way except at his tormentor, ignominiously scuttled out. But Leadbitter's demon remained unappeased. Arguing the toss with himself whether he should have another whisky, he approached the bar and said to the barman, who was a big, heavily built, pasty-faced fellow, with a slight foreign accent:

'Are you an American?'

'No,' said the barman.

'Well, what are you then?'

'If you want to know, I'm Dutch.'

'I thought you were an American,' said Leadbitter evenly. His voice made it sound like an insult, almost a threat: and a faint stir of interest went through the drinkers, the pleasurable anticipation of a quarrel, and they turned their heads, awaiting the barman's answer.

'It's written Dutch on my passport,' he said expressionlessly.

'Well, they should know,' said Leadbitter, inferring that such knowledge didn't matter much, either way.

The barman raised his eyes but didn't answer and Leadbitter, dropping the subject as if any interest it might have had was now exhausted, decided not to have another drink. For a moment, while his will clashed with the barman's, he had felt that life was worth living: it had been brought to the fine point of conflict that his nature craved.

Returning to his car he sat down behind the wheel. Sleepiness pressed upon him, his head nodded; but he didn't mean to be caught napping a second time, and he forced himself to glance, every minute or two, at the dark hole of the Cathedral porch. She'll be late, he thought, women always are. But the hand of his wrist-watch hadn't reached the half-hour when he saw her coming out into the sunlight, swaying a little as she walked. 'There must be a bar in that Cathedral,' he said to himself, and sprang out to open the door for her.

She took a moment to collect herself and then said: 'Oh lunch, of course. You must be starving. Let's go to the White Horse, I'm told that's the best. And get yourself a good lunch, won't you?'

Leadbitter, who often didn't get enough lunch to fill a hollow tooth, as he expressed it, promised her he would.

Chapter 5

AT last they were leaving Canterbury.

Pressed forward, Lady Franklin's underlip had the effect of pouting: it trembled a little, and somehow spoilt the contour of her face, making her look discontented. What right had she to be discontented? Leadbitter, who had seen tears on the faces of a good many women and had sometimes caused them, noted that there was a tear-mark on her cheek. She had made up her face without due care and attention because she had no one to make it up for, except him, and he didn't count.

She sat without speaking. First she talks my head off, thought Leadbitter resentfully, and then she hasn't a word to say to me. Well, two can play at that game. If she doesn't like it she knows what to do: so why worry? And he wrapped himself in a silence that stiffened his profile and could be felt through the car: a silence so loud and so insistent that it awoke Lady Franklin from her painful reverie.

Glancing at Leadbitter guiltily she said:

'Wouldn't you like to have the wireless on now?'

An imp of perversity entered into Leadbitter and he said with perfect politeness: 'By all means, my lady, but I rather thought –' and his hand, stretched out to the switch, stopped short of turning it. The irresponsive absorption of the wireless in its own concerns was no help to Lady Franklin, inextricably absorbed in hers. Feeling too much about one thing often means feeling too little about another. Outside the tender area of its activity a neurosis sometimes breeds a certain callousness: an inflamed conscience is not sensitive all over. 'What matter if he *is* bored?' Lady Franklin thought. 'I'm paying him.' But her thoughts were bolder than her words. She couldn't tell him that she was talking to him, at somebody's suggestion, to cure herself of an obsession; but one *must* apologize to people for boring them. Aloud she said:

'If you don't mind me talking –'

'Oh no, my lady.'

'Well, then.'

But what should she talk about? She could not tell him her story again: even at the confessional, she supposed, you did not confess the same sin twice, however heavy its burden of guilt and grief. Even the patience of a priest must have its limits. Suddenly she remembered what her friend had said: Make other people tell *you* their stories. They will, fast enough. Make them seem real to themselves, and then they'll seem real to you. Don't forget – what you need is, the sense of other people's reality. You mustn't go on living in your dream.

He's like the moon, she thought inconsequently. I only see one side of his face. And is there any life on it? Like the moon, with its shadows. The moon in its first quarter. . . . And yet not a moon face: anything but. Sensitive to looks she registered, without feeling it, the blend of strength and delicacy in Leadbitter's. For the first time she found herself wondering about him.

'Are you married?' she asked diffidently.

What did she want him to say? Yes or no? It was anybody's guess. And Leadbitter tried to feel in his broad palm, curved upon the wheel, the size of the tip that might reward each answer. Women didn't tip much anyhow, but it might make the difference between a half-crown and a florin. Most women would rather think he wasn't married, but not, he suspected, Lady Franklin, who was dotty about marriage. Lying, he spoke more quickly than when he told the truth, and his reply came pat: but he hadn't been able to rid his voice of the moment's uncertainty as he said:

'Yes, I'm married.'

'You don't sound very sure,' said Lady Franklin with a smile.

Blast her, she was sharper than he thought. How like a woman, to ask a question she had no right to ask, and then not believe him! Oddly enough he was touchier about having his word doubted when he told a lie than when he spoke the truth.

'Yes, well and truly married,' he said dryly, 'and three children too.'

'But you said not long ago you didn't mind the thought of dying!' Lady Franklin exclaimed.

'Well, Madam,' he answered reasonably, 'I'm not the first married man with three children to say that.' The 'Madam' was a slip but he didn't regret it: she was a madam, and no mistake.

I'm not married, thought Lady Franklin, inconsequently. Not now, I used to be. But how absurd, of course she was married, and so was the driver, though he didn't seem to like it. She glanced at him. She saw the shadows of fatigue beneath the natural healthiness of his complexion, the pallor on his cheek-bones, the hollows in his cheeks, and the smudges under his gun-metal eyes; and she remembered how irresistibly sleep had overtaken him.

'I'm so sorry,' she said, 'I'm so sorry! What is she like, your wife?'

Again Leadbitter hesitated, but this time he knew that it was safe to hesitate: she couldn't expect him to have a description of his wife on the tip of his tongue.

'My wife she is dying, hurray!
My wife she is dying, hurray!
My wife she is dying
I laugh till I'm crying,
I wish I was single again.'

Supposing he said that? But of course he couldn't; he had spoken out of turn even by suggesting that marriage wasn't what it was cracked up to be. He tried to think of the kind of wife that Lady Franklin would like him to have, and to endow her with an appearance and characteristics. Appearance – Lady Franklin would want to know what she looked like: women always wanted to know that. But no image came into his mind; all women suddenly seemed faceless, he couldn't even recall the face of the one he had last lived with, it was as blank as the photograph frame from which he had banished her image. All that he could see when he evoked it was his list of engagements. Why did women always want to mess one about with their feelings? He stole a look at Lady Franklin and suddenly had an idea. He liked it all the better for being mischievous.

'Why, she's a little like you, my lady, if I may say so,' he said slyly.

'Like me?' said Lady Franklin. 'Oh, I hope not!'

Leadbitter was not ignorant of the emotions; he was in flight from them, and he realized that Lady Franklin was sincere when she said she hoped that the fictitious Mrs Leadbitter was not like her. All the same she was fishing, the crafty Clara, like any other woman, and he would take his cue from that.

'Why not?' he asked. 'She might be like a lot of worse people.'

Lady Franklin considered.

'Worse people? I don't know, I suppose she might.' No doubt, thought Lady Franklin, there were worse women than she was, but were there many more unhappy? She shook her head impatiently; the idea of being in competition with other unhappy people was distasteful to her. It was an argument that her friends sometimes used, very delicately of course – that other people had more reason for grief than she had. As if grief could be measured by its causes, and not by the victim's capacity for suffering! And all this publicizing of her feelings, how was she the better for it? It went against her nature to speak of them. Why had she embarked on this shaming revelation?

'I didn't really mean that,' she said. 'I am glad you think your wife is like me. To look at, I expect you mean?'

'Well, yes,' said Leadbitter, feeling his way. 'But people

who look alike generally *are* alike, in my experience, making allowances for the way they are brought up, of course.'

Lady Franklin took the point. 'Well, she is lucky to have you,' she said.

'Lucky?' said Leadbitter, slowly. 'Yes, perhaps. I'm not sure if she thinks so, though, my lady.'

'Oh come,' said Lady Franklin. 'Every woman is happier with a husband.'

Leadbitter thought about this. 'And is every husband happier with a wife?' he asked.

Lady Franklin smiled. 'I couldn't tell you. I hope you are.'

'Oh yes, my lady,' he answered enthusiastically. 'I couldn't carry on without one. She ... she makes all the difference.'

'What difference?' asked Lady Franklin. 'What difference does a wife make?'

Again Leadbitter was flummoxed. His grievance against all women was so deep-seated, and supported by so many arguments in his mind that he couldn't, off-hand, think of a single redeeming feature that a wife possessed. The qualities that were supposed to recommend them – that they cooked, washed, mended and so on, he rejected, for what did Lady Franklin know about such things? And again for lack of any woman who would come into his mind he thought of Lady Franklin and tried to imagine what she would be like as a wife.

'They make a home for one thing,' he said.

Immediately Lady Franklin applied this to her own case. Had she made a home for Philip? No, he had given her one; all she had done was to occupy it decoratively and then, when he was dying, be away from it. She could not think of one wifely virtue she had displayed, but she knew that other women had them, and no doubt the driver's wife had.

'Yes, they can make a home,' she agreed, without much conviction. 'At least, some can.'

Leadbitter gave her good marks for this. Lady Franklin was not solid for her sex.

'And they can break a home,' he said.

To this Lady Franklin agreed without reserve, adding: 'But yours makes a home for you?'

'Oh yes, my lady,' Leadbitter said. 'She has her work cut out, though, what with minding the children and answering the telephone.'

'How old are your children?'

'How old?' echoed Leadbitter. He couldn't think of any age a child might be. 'Have you any children yourself, my lady?' he asked hopefully.

'No, alas.'

So his couldn't be the same age ... 'Let me see,' he said. 'The youngest's only two and she's a proper handful.'

'And the others?'

'The boy, he's the eldest, he's eleven, and the second, she's a girl, she's eight. Very good children they are, though I say it.'

'What are their names?' persisted Lady Franklin, determined to make Leadbitter and his family real to herself and incidentally to him, since this further mission was supposed to be part of her cure.

Leadbitter hadn't reckoned with this question.

'Why, I shall be forgetting my own name next!' he apologized. 'Donald, of course, and Patricia, that's the middle one, and Susan, that's the baby. Don and Pat and Susie, we call them.'

'What nice names!' said Lady Franklin.' And what's your wife's name?'

'Frances,' hazarded Leadbitter. It was the nearest sound to Franklin.

'Frances,' mused Lady Franklin, pronouncing it with a hard a, as he had; 'how strange, it's one of my names, though not the one I'm called by.' Did this coincidence make the driver's wife more real to her? She scarcely knew. But it made her more real to Leadbitter, for it gave her another link with Lady Franklin. Somewhere in his being a chord vibrated. But thinking that Lady Franklin might resent sharing a name with a mere driver's wife, he added:

'I don't call her Frances, though. She wouldn't know who I was talking to.'

'What do you call her?'

'Chips.'

He brought this out quite pat, for it had been his nick-name for his mistress: she had so many chips on her shoulder, he declared. But the next moment he regretted it and frowned, for it troubled his image of his wife as Lady Franklin. It troubled Lady Franklin's image of her too: she could not unite the two names in one person.

'And what does your wife call you?' she asked.

Oddly enough it took Leadbitter longer to answer this straightforward question than any of the others. Perhaps the switch from fiction to fact disconcerted him.

'Well, Stephen is my name,' he said. 'She calls me Steve.' Hoping to get something for nothing, Lady Franklin might say: 'Oh Steve, would you be kind enough to drop this parcel at Marshall & Snelgrove's on your way home?' It wouldn't be on the way home, of course, but he supposed he would have to. But no one called him Steve, and she never would.

'What are you going to do with the boy?' asked Lady Franklin.

'Put him in the Army,' Leadbitter answered promptly. 'I don't want him hanging about street corners at eleven o'clock at night, wearing a duffel coat.'

Lady Franklin agreed that this would be most undesirable. 'You don't like duffel coats?' she added.

'I wouldn't be seen dead in one, my lady,' Leadbitter said. 'And if my wife saw me wearing one, she would tear me off a strip.'

'I don't like duffel coats, either,' Lady Franklin said. 'I'm glad we have that in common, besides our names. Can you think of anything else we share?' And for the first time for years, it seemed, she found herself waiting for an answer, and wanting to compare herself with another human being – to find out something new about herself, to be outside the ring-fence of her grief.

'I'll try,' Leadbitter said. 'I'll try, my lady.'

He did try, and to such good effect that by the time they had reached the bottle-neck of Rochester he had thought of quite a number of points in which his wife reminded him of Lady Franklin, as, for example, that she would rather talk to him than listen to the wireless, that she affected the same colours, blue and white, that Lady Franklin wore, that she had rather the same way of walking. Also that she was kind and sympathetic and overlooked his faults of temper – for he supposed he was at times a tartar to live with. Attributing to his wife the good qualities women were said to possess, (though he did not think they did) he also attributed them to Lady Franklin. His imagination was ingenious in discovering these parallels; but he didn't realize, when every now and then he glanced at Lady Franklin to give him a new lead, that it was her presence that inspired him.

'But perhaps she isn't at all like you, my lady, except to look at,' he wound up, when he had completed the inventory of his wife's charms and virtues. 'You see I'm only guessing. I don't know you, except as I know my customers, but I do know her.'

'Thank you very much,' said Lady Franklin. 'I didn't want to think she was like me, and yet I'm glad to think I am like her.'

In the silence which had become habitual to her, unless she made a deliberate effort to break it, she contemplated the paragon whose image Leadbitter had set up. Was she at all like it? Leadbitter's guesses had not been wide of the mark; kind, gentle, patient, interested in other people and able to enter into their feelings – she saw how these epithets could, without too much flattery, once have been applied to her, though they did not fit her now. Now they were like the sound of lyres and flutes, or like the memory of a fortune-teller's prophecy (before her marriage she had frequented a fortune-teller), which had seemed plausible at the time, but to which events had given the lie. Yet something stirred in her, some interest that the chauffeur had kindled in her grief-laden, time-dimmed personality, even if it was only the interest of seeing herself mirrored in another woman.

The approaches to London have each their separate character but to Lady Franklin they all seemed alike – a succession of dull streets, often with ugly public houses at the corners, garish with glazed tiles. Automatically she asked herself: Will the traffic lights be green or red? That was the extent of her interest in the route. She did not take in, still less appreciate, the professional skill with which Leadbitter avoided the thronged main roads, steering his way through the 'back-doubles', to save time and petrol; and her whereabouts came to her as a surprise when the car pulled up at South Halkin Street.

A half-smile tilting the corners of his mouth, Leadbitter held the door open for her; crouching and ducking and a little dazed, Lady Franklin stumbled out, aided by his hand.

'It has been very nice,' she told him rather grandly, 'very enjoyable indeed. Thank you so much, Mr –' she tried to recollect his name, forgot it, and repeated: 'So much.' She opened her bag and fumbled.

'How much will it be?'

'That's all right, my lady, I'll send you an account.'

'How very kind of you,' said Lady Franklin, 'but –' Her hand still embedded in the bag, she looked up questioningly and shyly into his face, which had become as rigid and impersonal as that of a stone god about to receive a sacrifice. 'Don't forget to put your lunch on the account,' she said, playing for time. 'And thank you for the Canterbury Tale.'

Like an automaton he inclined his head. How much did one give a car-hire driver who had been with one – she glanced at her wrist-watch – for nearly seven hours? And whom one had bored with unsolicited information about one's own private life, and ill-bred curiosity about his? A doctor might have charged her several guineas for the first indulgence, and she might have lost any reputation she had as a talker for the second. She pulled out a pound note – it was green and larger than the brown ones – that was how she distinguished between them. For a moment it overflowed the fingers of her small hand, before it disappeared into the palm of his.

'Thank you very much, my lady,' he said, and waited dutifully to see whether she could let herself in with her latch-key – women sometimes bungled it. When the door yielded he saluted Lady Franklin's unresponsive back and retired into the car. As it slid off he hummed:

'My wife she is dying, hurray!
My wife she is dying, hurray!
  My wife she is dying
  I laugh till I'm crying,
I wish I was single again.
  I wish I was single
  My pockets would jingle
I wish I was single again.'

Taking one hand off the wheel, he felt in his pocket. Amid the jingle he heard the subdued crackling of Lady Franklin's note. All things considered, it hadn't been a bad day, but God, how that woman had talked! He had two more jobs to do but they were small ones: to pick up a party for the theatre and bring them back. With luck he would be in bed by twelve, not with a wife but with the more agreeable companionship of his telephone. And he sighed with relief, for though he would not have admitted it he was very tired.

That night Leadbitter dreamed that he was married. The dream began with a realization of his married state: it was a nightmare, he was trapped and longed to wake up. The woman, when she came into the dream, was not Lady Franklin but someone rather like her. She was getting him his supper, moving about in an assured, efficient way; he was sitting in an armchair with his feet up. The room was much larger than his own, and had floor lamps and table lamps dotted about it. 'How are you feeling, Steve?' his wife asked him, 'not too tired, I hope?' 'Oh no, my lady,' he was going to say, but realizing that she was his wife and that he needn't stand on ceremony with her, he grunted something. He was rather pleased that she had asked him if he was feeling tired. 'The children are in bed,' she said. 'Pat has a touch of toothache and been grizzling a bit; I'm taking her to the dentist tomorrow.' To his surprise he felt a twinge of sympathy for Pat. 'Poor little devil,' he said. 'I've promised her some chocolates afterwards,' said his wife. 'I've got them here: would you like one?' He said nothing but stretched his hand out and then savoured the sweet taste in his mouth. 'Give us another,' he said, and through the dream he again felt surprise, for his waking self never bothered with chocolates. His wife brought the box and put it on a table by his side. 'Yes, but leave some for her,' she said, and he laughed, and munched chocolate after chocolate until the upper layer was nearly gone. He thought his wife would scold him and was getting ready to resent it but she only said, half admiringly: 'I never knew you had such a sweet tooth.' Relaxed and appeased he decided to have one more, but at that moment there was a terrific commotion which gradually resolved itself into the rasping summons of the telephone. The pleasant sitting-room and his wife dissolved with the chocolate and in another moment, without waiting to switch the light on, he was holding the receiver to his ear. A voice that he recognized said: 'Is that you, Leadbitter? Look here, we're stranded at the Lotus Club, my wife and I. Can you drive us home?'

'I've got a small job to do first, sir,' Leadbitter said, to give himself more time. 'Then I'll be with you.'

The room, when it disclosed itself, looked small and bare, bristling with angles and sharp edges. It was half past one by Leadbitter's alarm clock. For night-work he charged more: the job would be a good one and put several pounds into his pocket. He glanced at the tumbled bed-clothes: between four and five he would be back between the sheets. But as he pulled his clothes on, and assembled himself in front of the looking-glass, he didn't feel his usual exhilaration. His imagination lingered in the pleasaunce of his dream, wife-ridden though it was; and he fancied he could still taste the chocolate's sweetness on his tongue.

Chapter 6

CATHEDRALS, country houses, beauty-spots – Lady Franklin was a passionate and indefatigable sightseer. Not so Leadbitter: to him they were not sights they were objectives, and if he looked at them it was with a soldier's eye, wondering whether they should be blown up or allowed to stand. He saw life as a campaign in which there was no real cessation of hostilities; opposition whetted his nature; agreement blunted it. Wherever he might be he wanted to take the next position, he had no interest in the terrain for itself, only in its possibilities for advance.

Lady Franklin was one of these possibilities; indeed she had become one of his best customers and as such he studied her with all the care of which he was capable. In a sense he regarded her as an enemy; she did not qualify for the category of old ladies and in a sense 'they', his customers, were all enemies. Such a being as the perfect customer did not exist, though some had more faults than others. Unpunctuality was one of the worst, and of this women were particularly guilty. They would make a point of his being there on time and then keep him waiting for an hour; they would expect him to pick up their friends and drop them again in distant places; they would challenge his choice of the route; they would want him to wait in streets where waiting was prohibited; they would ask him to turn round and go back; they would want to keep him long after he was due on another job. They did not or would not understand that time, which was as elastic to them as an accordion-pleated skirt, was a strait-jacket to him.

On the average, male customers were better about time, for like him they generally had an objective and did not dilly-dally making up and unmaking their minds. But a few, mostly businessmen, bent on some dubious deal or giving lavish entertainments on their expense accounts, were worse than any woman: they were capable of keeping him out most of the night, getting more and more sozzled themselves and occasionally wanting him to join them. He had a way with people of this kind and if they did not like it they knew what to do. Leadbitter was master of as many degrees of coldness as a refrigerator, he could modulate from a light hoar-frost to a deep freeze. But only with men did he adopt these tactics; women were to some extent non-combatants, and as such outside the arctic circle. Sometimes he said he would like to shoot the lot but in practice he treated his women customers with indulgence and seldom betrayed the irritation that they caused him.

Lady Franklin's chief fault was that she could not stop talking, asking him damn-fool questions about himself. Sometimes she returned to her own troubles, the grief and remorse she felt about her husband, whom Leadbitter still thought of as a lucky man. Shyly she would ask him for reassurance; did he honestly think she had behaved as badly as she felt she had? To which Leadbitter would reply that he couldn't see anything wrong in what she had done; after all, a woman had to go out sometimes, even his wife had to go out on occasions, tied though she was to the children and the telephone. Women needed a break, the same as anyone else. Men needed a break too – a break from women's tongues, he meant, but was too tactful to say so. Sir Philip, or whoever he was, must often have needed a break from Lady Franklin's.

'You may be sure, my lady,' he said, choosing his words, 'that your husband sometimes wanted, well ... time to look round and take stock of things, so to speak: every man does. He wouldn't be a man if he wanted you to be all the time waiting hand and foot on him. My wife doesn't, she looks after me, of course, but she'd go potty if I stayed at home all day. She's often told me so, when I've – when I've told her I was sorry I had to be out so much. It isn't nature for a husband and wife to be always together. Of course when a man's courting a girl he wants to be with her all the time; but when he's married half an hour a day's enough. And if anything happened to me, as it easily might, with the kind of drivers there are on the roads, especially some lady-drivers, who don't even know where the back of their neck is, well, it would be just too bad, but she wouldn't think she ought to have been waiting at the corner of Piccadilly Circus, or wherever it might be, in case I had a crash, and I certainly shouldn't want her to. It would be crying over spilt milk, for one thing. Life couldn't go on if people felt like that.'

'Yes,' said Lady Franklin, whose tormenting demon was tireless in finding arguments against her, 'but the two cases aren't quite the same, are they? Your profession automatically takes you into danger' (as she spoke a collision was only narrowly averted by Leadbitter's watchful eye) 'and your wife is, I know, a very busy woman. But I hadn't that excuse. I just went out to a party when I should have been –'

'But why should you have been, my lady?' broke in Leadbitter, heading her off. 'I'm sure if you could ask your husband, he would say, "I was having a jolly good time in your absence, only it just happened that my heart conked out" – it's like a car, you can't tell when it's going to happen, when the coil gets burnt out, for instance. That's what I should say to my wife, and she's just as fond of me as most wives are.'

'No doubt she's told you so,' said Lady Franklin, entering into the deepest shadow of her remorse.

'Oh yes, she has – but not all the time, you know, I really couldn't stick it if she did. It makes a man feel bad if a woman tells him she loves him – too often that is. I couldn't explain why.'

Lady Franklin thought about this. She had considered the incident from every possible angle, she believed, but it was a new idea to her that Philip might not have *wanted* her to tell him that she loved him. It couldn't be true! It couldn't be true! Her guilt rallied its forces and proclaimed an emphatic denial.

'Have you told her?' she murmured.

'Have I told who, my lady?' asked Leadbitter who, during Lady Franklin's self-accusing silence, had lost the thread of the conversation.

'Told your wife that you . . . you love her?' Lady Franklin brought out with an effort.

'Oh yes, often,' Leadbitter said glibly. 'But you know I think she takes it with a grain of salt.'

'No,' said Lady Franklin. 'No,' she repeated more firmly. 'Not if I know anything about women. They want to hear that, believe me – it's the only thing they really want to hear. And in spite of what you say, I think men are the same. Would you be as . . . as happy as you are, if your wife had never told you that she loved you?'

Leadbitter's face stiffened a little, while inwardly he prayed for patience.

'I think I should get over it, my lady,' he said.

Lady Franklin smiled, and the lip which had begun to pout, spoiling the contour of her profile, slipped back into place.

'I don't believe you would,' she said. 'Not altogether. I hope you would, of course, if the situation ever arose – which I devoutly hope it won't. But I beg you, don't take the risk. If there's anything you want to say to her – any message of love – any urgent message of that kind – say it at once – don't wait until it's too late, or it may spoil your life as it has mine.'

She's said that before, thought Leadbitter. But what he said was:

'I won't forget, my lady.'

Their conversations usually followed the same pattern: beginning with Lady Franklin and her obsession, they ended with Leadbitter and his fictitious home-life. Ask me no questions and I'll tell you no lies; but Lady Franklin asked a great many questions and Leadbitter told her a great many lies. He had no scruples in doing this because it was his principle to give his customers what they wanted. In practice the customer was often wrong, in theory the customer was always right, and theory dictated Leadbitter's behaviour. Except when 'they' annoyed him beyond bearing he himself did not come into it.

But underneath that stern, correct exterior there lurked, unknown to Leadbitter, the temperament and the imagination of an artist. Just as he could anticipate his adversary's next move, and might have distinguished himself as a boxer if he hadn't thought that getting knocked about was a mug's game, so in life he knew how to take advantage of a pressure, however strange and unexpected, that came to him from outside. Lady Franklin wanted to know about his private life, did she? Well, he would tell her. He who had had no emotional life for years, who had felt it an encumbrance and deliberately banished it, as he might have sent off parade a soldier wearing a button-hole, found a perverse delight in inventing a personal life for Lady Franklin's benefit. Instalment by instalment, as if composing it for the wireless, he built up a serial story of himself and his wife and their children, the story of an ideally happy family. Not that the Leadbitters were always happy; they had their ups and downs, of temper, health, and spirits, and they were chronically hard up. But whatever befell them – and Leadbitter did not shrink from reporting a death on the outer fringes of the family: for a whole week he supplemented the black tie he always wore by a black band on his arm – whatever befell them, it took place in an idyllic atmosphere, an atmosphere of gold and pink, with a never-empty box of chocolates on the table. For the whole fantasy owed its imaginative impulse to his dream – that dream in which someone rather like Lady Franklin was his wife.

By fixing his mind on it at bedtime he tried to make the dream come back. But the dream would not play, would not come to help him out, and the odd thing was that though while he was alone he could remember all the past incidents of the saga, he could not add to them; the traffic of his imagination was jammed, he was, as he would have said, in stuck-street. But no sooner was Lady Franklin by his side than the light turned to green and he glided forward into the world of fantasy.

He did not always talk to her about his home life, however. She had become a habit with him, he had got used to her, and sometimes he forgot she was a customer, forgot the 'my lady', forgot the special language and the special tone of voice he kept for customers, and talked to her as if she was a friend; but he didn't realize that his wish to tell her something was a sign he liked her. He talked of the jobs he had been doing, of his difficulties in being on time, of the drivers he had given work to and who had let him down. The tongue goes to the sore place; without a guard on it Leadbitter's tended to run on his grievances. Away from home, and the consolation of his family, life was an obstacle race and the world full of awkward, disobliging people, big-heads who were in for a dose of deflation when they encountered him. Lady Franklin was a good listener; she drew him out, she enjoyed the impact on her imagination of a nature which was so unlike hers. It was like watching a battle from a safe distance, hearing the shots fired, seeing the hand-to-hand encounters. In her world the men were as polite to each other as the women were, perhaps more so; the surface of social intercourse was seldom ruffled. But in Leadbitter's world a man had to stand up for himself, always with his tongue and sometimes with his fists. He could not afford to let another man get the better of him verbally; he had to have the last word, and if he couldn't, something in reserve more forceful than a word. But Leadbitter was too much of a man to vaunt his prowess in the ears of Lady Franklin. She had to be content with such understatements as, 'I gave him a birthday, my lady', or, 'I told him his horoscope'. When these exchanges took place with the driver of a passing car you had to be quick-witted to get in the word that stung. Leadbitter never treated her to an exhibition of his gift for repartee; his conception of correctness would not have allowed it. But using her eyes and ears, observing for herself, drawing aside the curtains that since her husband's death had shrouded the outside world from her view, Lady Franklin saw for herself that what he said was true. Motorists with set faces seemed bent on mowing down pedestrians. Cab drivers stuck their heads out and yelled at other cab drivers, owners of private cars raised their eyebrows and muttered angrily, bus drivers sneered from Olympian heights; and if time and opportunity offered, these gibes were returned in kind. It was a slanging-match.

'Are all motorists angry with each other?' she asked.

'Small wonder if they were,' he said, 'considering how they drive. Some of them would have us up the wall in no time. And the pedestrians! That woman seems to think that if she stands there with her legs apart I can drive between them.'

Was this the outside world?

'Let's go back!' cried Lady Franklin.

'Back, my lady?'

'Yes, to South Halkin Street.'

Chapter 7

'SHALL I shut the windows, my lady?'

'No, leave them open a little.'

'Shall I pull the curtains?'

'Isn't it a bit early?'

'The nights don't draw out as fast as they draw in, my lady, and there's a smog coming on.'

'A smog! But how exciting! I should like to see it. Please leave a chink between the curtains, Simmonds.'

Lady Franklin sat down with a book. She took out the marker, without which she couldn't find her place. She didn't read, however. Her eyes strayed to the gaps between the curtains, and her ears listened for sounds in the quiet street.

'But I thought that grief had quite gone out, with mourning and black-edged writing paper and plumes and mutes and such things. ... And it's so terribly unattractive, too. ... No, I suppose people still feel it a little, only nobody shows it, because they think that the deceased would have preferred in that way. Nearly everyone I know who lost relations and others near and dear to them in the war at once put on their nicest clothes and went to a theatre or a party. It was rather like jumping on a horse again when you've been thrown, and also to spare their friends embarrassment. And of course not to seem to mind is in the end the surest way of not minding. Two girls I knew lost their best friends in Italy, and you couldn't have told, you really couldn't have told, from the way they behaved, that anything had gone wrong at all. They talked about them just as if they were still alive; they laughed at anything there was to laugh at, especially anything to do with death (my dear, one can't help seeing the funny side of it) and very soon they were as gay as ever....

'Insensitive? Oh, I don't mean they didn't suffer; but if they did they kept it to themselves. The world has to go on, hasn't it, and a long face and puffy eyelids do no one any good. But of course they weren't rich like Ernestine. Grief is a luxury of the rich, and in rather bad taste, I think, like having a car when other people can't. Which of us can afford to put on black at a moment's notice? – though I own it's becoming to some people, especially the fair ones, and some of us would welcome the excuse. And about Ernestine I always think it's difficult to feel sorry for anyone who has enough to live on....

'Yes, but even religious people don't think you should give way to grief, it isn't Christian, when you're going to meet whoever it may be so soon in the next world. It shows such lack of faith. To really Christian people the dead are just as present as the living.... Is Ernestine religious? Well, more superstitious, I should say. No doubt she has sought the consolations of religion; she has tried everything, I believe, including obvious quacks.... But has she ever tried a man? Ah, that I shouldn't know, my dear; personally I should say not, not even when she was married to her Philip. Of course she's too loyal to his memory to say so; but look at that large family of his, all those long-nosed Franklins; between them have they ever produced a single child? The baronetcy goes to some distant cousin in Australia, I believe, whom no one has ever seen. No, I think a good man would do her a world of good, and when I say a good man I don't mean good in the moral sense. But is it likely that any man would dare, when she wears her grief like a *ceinture de chastité*? It sticks out all over her, and mourning is so middle-class and discouraging, if you know what I mean. No, I know she doesn't actually wear it, but all the same it's there....

'Her mother's in the bin, of course. You didn't know?

Oh yes, she is, and that's what makes us all so anxious about Ernestine. It makes her anxious too, I shouldn't wonder, although she doesn't say so, in case she should be going that way herself. For she must know it isn't normal, at least it isn't normal nowadays, whatever it may have been in the past. It's only in the Bible that people refuse to be comforted. And Queen Victoria – but think how bored the public got with her! For who is there that matters all that much? People don't count in that way now. Who does one want to see for longer than a meal takes – or for as long as some meals take? That's why so many of us would rather have acquaintances than friends – they aren't the strain, and they're more faithful in the long run. No one is irreplaceable. I couldn't answer for you, darling, but I'm quite sure I'm not, and I shouldn't like anyone to think I was. I shouldn't dare to die, if I thought somebody would cry their eyes out for me! Which of us is worth it? Certainly Philip wasn't. He was rather a stick, between ourselves, and too conscious of being a Franklin, as they all are – even Ernestine, poor sweet, in her grand moments.

'... No, she doesn't talk about her trouble as she used to. Perhaps someone told her, or she saw for herself how our eyes glazed with boredom when the record started – for with all the will in the world to help her, what could one say except, "You'll get over it, my dear, in time"? You might think she didn't want to get over it, but I'm sure she must, because of the example of her mother....

'Don't think I'm running her down. Ernestine is a darling person really, and we all want her back among us. And there's only one way to do it, *cherchez l'homme!* If we could find some nice upstanding fellow, somebody we all know and like, not a rich man, she wouldn't want that, but somebody she could take pity on. It sounds ridiculous to say it, but I think she married Philip out of pity. Pity is the way to her heart, pity and admiration. Whom do we know who might fill the bill? Jasper is a most deserving case and so is Archie, and even Hughie could be made to seem so, if

Constance would speak up for him. ... That's too much to expect? You never know with Constance. She runs him down to his face, but she defends him like a tigress when he isn't there – though of course he always *is* there! ... Not admire Hughie? Oh, I think one *could*; he's good-looking now and he'll always be promising. ... More like a caddish subaltern than a painter? Oh, I don't think that's fair; besides, it's part of his charm. We can't tell if he is generous; he's never had the chance to be, poor darling. But how can we get Ernestine to meet him or anyone else, when she never goes out? And when one goes to see her at her mausoleum in South Halkin Street, it's all so awkward. Lady Franklin's grief must be respected! We must be tactful, my dear, we must be tactful! We mustn't refer to it and yet we mustn't seem to be unconscious of it! It must be always in our thoughts but never on our tongues! Don't speak too loudly, it might startle her. Don't speak too softly, it might remind her of his death. Ernestine is a very important person in our lives and very dear to us all. Oh, I'm not alluding to the money Sir Philip left her. What good does it do her? She only uses it to protect her privacy, as a drug to deepen her slumber! Yet it is there, it is there! She has only to open her cheque-book. Her presence among us makes us feel safer. ... How safer? Well, safer financially, perhaps. For should anything happen, anything painful or unpleasant happen, Ernestine would ... well ... she would come to the rescue. That is why we must go and see her, at discreet intervals of course, and ringing up or writing first, to give her the chance to say, "No, no, I cannot receive you, I must be alone with my grief. With my grief I am hardly anything (Ernestine never had a high opinion of herself) but without my grief I am nothing: I exist in my grief."

'But all the same she is still one of us: we talk about her and think about her and want to help her to return to circulation. She is frozen, frozen like money in a foreign country. But her money isn't frozen, of course: it circulates, it's alive, much more so than she is; we can feel her bank-balance rubbing shoulders with our overdrafts, and it's a warm and comfortable feeling! So we don't mean to drop her, or let her drop us! Be an angel now and ring her up, and ask if we may come to tea on Thursday, or better still if she will come to a very small party, just a few friends, that we are having on Thursday week....

'But she won't come, of course. Jasper and Archie will come, and Hughie will come, he's never missed a party; and Constance will come, because she never misses a party that Hughie goes to. But Ernestine won't come....

'Is it very awful of me, darling, to talk like this? I thought you were looking down your nose at your old friend – are you ashamed of me? Have I been guilty of bad taste – do I sound what used to be called "common"? Of course I didn't mean a word of it. Dear, darling Ernestine, she's a bit wishy-washy but she is such a pet: is there anything wrong in trying to get her safely tied up with some nice man? We can't leave her to the mercy of the first adventurer who comes along, it must be somebody we know and trust.

'... Oh no, because she isn't happy with the Franklin set; they are too up-stage for her, besides, they remind her of the past and she knows they think she neglected their dear Philip – they make her feel guilty.... Of course, if she'd had a child! No, we stand a better chance with her, she hankers after people who do things, and nobody can say we don't! ... But seriously, wouldn't she be better off with Jasper or Archie or even with Hughie, who at any rate doesn't know what guilt is, than stewing in her own juice, living a totally unreal life, the life of a gilded cage which might at any moment turn into a padded cell? A romp with Hughie would blow away the cobwebs.... Constance would never let him? Oh, I think she might – good old Connie, but we mustn't call her that, she hates the Connie-Hughie jingle. She may be tired of him, we don't know; she may be tired of playing sheep-dog to his gambols. The question is, how are we to bring him and Ernestine together? – and that, I own, defeats me.'

Did these wandering voices, making free with her name, penetrate Lady Franklin's solitude? No, but a rumour of them did, the feeling if not the sense of them, like the distant buzz of an excited crowd, heard through open windows behind curtains that are not quite drawn. The threat and promise of life! What she saw and heard offended her; it rasped her tender unused sensibility, it blinded her inward-turning vision and shouted down her grief. Its very miscellaneousness confused and worried her; for she was used to seeing what she chose to see, and hearing what had been especially composed and orchestrated for her ears. Shut the windows, draw the curtains, keep the rumour out! How much safer Lady Franklin felt when this was done.

Chapter 8

AMONG the voices Lady Franklin heard, if she did hear them, was one which spoke in very different accents, accents which were harsh and unrefined, but she was familiar with them and would have recognized them, for they were Leadbitter's. At what moment it occurred to him that the thought of Lady Franklin's bank balance was a comforting thought, he couldn't himself have told; he knew that she lived in Easy Street, but then so did most, if not all, of his customers. He was glad they did, for otherwise they could not have hired him. But in no other way was their wealth of any interest to him; they did not propose to share it with him. Some of them tipped him better than others, and this he remembered in their favour. But when he left the Fire Service, and started on his own – that death-defying leap which they all knew about, for he had both told them personally and circularized them with his Trade Card 'Leadbitter's Garages Ltd, Cars for All Occasions' – had one of them offered to 'help' him? Yes, one had, an old lady: with great diffidence and delicacy, she had offered him a pound, and he, with equal diffidence and delicacy, had refused it, because he thought she couldn't afford it. But none of the others, however rolling in riches, had offered him a penny; they had left him to sink or swim. They might be coated in money, but the money didn't rub off. On the contrary, quite a number of his customers wrote to him, querying this or that item in their accounts. He had told them that his charges would be less than those of other firms and so they were; but the malcontents professed to find them heavier. Leadbitter didn't like these letters: his nervous tension showed itself in an exaggerated fear of losing his customers.

But he wasn't afraid of losing Lady Franklin: he realized that it was not in her nature to take offence, and that even if it had been, she was too much wrapped up in herself to mind what other people said or did to her. Her heart was in the grave. Probably, he thought, she never even checked her monthly account. He did not envy her her indifference to money, but it was a fact, and a fact to be reckoned with.

And yet, indifferent as she was to money and to most other outside circumstances, she wasn't indifferent to him. Never a drive passed but she asked him for the latest instalment of the Leadbitter saga, she listened like a child and like a child asked questions. What 'The Archers' and 'Mrs Dale's Diary' were to other people, so was his narrative to Lady Franklin; only to her of course it was true. Nearly all women were interested in people, just as nearly all men (including himself) were interested in money. And as long as she was with him he had no difficulty in making the supply of facts meet the demand.

One showery afternoon in March they were motoring back from Chichester. Lady Franklin still believed that the answer to her problem could be found in a cathedral: its atmosphere always promised relief, there was always a moment when relief seemed to be coming, and though in fact it never came, she went on hoping. Disappointment made her silent and abstracted during the first part of the homeward journey: her lower lip came forward, trembling, and her face wore its shut look. On this occasion, as on others, Leadbitter waited for her distress to spend itself and then he said:

'I've had some bad news since the last time we went out, my lady.'

'Bad news?' repeated Lady Franklin from the depth of her brown study, and it might just as well have been good news, by the expressionless way she said it. Then the meaning of the words seemed to penetrate, she shook her head, and turning to Leadbitter said in a very different voice, 'Bad news? Did you say you had had bad news?'

'I'm afraid so, my lady.'

Lady Franklin hesitated. 'Can you tell me what it is?'

'I dare say I could,' said Leadbitter, 'but I don't want to bother you with my affairs.'

He looked straight ahead of him.

Almost for the first time, it seemed to Lady Franklin, she was brought up against Leadbitter the man. Hitherto he had been her Chaucer, beguiling her with Canterbury tales, tales to be continued in our next, tales that had always had a happy ending. But for that one bereavement, the Leadbitter family had seemed to bear a charmed life. And now misfortune had overtaken them. A chill went through her, a shaft of cold like nothing she had felt for years, piercing the matted wadding of her self-generated emotions. She felt the embarrassment, the slight resentment that we feel when someone whom we have always known on one plane of acquaintance and at the same remove from us, steps out in front of us and blocks our way.

'Is there anything I can do to help?' she said, and blushed for the inadequacy of the words.

'Oh no, my lady,' Leadbitter said. 'I oughtn't really to have mentioned it.'

The harshness of his voice seemed to be a measure of the disaster he was up against: from that she gauged its seriousness. She was used to a society in which troubles spread and softened themselves in words; with articulate people of her own sort they reached out and clothed themselves in phrases, emollient phrases to which sympathy could respond. They used a conventional language for calamity which Leadbitter did not know.

Lady Franklin felt utterly at a loss. How much did Leadbitter count with her as a human being? Should she press him to tell her? It seemed inhuman not to; but his trouble, whatever it was, seemed to have cased him in steel. She must be as sincere with him as she had it in her to be, stop thinking about herself, give him her unalloyed attention, as the Good Samaritan did to the traveller who had fallen among thieves.

'Has it anything to do with your wife?' she hazarded.

'It affects all of us,' he said.

It affects all of us. . . . This laconic statement moved Lady Franklin strongly. The whole Leadbitter family whom she knew so well, whose life had become so much a part of hers that it was as real to her as anything outside herself could be, was threatened.

'Please tell me,' she said. 'If I can't do anything to help, I can at least say how sorry I am.'

Leadbitter shook his head.

'I'm afraid I can't, my lady. What's the good of upsetting you? It's just one of those things.'

Lady Franklin was baffled. Her instinct was to say no more, to intrude no further on the driver's unhappiness. But that was cowardly. She felt a new respect for Leadbitter; she saw him as a soldier on the battlefield defending himself against overwhelming odds, disdaining help; driving the car, doing his job as though nothing had happened. Whereas she – she had thrown up the sponge, beaten a retreat, let life get her down. She wouldn't desert him, even if he wanted to be deserted. Besides, she was beginning to feel the prick of curiosity.

'They say,' she ventured, 'that it does one good to tell one's troubles. It's somehow strengthening. . . . I've . . . I've told you mine, and I've felt stronger for it, anyhow for a time.'

'I don't agree, my lady,' Leadbitter said. 'I think it's weakening. And if other people know they take advantage, they don't let you forget it – begging your pardon, my lady.'

The very ungraciousness of this speech piqued Lady Franklin. Supposing it was another kind of trouble, something he was ashamed to tell her, trouble with the police?

In that case she had been very tactless, probing him. She tried to revise her estimate of the whole situation, and said as lightly as she could:

'Well, perhaps you'll tell me the next time we go out.'

'I'm afraid not, my lady,' Leadbitter said promptly.

'Why not?'

'Because there won't be a next time. I shan't have the car.'

'Won't have the car? Why not?'

'Because I only have it on the H.P. and now they want it back.'

'The "H.P."?' asked Lady Franklin.

'The glad and sorry system. Well, I'm the one that's sorry.'

Still Lady Franklin did not understand, but she was on her mettle and did not mean to leave the tooth half-drawn. At length she got the story out of him. Leadbitter was paying for his car by monthly instalments. He had also paid a preliminary deposit on it. Now the firm which was supplying it had got into difficulties and had informed him that unless he paid the whole of his remaining debt, or a large proportion of it, in a lump sum there and then, he would have to forfeit the car, and not only the car, but all the money he had already paid.

'But can they legally do that?' asked Lady Franklin.

Leadbitter took a chance.

'Unfortunately they can, my lady.'

Lady Franklin tried to see what this would mean to him.

'And what will you do?'

Leadbitter shrugged his broad shoulders.

'Try to get a job as driver with another car-hire firm. It won't be very easy because they don't like a man who's been on his own. I've got my customers of course, and they're an asset – some of them would go with me to the new firm. But I shouldn't be able to serve them personally, same as I do now. For instance, I shouldn't be able to serve you, my lady. You'd have to take whoever they sent, it might be me, but ten to one it wouldn't be.'

'I should be very disappointed,' said Lady Franklin, rather grandly, 'and so I'm sure would all your customers.'

'Yes, I think they would be. They've got used to me, you see, and I've got used to them. Getting used to someone means a lot, and it takes time. I was working up a nice little business; in three years I should have had my own car, and in another couple of years I could have bought another car and hired a man to drive it. Seven years from now, if things had gone well, I might have had two men working for me. Now I've got to go back to being a hired man myself at four pound ten a week, and no prospect of starting again for years, if ever. The little bit of money I'd put by, my war gratuity it was, I've lost. Well, it's just too bad. A man doesn't like to think himself a failure but I'm not the only one. Several fellows I know have started on their own and had to go back to wage-earning, because they couldn't stand the pace, but I thought I'd be lucky.'

The saga of the Leadbitter family life unrolled itself before Lady Franklin's eyes, the touching scenes, the developing domestic happiness, suddenly ending – how?

'Will this make a great difference to your life at home?' she asked.

'Indeed it will, my lady,' Leadbitter said grimly. 'We shall have to look for cheaper quarters right away. I haven't told my wife yet, though she's guessed something is wrong, because I couldn't eat my breakfast.'

'When will you tell her?' Lady Franklin asked. She couldn't help identifying herself with Mrs Leadbitter, and wondering how many hours of blessed ignorance the poor woman still had.

'Tonight, I shouldn't wonder, when the children are tucked up in bed.'

Lady Franklin had a vision of their rosy faces half hidden in the deep dents of the pillows, and thought of the imminent fall in their standard of comfort. They were too young to take it in, perhaps; but Mrs Leadbitter –

'Will your wife mind very much?' she asked.

Leadbitter's chin dropped a little.

'She will, my lady. It'll half kill her. She never wanted me to take the plunge, of starting on my own, I mean. She thought it was too risky. She's one of the cautious type. But when I'd taken it she was as pleased as Punch. She won't say "I told you so", she'll stand by me, of course. But it'll break her heart. For myself I don't mind so much. I'm used to roughing it, and I don't mind what the neighbours say, let them get on with it. But she will, she won't like dropping in the social scale, no woman does. She's rather house-proud, but I told you that.'

Tears came into Lady Franklin's eyes, and for the first time for many months they were not tears for herself. Through the thick defences of her own sadness she was pierced by the sadness of the outside world, a sadness unrelated to and greater than her own. It was for Mrs Leadbitter that she felt the most; men were still shadows to her. But she felt for Leadbitter too, wounded in his masculine pride, but taking it all so stoically.

He saw her distress.

'I oughtn't to have told you, my lady,' he said. 'I didn't really mean to. But when you get used to somebody, things – well they just slip out. You'd have had to know sooner or later, though, when I didn't turn up with the car.'

This was Leadbitter's boldest throw. How he was going to account for the fact that he would turn up with the car the next time Lady Franklin ordered it, if she did order it, he himself didn't know. It was also, for its effect on Lady Franklin, a master-stroke. Suddenly she felt deprived, deprived of something whose importance she hadn't realized, her expeditions with Leadbitter, a streak of vivid life within the greyness. She had begun to look forward to these outings and to the vicarious form of living which consisted in listening to the annals of the Leadbitters. Now she had nothing to look forward to – nor had they. Am I a *porte-malheur*, she wondered, do I bring bad luck? The horrible thought began to slide into her being; she felt it dropping, like a wicked seed, into that steaming hot-bed which nourished such monstrous growths. The fear was physical; she moved, she clutched her bag, she opened it – anything to distract herself – and her eyes lit on her cheque-book, that long, thin, pale-green talisman.

'May I give you something?' she said to Leadbitter. 'Would you accept a present from me?'

He thought a moment.

'I should be a fool, madam,' he said, forgetting the 'my lady' though his voice was steady, 'if I didn't. I hope I'm not such a fool as that.'

'I've no idea how much would be any use,' said Lady Franklin. 'Ten pounds, fifty pounds, a hundred?'

Leadbitter didn't lose his head.

'A hundred pounds would be a help,' he said.

Lady Franklin heard the reservation in his voice. Of course a hundred pounds wouldn't be enough. What was a hundred pounds? It wouldn't keep her two houses going for a week. What a paltry sum to offer a man whose livelihood was at stake! Whose wife and children, whom she knew as well as if she had seen and talked to them, were threatened with privation? What could have possessed her to be so mean? Her heart swelled with the joy of giving, swelled almost to bursting, like a fruit when ripeness overtakes it. She seemed to feel vents and fissures opening through which her spirit breathed. The relief of action became imperative: she couldn't even if she had wanted to, have delayed it. They must be running into London, for houses lined the road: otherwise she had no idea where they were.

'May we stop?' she asked. Despite her regal moments she had never learned the habit of command: her habit was to ask permission.

Leadbitter didn't answer, but the next thing she knew the car was at a standstill.

What am I going to do? she thought. She was paralysed, she could not move, and why? Because she had the Franklins up against her, her solicitors and her trustees against her, her own youth with its straitened means, against her. She had signed large cheques many times, of course, but only when she had been told to. Wealth had not exorcised her fear of money; she thought in terms of petty cash, not large lump sums. She had sometimes given such sums to charity, but charity was a collective object with a headquarters somewhere, not one man sitting beside her in a car. What would they say, this cloud of hostile witnesses, to her mad act of extravagance?

The conflict deepened in her, seemed to split her in two. She felt as if her childhood was being torn out of her. She lost sight of the issue; she only knew that she was fighting for her right to be herself. She triumphed, she looked out through other eyes, the eyes of a freed slave. They lighted on the cheque-book and the pen. But all else fled from her mind, even the driver's name.

'Whom shall I make it out to?' she said, flushing at the absurd contretemps.

His eyes released from the tyranny of the road, he turned and looked at her. How pretty she was, with this new warmth in her voice and the softness in her face.

'Were you going to write a cheque, my lady?' he asked, in a neutral voice and as if he was not concerned in it.

'Well yes, to you.'

'The name is Leadbitter,' he said.

'Oh yes, of course.' How could she have forgotten? 'I meant your initials.'

'S.'

'What does "S" stand for?' she asked him, her pen poised.

He hesitated.

'Stephen. You asked me once before, my lady, and I told you.' He sounded hurt.

Lady Franklin was horrified at herself. To have asked his name, to have been told his name, and to have forgotten it! Contrition pricked her; the sum she had in mind now didn't seem enough; she added to it. Released by the act of giving, a sudden rush of love for the whole world possessed her. Her heart melted. She felt as if she had found a treasure, not bestowed one. Signing the cheque with the initial E before her name, as was her habit, she folded it across the middle and put it into Leadbitter's hand.

'With my best wishes,' she said.

'Thank you very much, my lady.'

To her surprise and rather to her disappointment he did not unfold the cheque to see how much it was for, he slipped it into the slot behind the driving-wheel, as unconcernedly as if it had been the confirmatory copy of a telegram. But when they had gone a little way he slowed down and drew Lady Franklin's attention to a vast, grey, many-balconied building that was rising on their left. 'Those are some new flats the Council is putting up,' he said. 'They've got all the latest gadgets. When my wife saw them she went hopping mad with envy.' And while Lady Franklin was straining her eyes and trying to imagine what it would be like to live there, he deftly unfolded the cheque and saw the figures in the lower right-hand corner, and turned pale.

Having satisfied her scrutiny Lady Franklin turned her head, meaning to make a comment; her great blue eyes, surprised at last into seeing, rested on Leadbitter's gun-metal ones.

'Why, you look as if you had seen a ghost!' she said, with the new intimacy she was beginning to feel with every living thing.

'Perhaps I did, my lady,' Leadbitter said.

'I hope it was a nice one?'

'I wouldn't mind seeing another like it,' said Leadbitter, with more than his usual gruffness.

Lady Franklin sighed, happy in her happiness and his.

For the rest of the journey their conversation flagged. Leadbitter said nothing about the cheque and therefore could not allude to the change it was going to make in his domestic situation. Inwardly he was much too excited to have invented a new instalment to the family saga, and in any case Lady Franklin wouldn't expect one until he had had time to break the news.

The same evening Leadbitter rang up the agency to which he was paying the instalments for his car and announced that he was now in a position to buy it outright. He was all impatience to have the deal concluded, but there were certain formalities to be gone through first, and it was not until three days later that he was able to call the car his own.

Chapter 9

THE telephone bell rang and a voice which Leadbitter recognized with the immediate certainty of dislike said:

'This is Lady Franklin's butler speaking. Her ladyship says would you be good enough to call for her with the car next Tuesday morning at ten o'clock.'

'Ten o'clock!' said Leadbitter. 'That's rather early for you to be about, isn't it?'

'Those were her ladyship's wishes,' said the butler, ignoring this. 'Shall I tell her ladyship that you will be able to comply?'

Leadbitter consulted the engagement-sheet in the photograph frame. At half past nine on Tuesday morning he was to take a fare to the Airport. It was a new customer whom he didn't want to disappoint. The claims of new customers were brighter than the claims of old ones, and he was always having to weigh the one against the other. But Lady Franklin had a special claim and he would give the Airport job to someone else.

'All right,' he said. 'I'll be there, if you are. How long does Lady Franklin want me for?'

'Her ladyship didn't say.'

'That's all right,' grumbled Leadbitter, 'but I have my living to earn. I don't just stand and wait. Couldn't you find out?'

After a pause the butler came back. 'Her ladyship would like the car for the whole morning if' (he added grudgingly) 'you are free.'

'Do you know where she's going?' Leadbitter asked.

'Her ladyship has not informed me,' said the butler, 'but I think she intends to do some shopping.'

Shopping, thought Leadbitter, that's a new one on me. In

all his experience of Lady Franklin she had never taken him shopping. It was one of her merits as a customer, for he did not like to take women shopping. Shopping, they were at their worst, slow, undecided, changeable, exacting, and above all unpunctual. As a sightseer Lady Franklin was not too bad, but as a shopper! And she would expect him to tell her how his family had reacted to her gift, the threats of suicide it had removed, the blessings it had called down on her. And how was he to do this, dodging in and out of Bond Street? Why, it was murder, even without a customer. Yet she would certainly want her bed-time story, and in a way, he had to admit, she was entitled to it. Well, he would have to do his best, and keep a double guard on his irritable tongue.

But it was another Lady Franklin, not the one he knew, who came tripping down the steps, her face alight with smiles. The smiles were there before they reached him, but when she saw him they multiplied and broadened, as if he, Leadbitter, had called them into being. He felt his own face relaxing as he gave her his best salute. Yes, she was transformed. He could hardly remember her shut-up look; she was full of herself – the glum, dumb parasite that fed upon her spirit, had been banished. How could he have known that all this radiance was not so much for him, as for the gift which had somehow given her back to herself? He didn't know, but for a moment he watched her narrowly. When she had told him where to go she said:

'Is everything all right now?'

At this he gave her one of his rare smiles, and said:

'Well, it ought to be, my lady. I didn't know there was so much kindness in the world.'

'Oh, please don't speak of it,' cried Lady Franklin, gratified beyond words. She, the source of the world's kindness? Oh no, the sin of pride! Think quickly of someone else. 'And your wife?' she asked.

Leadbitter looked again at Lady Franklin before he answered, as though to take his cue from her.

'Oh, she's all over herself, my lady! You wouldn't recognize her – it's all the difference between a long face and a round one. But' (even at this moment his misogyny got the better of him) 'you know what women are, she isn't *quite* content –'

'Of course not,' Lady Franklin said, as if to be quite content would have been a fault, 'how *could* she be? If you get rid of one set of troubles, another takes their place. *I'm* not quite content either – I'm like your wife in that way, too – though I feel better this morning than I have for years – better in *myself*, whatever that means! As if one could be better in someone else! And yet,' she mused, 'I suppose one could, I suppose one could! You have done me a lot of good, I don't know how, but you have! I could almost say I was better in yourself, but that would be nonsense, wouldn't it? But I know that when I say the word "myself", or think it, both of which I do all too often, it means something quite different to me now from what it did a week ago! It used to be a terrible bugbear to me, that word, my heart sank when I said it or thought it! Myself! It was like saying my prison, my torture-chamber almost, or does that sound too dramatic? – but something I was condemned to stay in, and never should get out of! But you have never suffered from your nerves, have you?'

'I should hope not, my lady,' Leadbitter said, little realizing how much he suffered from them. 'But I once knew a chap whose nerves stuck out eight inches and were curly at the edges.'

Lady Franklin smiled half-heartedly. 'Then you won't understand, and I hope you never will, what it means to be the prisoner of oneself, a self one doesn't like and that doesn't like one! One's self is a blackmailer that can never be paid off. I'm sure you know what I mean. But now I can get away whenever I like – touch wood,' and Lady Franklin looked for a piece of wood. It seemed to be all painted tin, cold to the touch; but she only laughed. 'And do you know where I can escape to most easily? It sounds fantastic to say it, and you'll never believe me, but it's into *your* life, the life you've been telling me about, your life with your family! Somehow it's become as real to me as my own, perhaps more real, your trials and triumphs and so on! You've done that for me and I'm infinitely grateful!'

'And I'm very grateful to you, my lady,' Leadbitter put in, soberly.

'Oh that, oh well! But what is money? Excuse me, I know it is a great deal, but it isn't everything, it doesn't unlock the door of the prison, in fact it sometimes locks it! When you get rich, as I hope you soon will, you may even find that yourself, so be warned.' (It would take a good deal of money to lock the door on me, thought Leadbitter.) 'But don't imagine,' she went on, perhaps sensing something critical in his thought of her, 'don't imagine that just because I can escape ... well, to you, as it were, that I'm going to be a permanent visitor, a sort of paying guest, or paying ghost' (she reddened at the reference to money) 'in your home circle, just because you've made my thoughts at home there! I'm going to inflict myself on my other friends as well. The day after tomorrow I'm going to a party, the first party I've been to since my husband died, and I'm really looking forward to it! That's why I'm going shopping now, to try to make myself a little presentable!'

She broke off, and Leadbitter found that the thought of Lady Franklin going to a party didn't altogether please him.

'When will that be, my lady?' he asked practically. 'And shall you need the car?'

'Oh I don't think so,' said Lady Franklin. 'It's so near I could almost walk. It would do me good to walk.'

Leadbitter didn't like the idea of Lady Franklin on foot.

'I'm afraid you'll have to walk now, my lady,' he said a little crisply, 'because they won't let me wait here. You'll find me in Park Street, but they'll only let me wait there twenty minutes.'

'Oh why must people make things so difficult?' moaned Lady Franklin, pretending despair but really made more radiant by the difficulty. In her new mood, any setback seemed the greatest fun. 'I won't be more than twenty minutes, I promise you.'

Leadbitter helped her out and went off to the meeting-place. The twenty minutes passed, the police moved him on, and he began to cruise round the neighbouring streets, a way of killing time that he especially loathed. When, three-quarters of an hour later, he drew up at the kerb where Lady Franklin was standing, smiling ruefully, he didn't think he would be able to smile back; but found he could.

The days passed and he saw nor hide nor hair of Lady Franklin. What had happened to her? She was doing a round of parties, he supposed. Well let her get on with it; he had plenty of other customers, though he still had gaps in his engagement list which a country jaunt with Lady Franklin would have conveniently and profitably filled.

But he couldn't put her out of his mind. Had he 'done anything', he asked himself, to annoy her? No; in spite of a good deal of provocation, his behaviour when he had taken her out shopping had been, he knew, exemplary. At these parties that she went to, blast them, had she been recommended another driver who pleased her better? Customers were notoriously fickle. Had her butler rung him up when he was out, or when the man he paid to answer the telephone (the clerk was a new departure, made possible by Lady Franklin's bounty) was off duty? Did she feel she had done enough for him, or too much, and now avoided him because he reminded her of her folly – once bit, twice shy?

The fact of owning his car no longer elated him as once it had, but it did remind him, on and off, of Lady Franklin. It was like a substitute for her in terms of money. Well, what of that? The first time he was alone with her cheque he had felt as clever, as trimphant, as pleased with himself as if he had stolen the car from her – as in a way he had: he had certainly got it out of her on false pretences. The Leadbitter family chronicle! How greedily she had swallowed that bait! And how, for a day or two, he had despised her for it – no, not exactly despised her, but seen in the whole episode a too easy vindication of his cynicism. It had been as simple as falling off a log. So why did he now feel aggrieved with her, as if after making him this handsome present she had no right to remove herself, as if by giving him the car she had actually put herself in his debt and owed him something? Owed him what? Her presence, he supposed, her continued custom. But why on earth –! All the same when he thought of her at those parties, tripping about with this glad new smile on her face (which he would gladly have wiped off) calling and being called darling by a gang of socialites, he felt not only disgusted but hurt. That smile, which he (so she said) had put there, was the beginning of the trouble. Smiling on parade! With that smile she had dismissed him, signified that she had no further use for him. Good-bye, Mr Chips! It haunted him, her smile.

Chapter 10

One day he received a telephone call (or rather his man did, Leadbitter was out) asking him to pick up a party at an address in Chelsea, take them out to Richmond, wait while they had dinner, and bring them back. Quite a good job: his clerk had booked it for him.

Leadbitter called for the man first. He was the artist type, tall, young, loosely built, with greenish eyes and auburn locks and a beard. Leadbitter took against him at sight, but he was an impartial judge of a man and he had to admit that as a man, if you cared for that type, this one made the grade. He had a pleasant, musical voice, cultivated without being affected, and an assurance of being liked which showed itself in his movements. He asked Leadbitter to go to an address on Campden Hill, and there he got out, rang the bell, and waited on the doorstep. Here he was joined, as Leadbitter expected, by a woman. She, too, was tall, nearly as tall as he, with bronze hair, wide, high cheek-bones and an air of breeding. (Leadbitter prided himself on being able to pick out the blue-blooded ones.) From the moment of their greeting Leadbitter took for granted that the two were lovers of old standing, there was just that amount of passion in their kiss. In the woman's he detected something maternal; in the man's an uncertain ardour. She's older than he is and she wears the pants, he thought, and yet she isn't too sure of him. Indifferent as he was, in a sense, to human beings Leadbitter had seen so many embraces, so much face-tasting, as he termed it – that he knew exactly what degree of intimacy each implied.

The man gave him the name of a hotel in Richmond.

'Well,' said the woman when they were both settled in

the back seat, 'this is a surprise – a delightful surprise, of course. But why the extravagance, Hughie? Why the car? Since when have you become a millionaire?'

Hughie (Cantrip was his surname, Leadbitter remembered) laughed and said:

'I've had a stroke of luck since we last met.'

'I wondered if you had, but knowing your impulsive temperament –'

'Nothing's too good for you,' he said.

She sighed. It was a happy sigh but with a touch of impatience in it. Women are never satisfied, thought Leadbitter, who could see the couple in his mirror.

'I'm not looking the gift-horse in the mouth,' she answered. 'It's sweet of you and I'm not going to scold you. But tell me about this stroke of luck: where did it happen, and how?'

'It happened at a party,' Hughie said. 'As a matter of fact, you were there, too.'

'Was I?'

'Yes, Connie, you were.'

'Don't call me that awful name, or I shall think you hate me.'

'Well, Constance, then.'

'That's better, but you haven't told me.'

'I was coming to it when you interrupted me. It was at the Portingsales, that party that they gave for Ernestine.'

'To celebrate her return to the world?'

'Yes,' said Hughie. 'That was the idea. You were there, too. You know her, don't you?'

'I used to know her a little in the old days, before she became rich, and then I saw her once or twice before her breakdown. I could never take her quite seriously as a person: she never seemed quite real to me. Rich people never do.'

'Why not?'

'Oh, I don't know. Their problems are not the same as ours, and all that freedom of action – it's like a fairy-tale.

They float around, they don't belong – there are not enough of them, now, to make a social unit. They are an anachronism, a vestigial survival, like one's appendix, or one's tail, if one had a tail. Besides, thinking of her case, anything to do with nerves is unreal, really.'

'What do you mean by "unreal, really"?'

'Darling, you know quite well what I mean. And her name, Ernestine, isn't a real name, somehow.'

'It's real at the bottom of a cheque.'

'Oh, so you've seen it there?'

'No, not her name but her initial.'

'Don't keep me on tenterhooks, please, Hughie.'

'Well, I was introduced to her.'

'But I thought you knew her? You spoke of her by her Christian name.'

'But don't we all, nowadays? You are old-fashioned, Constance. I was introduced to her and I told her I was a painter.'

'You said that was your line?'

'Don't tease me,' Hughie said. 'And she seemed, well ... she seemed to take an interest.'

'I don't suppose she knows many painters.'

'She said she didn't. She said she was quite excited meeting me.'

'I can't make any comment on that.'

'You don't remember what it was like, to meet me for the first time.'

'Oh yes, I do,' said Constance. 'And then she asked you to paint her?'

'No, she didn't.'

'Wise woman.'

'How horrid you are, Constance. I'm tired of asking you to let me paint you.'

'You can do anything you like with me except paint me, Hughie dear. I have to draw the line somewhere. But that's just what you *can't* do – draw a line, I mean. I like you in every way, as you well know, except as a painter. You would have been a good painter if you had never painted – did I invent that?'

'No,' said Hughie promptly. 'You had the help of Tacitus. I could put it into Latin for you: *Omnium consensu, capax pingendi, nisi pinxisset.*'

'How clever you are!' breathed Constance admiringly. 'What a promising classical scholar was lost in you.'

'That's another buried Latin tag – Nero, this time. You're not very original. Couldn't you even pretend to like my painting?'

'I can lie about anything,' said Constance energetically, 'but not about Art. There I must speak my mind. But if she didn't ask you to paint her, why the cheque?'

'I was coming to that when you started insulting me.'

'I'm sorry. Please go on – I'm all attention now.'

'She asked me to paint her husband.'

'But he's dead – that's what all the fuss has been about.'

'I know, she told me. She seemed rather ashamed of it – the fuss, I mean. She said her friends had been very patient with her. She's extraordinarily forthcoming, isn't she, bubbling over, uncontrollably effervescent?'

'She was once, then she shut up like a clam.'

'She was most forthcoming with me. Almost embarrassingly so. She seemed quite light-headed.'

'That was the cocktails, perhaps.'

'I think it was me. . . . Anyhow, she asked me to paint her husband.'

'Is she going to have him exhumed?'

'No, from a photograph.'

'A spirit photograph, of course?'

'No, a real one.'

Constance registered horror. 'You couldn't sink as low as that!'

'Why not? Many better men than I (as you'd agree) have painted from a photograph. Sickert, for instance.'

'That was all right for Sickert.'

Hughie said rather sulkily, 'Anyhow, she gave me the commission.'

'Well, I do congratulate you, Hughie darling,' Constance said, with sudden warmth. 'It's really marvellous, isn't it? I couldn't be more pleased. And you'll have all the advantages and none of the drawbacks. You won't have to gate-crash somebody's house, you can sit quietly in your studio with a subject that doesn't move –'

'But I'm going to paint it in her house,' Hughie said.

'Oh, in her house?'

'Yes, in the room where the photograph was taken. She's kept it exactly as it was.'

'I see.'

'I'm to begin tomorrow.'

'I see. ... But why has she paid you in advance? Is that usual?'

'No, sometimes they don't pay at all. But she gathered I was hard up.'

'She gathered?'

'Well, you only have to look at me.'

Constance did look at him, and they embraced, as Leadbitter felt sure they would. Indeed, he thought the moment had been unconscionably delayed. When it was all over, Constance said:

'I feel a little bit jealous. You mustn't fall for her, you know.'

'Fall for her? It wouldn't be any good. She's quite, quite unawakened.'

'How do you know?'

'I made inquiries ... besides, I could see for myself.'

'Darling, I must admit that for *some* purposes you have a painter's eye.'

Again they fell into an embrace. When they came out of it, Constance, arranging herself, said brightly:

'What a nice car this is.' She spoke with surprise, as if she hadn't realized until now that they were in a car. 'How did you discover it?'

'Somebody told me – a chap called Fullerton. You know him, don't you?' he added, addressing the back of Leadbitter's head.

'Yes, sir, I do his driving sometimes.'

'Well, he put me on to it.'

'Well, I'm grateful to him, and grateful to you, darling, and grateful to Ernestine. What a lot of gratitude! We must drink her health when we get to Richmond.'

To all this Leadbitter listened with half an ear, as he generally listened to the conversation of his customers when it was not addressed directly to him. He didn't listen all the time, nor did he connect the Ernestine that they were talking about with anyone he knew.

Chapter 11

THE telephone bell rang, and a woman's voice which he recognized yet couldn't quite place, said:

'Is that Mr Leadbitter?'

'Leadbitter speaking,' he answered.

'Oh, Mr Leadbitter, this is Lady Franklin.'

Of course it was and he should have known. Yet never before had she rung him up herself; and her voice sounded different from the voice he used to know, the dull, tired voice; it was happy and excited.

'Oh good morning, my lady,' Leadbitter said, and was surprised by the warmth in his own voice. And then he allowed himself a phrase he rarely used to customers. 'Nice to hear you,' he said.

'And very nice to hear you,' said Lady Franklin, with a slight emphasis, he thought, upon the 'you'. 'I was afraid you'd think I had forgotten you – not' (she hastily took herself up) 'that I flattered myself that you would regard that as a great disaster, because I know your customers are falling over each other, but all the same I shouldn't like you to think I'd forgotten all the pleasant times we'd had together – besides, they did me so much good. Frankly, I owe you more than I can ever say. It may sound exaggerated, but you brought me back to life. I'm a different creature now.'

'Very glad to hear it, my lady,' Leadbitter said. 'Not that there was much wrong with you before, that I could see.'

'Ah, but there was. Now there were two things I wanted to ask you. First, how is the family? It seems so long since I had news of them.'

Leadbitter looked helplessly round his bachelor apartment, where dearth of domesticity amounted to a famine.

Lacking Lady Franklin's physical presence, he could think of nothing new to say about his family. Their shapes refused to take material form: his mind's eye could not see them.

'They're fine, my lady,' he said. 'They couldn't help being, after what you did for them.'

'Oh, that was nothing. I want to hear all about them, but that must be for another time, which brings me to my second question. Can you take me out again tomorrow week? Thursday, that is? I want to go to Winchester – it's the only cathedral within reach that we haven't seen. I know you don't care about them very much, but . . .'

'Just let me look, my lady,' Leadbitter said, ignoring the question of cathedrals. He knew that Thursday was free; but it was never wise to seem too eager or give a customer the impression that he was disengaged; so he consulted the sheet on the photograph frame before he answered.

'Thursday will be all right, my lady.'

'I'm so glad,' said Lady Franklin, and by her voice she did indeed sound glad. 'Could you come at ten o'clock? I get up earlier now – that's another thing you've done for me. I owe you my virtues, you see, as well as my happiness. And don't forget to bring me the latest, stop-press news about your family.'

'I won't forget, my lady,' Leadbitter promised her.

Lady Franklin was rich, Lady Franklin was lonely – did she feel herself neglected as regards male attachments? Was she in love with him? During his career as a driver two or three women customers had fallen for Leadbitter, and declared their passion; but they had not paid him in advance for his services, and in any case he would have turned them down. Sex played little part in his life; he wanted to get on in the world, and how could he get on with a parcel of women hanging round his neck, making scenes and accusing him of cruelty? Most of them, after one rebuff, had ceased to employ him, and except by chance, they never crossed his path again. They were, as customers, a dead loss; even more of a loss than those who would not take 'no' for an answer, these were, from the point of view of building up a connexion, still more undesirable in the long run. The gain, if there was any, was out of proportion to the trouble and embarrassment. With what relief, after such an irksome encounter, did he return to himself and his invulnerable heart! He was aware of possessing it only when someone, greatly daring, tried to thaw it.

But Lady Franklin was different, or seemed to be. She had made no overtures to him; he was an expert in such matters, but he hadn't noticed a trace of flirtatiousness in her manner when she gave him the cheque. Yet she was always thanking him, always letting him know how much she owed him, and somewhere, he believed, she had a tender feeling for him; she wouldn't have parted with so much money unless she had. But strangely enough, the idea that Lady Franklin was in love with him didn't bore and exasperate him as it would have in the case of other women.

His motto was to give his customers what they wanted. If Lady Franklin wanted what she seemed to want, why shouldn't she have it? If another cheque was the result, so much the better; and if it wasn't, no great harm would have been done.

All the same, when Thursday came, Leadbitter, who was accustomed to execute his own orders as promptly as he executed other people's, found himself hesitating. He was a man who often changed his mind, for a soldier has to change his mind when circumstances demand it: he may even have to retreat when the odds are against him. But he was seldom in two minds at once, for a divided mind is fatal to a military operation. If an enemy position has to be taken, it must either be attacked or left alone. Lady Franklin was that enemy position, and he couldn't make up his mind about it.

Her greeting had been all that he could have wished for.

Even under the cold, disapproving eye of the butler whose face always seemed to contract when Leadbitter appeared, she had not disguised her pleasure at seeing him again. And how differently she was dressed! Gone was the blue and white uniform, suggesting convents, hospitals; under her fur coat she was all done up (he thought) like a dog's eye-brows. And her shoes, that showed her toes! Half shrinking, half desiring, his skin reacted to them. If all this was not for him, who was it for? 'Isn't it three weeks,' she prattled when she was seated at his side and the car had glided off, 'three weeks since you last took me out?'

'Three weeks and two days, my lady,' Leadbitter replied.

'How nice of you to have counted the days!' said Lady Franklin. 'They have been such busy days for me. Well, perhaps I oughtn't to say busy, when you are so much busier than I am, in the true sense of the word. But they have been very full days, full of social engagements, going here and there. But they have been very happy days, too, very happy.'

For some reason Leadbitter wasn't pleased to be told that Lady Franklin had been spending happy days, but he dutifully answered:

'I'm very glad to hear it, my lady.'

'Oh yes. Oh well, you know what it is when one comes back to something after a long absence, something that one used to enjoy, but for one reason and another hasn't been able to enjoy – social life, I mean. It's quite gone to my head, seeing all my friends again and finding them unchanged and still fond of me, or saying so, at any rate. You know they've made quite a fuss of me,' she said, turning on Leadbitter her great blue eyes, which now looked larger than they used to.

'I'm very glad to hear it,' repeated Leadbitter.

'Oh yes, and they might have been rather chilly with me, or at any rate distant and uninterested, because I hadn't wanted to see them because – well, you know why. They must have thought me unfeeling and even rude, but somehow I couldn't. I see now it was wrong to have wrapped myself in my grief – selfish really. What would happen to the world if everyone who had – well, lost someone who was dear to them – shut themselves up and moped? Life would come to a standstill. I'm sure that you, for instance, would put a good face on it, however much you suffered.'

For a second Leadbitter tried to think of someone whose loss might make him suffer, and he nearly laughed. A lost customer, yes, a lost customer did upset him, but only for a time.

'I expect it's just a question of getting used to it, my lady,' he said.

Lady Franklin gave him a sly smile.

'That's your panacea, isn't it?' she said. 'But you know, I think you're wrong. I *was* getting used to it; that was the trouble: I *was* getting used to my – well, my unhappiness, let's call it. I was getting used to it and I didn't really want it to end! In a way, I'm sure you can understand? – it was a sort of protection to me. It seemed to answer every question, in the negative, and I'm lazy, I hate answering questions! At least I did then. And it was an excuse for everything, for everything I didn't want to do, and there was nothing that I wanted to do! It was a sort of labyrinth,' she said, frowning, 'a labyrinth without a clue, and as you were saying, I got used to it. But you showed me the way out,' she added, brightening, 'and I can never tell you how grateful I am.'

'That's all right, my lady,' Leadbitter said.

'Yes, but it isn't. I wish there was something I could do for you.'

'You've done a great deal for me,' said Leadbitter. 'I shouldn't be sitting where I am, sitting pretty, to coin a phrase, if it wasn't for you. I shouldn't be' – he was going to say 'owning my own car' but stopped and substituted 'my own master' – 'if it wasn't for you. And I shouldn't be driving you, either.'

'I gave you money,' Lady Franklin said, 'that's easy. But

you gave me happiness, which isn't easy. How can you compare the two?'

'You saved me from unhappiness,' said Leadbitter. 'Isn't that the same?'

'Well, perhaps it is. I shall try to think it is. You know, I've missed you very much these last few weeks.'

'Missed me, my lady?' Leadbitter said.

'You sound so surprised,' said Lady Franklin. 'But don't heaps of people miss you? Your wife, for instance, and Don and Pat and Susie? I'm sure they miss you all the time. And now, please tell me about them. Tell me everything – I can't wait to hear. Just one more Canterbury tale. I'm dying of news-starvation.'

Leadbitter's gun-metal eyes narrowed. He tried to jerk his mind back from other things that were nearer and more real, to the contemplation of his fictitious family. Not a word would come. Hoping for inspiration he glanced at Lady Franklin.

'Well my wife –' he began uncertainly.

'Yes, Frances,' Lady Franklin prompted him.

'Well, Frances –' he looked at Lady Franklin again, almost bewildered, and waited for the electric spark to leap between them.

'Yes, Frances,' Lady Franklin repeated, amused and half impatient. 'I see I shall have to jog your memory! But,' she added, suddenly contrite, 'it's so long ago! No wonder you've forgotten. All my fault! Lunches, cocktail parties, dinners, it didn't seem worth while – worth your while, I mean – to drag you out for them, when you might have been doing much more interesting things, more profitable too, I'm sure!' She gave Leadbitter's stern profile an appealing look. 'And how could we have talked? It would have been so disjointed – you couldn't have got going! And I should have felt so frustrated! But I can tell you just where you left off: things at home had been easier, you told me, easier in a way, but Susie had got chicken-pox and now your wife was worried in case the others caught it. You said

I needn't be afraid of you, of contact with you, I mean – because you'd had it.'

'That's right,' said Leadbitter, to gain time. 'I've had it.'

The words had an ominous ring.

'Well, did they catch it?' Lady Franklin asked.

'No, they didn't,' said Leadbitter. 'They didn't,' he repeated more confidently. 'They . . . they just escaped.'

Lady Franklin laughed.

'How do you know they "just" escaped? Still, a miss is good as a mile. So now your wife is happier?'

'Oh yes,' said Leadbitter lugubriously. 'She's as happy as a sandboy.'

'But don't you want her to be happy?' Lady Franklin asked.

'Of course I do,' said Leadbitter, who hardly knew what he was saying. In another minute he would give the whole show away. Furtively he stole another look at Lady Franklin, as a schoolboy might at his crib, and at last his imagination began to work. 'I do want her to be happy,' he said, 'but not too happy, if you see what I mean.'

'I'm not sure I do see,' Lady Franklin said.

'Well, she thinks that because we've got this money – I didn't tell her where it came from, of course –'

'I thought you did tell her,' said Lady Franklin, puzzled.

'No,' said Leadbitter firmly. 'I told her I won it at the football pools.'

'But why?'

'Because she might have been jealous.'

'I see,' said Lady Franklin. 'I hadn't thought of that.' She glanced at Leadbitter to whose appearance one could only deny the word beauty because the soldier in him repudiated it – and realized, perhaps for the first time, that he was a man of whom a wife might well be jealous.

Leadbitter waited for her reaction.

'Perhaps you were right,' she said. 'I . . . I . . .' her voice faltered and died away. How explain that Mrs Leadbitter the chauffeur's wife, had no need to be jealous of Lady

Franklin? Leadbitter noticed her hesitation, but did not guess its cause.

'My wife is of a jealous disposition,' he said, 'I shouldn't know why. But what I was going to say to you, my lady, was that now we're so much better off, thanks to you, and not the football pools,' he added jokingly, 'she thinks that everything in the garden's lovely. She's forgotten about Stuck Street. She's bought new sprauncy clothes for the children and herself, she calls on the neighbours, she's out half the time and doesn't answer the telephone, and when I start cribbing she just laughs – that's what I mean by being too happy.'

'I see,' said Lady Franklin, not seeing that the parable was meant for her but aware of the cloud on Leadbitter's strong features. 'I told you, didn't I – I think we agreed – that money only alters the form of one's troubles.'

'Don't think I'd be without it,' said Leadbitter, hastily. 'It's made all the difference to me, my lady. What I meant was, that being so happy, I can't do for her what I used to do, she's grown a bit independent, so to speak. Whatever *I* feel like, she's still happy.'

Lady Franklin thought a moment and saw to her dismay that her happiness might not be a boon to others, to Leadbitter, for instance, to whom she owed it. Smitten with contrition, she exclaimed:

'Oh, but you mustn't think that! Happiness does make people selfish, I dare say, but so does sorrow. Wasn't I selfish when you first met me?'

It was the most intimate thing she had ever said to Leadbitter.

'I wouldn't say that, my lady,' he said carefully. 'You were a bit shut up in yourself, like we all are at times, and I...'

He paused.

'Go on,' said Lady Franklin.

'I sort of tried to help you out of it.'

'You did indeed,' said Lady Franklin, thinking again of

Leadbitter the liberator and unaware of the warmth of her words. 'And now that I am out of it, don't you like me better?'

'There's not so much for me to do, my lady, now. It isn't quite the same.'

'But of course it is! I rely on you more than ever!' cried Lady Franklin, conscience-stricken, feeling she had treated Leadbitter very badly. Just because his feelings seemed so hard to hurt, she was the more afraid of hurting them. 'I want to hear about everything that has happened to you since ... since we were last together.'

Put like that, it sounded very intimate. Again the Leadbitter family history fled from his mind.

'Where was I?' he asked gruffly.

'Don and Pat had just escaped chicken-pox, and Mrs Leadbitter – Frances – was being a little bit more social than you liked.'

'Oh yes,' said Leadbitter, in a discouraged voice. 'Well, after that –' he began heavily.

The recital dragged. In spite of, or perhaps because of, Lady Franklin's nearness, his imagination would not feed his tongue: it halted: and Lady Franklin, though she listened with ardour, prompting him with her eyes, was secretly a little bored.

But all the more did she feel guilty towards him; he was her benefactor and she had neglected him; and when they got to Winchester she said, on a sudden impulse:

'Now this time, please, you really must come with me into the Cathedral. I insist on it! I shall feel quite hurt if you don't!'

He took off his peaked cap and dropped it between the front seat and the back seat, out of view. Lady Franklin had not noticed this manoeuvre; as he opened the door she looked up and saw him standing bare-headed.

'Why!' she exclaimed staring up into his face, 'I've never seen you without your cap before! I shouldn't have recognized you! You look quite different!'

'Do I, my lady?' Leadbitter fixed on her his riot-quelling eyes. Then with a burst of confidence he said, 'I've worn a peaked cap nearly all my life. As I was going to be with you, I thought –'

She finished the sentence for him.

'You'd rather be in mufti?'

He nodded.

'Well, I must say it suits you!' Lady Franklin said, not disguising from Leadbitter the man the admiration she owed to Leadbitter, the Perseus, the deliverer. 'Not that your cap doesn't suit you, but now –' What should she say? – 'Now I feel I really *know* you! It's a great shame,' she added, 'when anyone has hair as nice as yours, to cover it up!'

Leadbitter's dark hair waved naturally and grew down to a peak on his forehead. Like the rest of him, it was subjected to rigorous discipline, and only waved on sufferance.

Still feeling she had hurt his feelings and must somehow make amends, Lady Franklin said:

'You look quite another person! More, more ...' 'human' she was going to say but stopped herself and took another tack. 'Less, less – as if you had all the cares of the road on you!' And as they began to walk together along the street she added: 'How confusing it must be for your wife, to keep your two selves separate, or should I say, keep them together!'

'I expect she gets used to it, my lady.'

'You always say that! But hasn't she ever told you the difference it makes?'

'Well, she has said something about it once or twice. She did this morning. I think she likes me better like this.'

Lady Franklin studied him again.

'I think I should, if I were she.'

'Well, that's another thing you have in common with her, my lady,' Leadbitter said smiling.

'Sometimes I almost feel,' said Lady Franklin, 'that we are the same person!'

‘If that’s all right by you, my lady,’ Leadbitter said, ‘it’s all right by me.’

Lady Franklin was going to answer when the vast, sprawling bulk of the Cathedral blocked her view, and awed her into silence.

Chapter 12

WINCHESTER was the first cathedral that Lady Franklin had visited since her deliverance. Overwhelmingly it was borne in on her, with that thrilling enlargement of the spirit that the moment of entrance to a cathedral gives, that this visit was different from the others: it was a visit of thanksgiving, not a visit of intercession. But how could she give thanks, with Leadbitter towering over her, on a scale with the Cathedral itself, stiff as a soldier on church parade, and as resentful? He was looking towards the High Altar as if it was an enemy position that he wanted to blow up. Why had she enticed him inside when he would so much rather have stayed outside? A centaur on four wheels, he was utterly out of place in a church. She could not ignore him, or leave him to ramble about by himself; he had not the most elementary notion of sightseeing: he was waiting for orders. If she dropped on her knees to ease her heart of its burden of gratitude and thankfulness, would he follow suit? She could not imagine him kneeling; and how could she pray against his prayerlessness? But there he was, and but for him, she reminded herself, she wouldn't be free and happy as she now was, in the clear, able to refresh and renew her spirit with every chance impression and emotion that played on it; she would still be her own prisoner, condemned to think only one thought and feel only one feeling. Had Leadbitter been the answer to her prayer? If so, Heaven had chosen a strange agent to rescue her, but what more appropriate than that he should now be at her side?

'Would you like,' she asked him timidly in a church voice, 'to . . . to take a look round?'

'Certainly, my lady,' he answered promptly and loudly. 'Anywhere you say.'

Thus given the freedom of the whole building she couldn't think of anywhere to go.

'Well, this is the nave,' she said, 'it's one of the longest in England, if not the longest. The whole Cathedral is the longest, that I do know. . . .'

The notion of length, how abstract, how geometrical it was! For any idea of beauty or religion it evoked she might have been speaking of a clothes-line.

'It does look pretty long, my lady,' Leadbitter said, measuring the great vista with his practised eye. 'I should give it a couple of hundred yards at least. I'm judging by a running track, of course.'

'How clever of you to know,' said Lady Franklin.

'I *could* tell you the exact length,' Leadbitter volunteered.

'How?'

'By stepping it.'

Lady Franklin realized that the need for action had become imperative to Leadbitter.

'Oh do,' she said.

Off he strode, and she sank down on her knees, nor did she omit Leadbitter from her offering of praise and thanksgiving. Indeed, she might have been praying to him as well as for him; for when after a timeless interval during which her thoughts had wandered in many directions and sometimes faded out altogether, she looked up and saw his tall figure approaching, he seemed to incarnate the mood and intention of her prayer. She rose to her feet guiltily as if it was unseemly to be caught praying in his presence.

'I make it a hundred and eighty yards, my lady,' he said. 'Not bad, considering those old monks had none of the facilities that we have, and it was all done by strong-arm stuff.'

Lady Franklin made a mental note to tell him it was not all done by strong-arm stuff, but in the meantime she must try to initiate him into the joys of sight-seeing. The dimensional interest of the building was exhausted: besides, cathedrals are not made to measure, but for the greater glory of

God. For the greater glory of God! How that phrase thrilled her! A month ago it would have meant nothing to her: it would have given out the dull, muffled sound that all her thoughts gave. Now each thought had its own value, its special contribution to her happiness. Surely among them was one that she could share with Leadbitter?

'Jane Austen is buried somewhere here,' she said, 'at any rate there is a tablet to her. Shall we go and look for it?'

'By all means, my lady.'

How accommodating he was!

They searched in vain and had to ask directions from the verger.

'Oh thank you, thank you,' Lady Franklin said and after some fumbling, for her money was never quite where she thought it would be, although spread over continents there was so much of it, she pressed a coin into his hand.

'I expect these chaps do pretty well,' Leadbitter observed, 'what with Americans and so on. All the same, if it meant spending all my days in here –'

'Really, you are incorrigible!' Lady Franklin said. 'Now read me what it says about Jane Austen.'

Putting one hand behind his back, he squared himself in front of the tablet. When he had finished reading, Lady Franklin said:

'I don't think she was kind-hearted, do you?'

'I couldn't say, my lady,' Leadbitter said cautiously. 'It wouldn't surprise me if she wasn't.'

'Why?'

'Because with one or two exceptions,' and his voice faintly underlined the words, 'ladies aren't very kind-hearted, in my experience.'

'Oh, would you say so?' Lady Franklin said, made thoughtful by the compliment. 'Perhaps we haven't a very good name for it.'

'It makes the others stand out,' said Leadbitter obliquely.

Lady Franklin couldn't but lap up this repeated dewdrop.

'How sweet of you!' she said. 'I'm afraid I don't deserve – But Jane Austen had many qualities more valuable than kind-heartedness. At least, more valuable to posterity.'

'I expect she was a tartar in her time,' ventured Leadbitter.

'Do you rate kind-heartedness very high?' asked Lady Franklin, and knew that she was fishing for another compliment.

'I do, my lady. I rate it very high, higher than' – he looked round for something to compare it with – 'higher than . . . well . . . a cathedral, for instance.'

Lady Franklin shook her head, but saw herself, fleetingly but most agreeably, as something of greater value than Winchester Cathedral or Jane Austen.

'Come on,' she said. 'I'm not going to let you off. Let's go down to the transepts – they're older than this part – less rigid, freer, grander somehow. I'm sure you would enjoy the transepts.'

'I'm sure I shall, my lady,' Leadbitter said. He doesn't know what transepts are, thought Lady Franklin, as side by side they moved towards the crossing, so how can he enjoy them? But he will know, in a minute, and I mustn't forget how many things he knows that I don't know!

The thought that Leadbitter knew more than she did filled her with happiness – such happiness as in her schooldays she had felt when she knew something that the other girls did not know. How is it, she asked herself, that every experience I have now turns to happiness – even this unhopeful one of trying to make Leadbitter enjoy the transepts? Am I entitled to it? Would Philip mind, that I can think of him and not grieve for him? Have I become heartless? Am I wicked? Is this euphoria as groundless as my depression was? – more groundless, since I then had something to feel depressed about and I have nothing, really, to feel happy about? Is it the conviction of wellbeing that sometimes goes before an illness?

Experimentally she summoned up her black mood but it

would not come: as little could she raise a cloud in her own sky as she could have raised one in the heavens. And now the Norman arches were spreading to right and left.

'You see what I mean?' she whispered to Leadbitter. 'These arches and pillars aren't made to a pattern like those others in the nave – those are Perpendicular, as I expect you know, and too cold and uniform for my taste. But these don't repeat themselves, or not exactly. There's a kind of living relationship between them, if you see what I mean, as there is between human beings, not just structurally, but spiritually as well, the likeness and the unlikeness, which somehow draws us to each other – the contrast you sometimes see between ill-matched couples which helps to make them one.'

She looked up at Leadbitter anxiously, to see if he was following her thought: his head thrown back, he was staring at the massive triforium as if trying to trace in it the emblems of love which Lady Franklin had professed to find there. He looked down at her enigmatically and said:

'I see they are different, but don't you think those old monks were trying to make them alike and didn't know how to?'

'Oh no,' Lady Franklin said, decidedly. 'They could have copied – anyone can copy. No, they liked the feeling of the difference.'

'Does everyone, my lady?' Leadbitter asked.

'Like the feeling of difference? In other people, do you mean?'

'Well, yes.'

'I do,' said Lady Franklin. 'I like people to be different from me. There's nothing to find out when they're just like yourself. No surprises. I like people who give me a surprise. There must be a basis of agreement, of course. That's chemical, I believe.'

'Anyone might have it for anyone?'

'Why, yes.'

'And doesn't class make a difference?'

'Oh dear no,' said Lady Franklin, horrified by what she thought was in his mind. The titled lady and the chauffeur! 'No,' she repeated, 'class-distinctions add richness to life, I think. They make the kind of difference we were speaking of – the right kind. At least they used to, but there aren't any now.'

Leadbitter shook his head.

'Most people wouldn't say so, my lady,' he said.

'Well, I do,' said Lady Franklin, feeling it was the greatest fun in the world to abolish class. 'I never know what people mean when they –' she stopped. 'I've always had the happiest relations with my –' she stopped again and substituted 'staff' for 'servants'. 'I've had a different kind of upbringing from you, I suppose,' she went on, 'but I've never felt it a barrier and I hope you haven't.'

'Can't say I have, my lady,' said Leadbitter in a rather thick low voice, which Lady Franklin attributed to a suddenly-remembered reverence for the sacred building.

'Then may I call you by your Christian name?'

'Yes, my lady, but hardly anyone does.'

'Then I shall be one of the privileged few. Stephen. . . .' But while she was thinking of something to follow Stephen, something that should be as intimate as his name, a panic seized her, a cold hand gripped her throat. What would the Franklins say? Eyebrows raised, they were all round her. 'A chauffeur? No, my dear, you mustn't.' Resentful, protesting, but inhibited, she struggled with them.

'Unless you'd rather call me Steve,' said Leadbitter, suddenly.

'Steve,' she repeated, 'Steve.' She lingered lovingly upon the name, but couldn't frame a sentence to go with it. 'Steve?' she said again, as if it were a question.

'Yes, my lady?'

'Oh, nothing.'

'Nothing, my lady?'

'I meant it's such a nice name.'

'It sounds nice when you say it.'

But this time the Franklins had won. She knew she wouldn't, couldn't say his name, but Leadbitter did not know and from that moment he began to listen for it. Steve . . . Steve . . . Who had last called him Steve?

In silence they passed out of the Cathedral.

'Now we must be thinking about luncheon,' said Lady Franklin in an open-air voice. 'And afterwards we'll come back here for a bit. At least I will, perhaps you would rather be excused.' She smiled, but Leadbitter to her surprise said:

'That's all right, my lady. I'll come back if you want me to.'

'That will be very nice,' said Lady Franklin in her regal manner. 'Let's meet at the West door at half past two.'

Chapter 13

To Lady Franklin their second visit to the Cathedral was more rewarding than the first, for this time the great building did not seem a barrier between her and Leadbitter, it seemed a bond. It was no longer a piece of hostile territory that he had rather unwillingly to subdue (she was getting used to the military cast of his mind); he had either conquered it or accepted it as friendly. It was still alien to him, that she saw; a survival from the past with no meaning in the present: its enduring religious aspect was quite hidden from him. But the fact of its great age impressed him, and the engineering feats, the 'grouting' which the guide told them had saved it from sinking down into the mud. Indeed the application of modern methods to preserve it interested him much more than the spirit that had raised it: he saw it as a problem which posterity for some reason had taken on itself to solve.

There was something touching, something to be grateful for, in the way he gave his mind to a subject which had no natural attraction for him – consenting to appear, in the guide's eyes, uninstructed and pleased to learn, an attitude which she guessed didn't come easily to him, for in ordinary circumstances he was far readier to tell than to be told. He is doing this for my sake, she thought – nor was she wrong.

Another smaller thing that touched her was that he had subdued the natural resonance of his voice, which before luncheon might have awakened the dead and ordered them to fall in, to a reverent huskiness, and this did not wear off even when they were in the car and speeding back to London.

Yes, it had been a success, Lady Franklin thought, a definite success, and brought her nearer to him than at any other time in their relationship. Why did she want to be brought nearer to him? Because, she told herself for the hundredth time, he had done something for her that no one else could do: he had saved her from herself. She didn't realize that she had found herself in giving; she put it all down to Leadbitter's good-nature, his patience in telling her about himself and his family. During the last weeks, she had heard so many other stories, stories much more scandalous, or intriguing, or amusing, about people of her own set, that the colours of his story had grown somewhat faint: she could not be as excited as she once had been to hear that Don and Pat had just avoided chicken-pox. But this had made her feel more guilty towards him and more anxious to make amends, for how without his story, and the window it opened on reality, would she have ever heard, or wished to hear, these much more entertaining stories that were circulated at the luncheons, cocktail parties, dinner-parties which she had been frequenting? She did not believe – she did not try to believe – that the mere signing of a cheque had paid her debt: she owed him payment in another coin – a currency of the spirit.

She had another reason for wishing to be extra kind to Leadbitter. In future she would not use his car so much, having no need for pious pilgrimages. The patient had been cured and the physician had become redundant. It would be nice to feel that she had parted from him on a note of understanding, of shared experience, with something outside themselves to give the memory substance. But parting from him, no, she wasn't parting from him, she put that thought away from her, it made her feel guilty, as if she had made herself responsible for him – and how could she have – a man with a wife and family, who was so well able to take care of himself, and them?

Cramped for them both by Steve-suppression, and perhaps by their fear of rubbing the bloom off something, the conversation had been desultory and they were more than half-way to London, when she said, with some idea of making the occasion still more memorable, both to him and to her:

'You know, St–' (she smothered the name as if it had been a stammer) 'seeing the Cathedral reminded me of a book I once read – I don't know if you've read it – called *Mt St Michel and Chartres* –'

'I don't think I have, my lady,' said Leadbitter, still in his husky voice. 'I don't get much time for reading.'

'Of course you don't. Well, it's mostly about the great Cathedral of Chartres, which has the finest stained-glass in the world, and about the other French cathedrals as well, and in it he tells how they came to be built. It wasn't just a task that people set themselves, as if the Church had ordered a cathedral here and there; they sprang up to supply a kind of need, as cinemas and skating-rinks do nowadays. It wasn't a question of urging people on to build them, they couldn't be held back, and all because, he says, it was just then, in the twelfth century, or the thirteenth, that the idea of the Virgin Mary first got hold of people's minds. You see, till then Christianity had been a good deal a man's affair – the Trinity is vaguely masculine I think – and terribly serious, martyrs and dogmas, heresies and all that. It hadn't a softer side, if you see what I mean. Well, suddenly the Virgin Mary came into it – she'd been there all along, of course – and gave it something new. I know you don't think too well of women –'

'Only some women, my lady,' Leadbitter said. 'There are exceptions –'

'Yes, your wife for one. Well, she was like a wife and a mother and a . . . a girl-friend to every man, every man could see his ideal woman in her, and every woman wanted to be like her, and look like her, and she brought, or the cult of her did – into religion all sorts of qualities that hadn't been there, like tenderness and gaiety and earthly love and home-making – you wouldn't deny those to all women, would you?'

'No,' said Leadbitter smiling, 'not to all.'

'Well, men's minds became – I won't say feminized – it's such an awful word – but more alive to a feminine element in religion and it took on tremendously and burnt up in their hearts like a flame and so they couldn't stop themselves from building in her honour – it was a craze, she was like a universal film-star, or pin-up girl, if that doesn't sound blasphemous.'

'I'd like to know which film-star,' Leadbitter said.

'Well, your favourite, if you have one. And this ideal, working in their minds, sprang up in stone and glass all over France, and England too, and all in praise of us – us women, if I may say so. The greatest compliment we've ever had.'

'That was a long time ago,' said Leadbitter.

'And women have changed for the worse since then? Well, perhaps they have. Perhaps we all have. Work is measured by money now, isn't it? It was then, too, to some extent. Building was always being held up, and given up, for lack of funds. I don't know how much the cathedrals cost, but Henry Adams, when he wrote, valued them at £600 million, just the French ones.'

'That's a lot of money,' Leadbitter admitted, still with a frog in his throat.

'Yes, and now they would be worth a great deal more. But one doesn't think of the money – one thinks of all it meant in terms of enthusiasm and the joy of creation – not feelings turning into stone, but stone turning into feelings, and the abstractions of religious thought, which can be so dividing, turning into feelings too: all that surge and uprush of devotion not spending itself in wrangling or money-getting, but perpetuating itself in things of lasting beauty. Most art is the work of individuals, and often of individuals at odds with their lot: it's the fruit of loneliness and separation. The cathedrals were a collective effort, a family affair – the result of an epidemic, not a personal, non-infectious illness.'

Lady Franklin laughed to think where the metaphor had

landed her, and rather to her surprise, Leadbitter laughed too.

'I meant to be so cheerful, and I felt so cheerful,' she apologized, 'and I've ended up with plague and cancer, or something like them. Why are so many metaphors drawn from unpleasant things? What was in my mind when I started on all this, which must have been very boring for you, was that my happiness – which I can't compare to a cathedral or even the smallest parish church, but still it means a lot to me – was something I couldn't have achieved by myself: it was the result of our combined effort – I owe it to you.' She didn't realize she was repeating what she had often said to Leadbitter; she felt she was surging forward on a great wave of gratitude, foam-crested, translucent. 'Thank goodness, you don't know what it means to live in solitary confinement with a single thought and that a painful one. Besides your other customers, who no doubt plague you with their grievances as I do (or perhaps they don't, perhaps they have more consideration), you have your family, your wife and Don and Pat and Susie, all of whom suck the poison from the wound – for I suppose we all have a wound? I hadn't anyone to help me, or anyone who did help me – that was part of my trouble – until you came along.'

'I'm very glad if I've been a help to you, my lady,' Leadbitter said.

'You have, and more than a help, you've been a mental standby, a consoling thought, even when you weren't with me. I realized that you had been through far more than I had – in the war, and so on – and hadn't let it affect you: you had made yourself fit for peace as well as war, which isn't easy for everyone, I know.'

'I suppose I'm pretty tough,' said Leadbitter.

'Yes, that's what I liked, and somehow you passed it on to me. I felt that here was someone I could rely on absolutely, who responded to the true values of life, whose experience wasn't spurious and self-induced, like mine. You were real and so was everything about you – your wife, your family, and the way you lived – and gradually they built up in my mind the impression of a reality outside myself, which was what I needed. I got it through your companionship; you gave it me. Loneliness is something you don't suffer from – how could you? Perhaps it's just the opposite with you, perhaps you sometimes want to be alone.'

'I do feel lonely sometimes,' Leadbitter said, 'I do feel lonely,' he repeated.

'In spite of your busy life and your family all around you, growing up?'

'Yes, in spite of them,' said Leadbitter. 'But you don't feel lonely any more, my lady?'

'Oh, I wouldn't say that. I do feel lonely but in quite another way. I want companionship now; I didn't before.'

'I want it, too,' said Leadbitter.

'In spite of having so much?'

'It isn't the same,' he muttered, 'it isn't at all the same.'

'When do you feel lonely?' Lady Franklin asked.

'When do I feel lonely?' Leadbitter repeated. 'You wouldn't believe it, my lady, but I feel lonely when you are not there.'

'Oh, I'm so glad,' said Lady Franklin, and then, seeing from his face that she had said the wrong thing, she corrected herself, 'I mean I'm glad that you . . . well . . . like me enough to miss me.'

Leadbitter ignored this.

'I miss you when you are not there,' he told her, spacing out the words.

'Oh, but I'm sorry!' Lady Franklin said, doubling like a hunted hare. 'I'm glad that you miss me, sorry that you miss me – oh, what *do* I mean?' She looked at him despairingly. Accustomed to thinking of herself as missing someone, she could not imagine someone missing her – least of all Leadbitter, the man of many customers, the family man.

'Don't you think I ought to miss you?' he challenged her.

Then she knew that something was the matter, but she only knew it from the tone of his voice, and didn't really link it to his words. So she answered the words rather than the voice.

'I'm very sorry if you miss me,' she said, trying to take the me-ness out of 'me'. 'We've been a lot together, haven't we? But I thought your wife –'

'Forget her.'

'And your family –'

'Forget them, too.'

'But how can I forget them,' protested Lady Franklin, 'when you've told me so much about them? You even promised me that I should meet them.'

'Forget them,' Leadbitter said, violently. 'They don't exist – they're all ballyhoo.'

'Don't exist?' She didn't understand him.

'No, but you and I do.'

A naked, nameless need shone in his eyes. It might have been a cry for help, it was so urgent. It loosed the springs of pity in her; pity loosed her tongue; she cried:

'Can I do anything for you?'

'Yes, you can.'

The car slowed down, turned into a side-road and stopped. Leadbitter was no bungler in the arts of love. He tried no cave-man methods, but he well knew how to make a shock delicious, and make deliciousness into a shock. The shock and the delight were there, divinely blended; and Lady Franklin had closed her eyes in rapture before she opened them in outrage.

'I must get out,' she said.

Leadbitter didn't answer.

'I must get out,' she repeated. 'Please let me out, Leadbitter.'

Even in the bewildering tumult of his feelings, the surname struck him like a blow.

'But you can't get out here, my lady,' he said. 'We're still ten miles from London.'

'It doesn't matter,' Lady Franklin said. 'I can walk, or someone will give me a lift.'

'At least let me take you to a taxi,' he said.

'No, thank you,' she said, still looking away from him. 'I'll find my own way back.'

'Lady Franklin,' he said, using her name for the first time, 'is there nothing I can do?'

'Nothing,' she answered, 'except let me out.'

Awkwardly unfolding his long legs he clambered out of the car, went round behind it so that he should not see her, opened the door and stood beside it, with squared shoulders and a wooden face, staring down the road.

'Thank you,' said Lady Franklin. 'That . . . that will be all,' she said.

Dismissed, Leadbitter regained the car, and backed it at a dangerous speed towards the main road. As he turned into it his eyes caught sight of her, moving slowly in his direction. She had nothing in her hand or under her arm; and suddenly he noticed her handbag and paper-bound guide to Winchester Cathedral lying on the seat by his side. For a moment he thought of driving on, so little did he want to encounter her again; but remembering the complications that would follow, if he did not at once return her property, he took it and went back to meet her.

'You left these in the car, my lady,' he said.

She looked up at him, startled, startled into a sudden nervous smile 'So I did, so I did,' she said, 'thank you for remembering.'

Saluting her, which he had forgotten to do the first time, he strode off. Then he turned back once more.

'Sure I can't take you anywhere?' he said.

'No, thank you,' she answered. 'I shall be quite all right.'

'I should be happier if you'd let me take you somewhere,' he said, forcing out the words.

Not trusting herself to speak, she shook her head and he retreated.

Chapter 14

'My wife she is dying, oh then –
'My wife she is dying, oh then –
  My wife she is dying
  I laugh till I'm crying
I wish I was single again.
  I wish I was single,
  My pockets would jingle,
I wish I was single again.'

THE song haunted Leadbitter for days, and he sang it in his harsh voice, and deliberately out of tune, for he had an excellent ear, to do dirt on art, to do dirt on his feelings, to do dirt on Lady Franklin. For his first reaction was to be furiously angry with her. She had led him up the garden path, she had given him the soft flannel, and then when it came to the point she had turned him down. She had pinned his ears back for him, she had wrapped the rolling pin round him, and all because he wasn't her class. She had talked a lot of blah about classlessness, and how it brought people like him and her together, but when it came down to brass tacks, she had disdained the opportunity of non-chastity that he offered, oh no, oh no: 'unhand me, varlet.' Well, let her get on with it. He would know another time.

They had deceived each other, but of the two, and at a deeper level than she, he was the more deceived. The wound to his male pride went very deep and there was no one to suck the poison from it. When he thought of the advances which his women customers had sometimes made to him, for which he had given them no excuse whatever, and which he had turned down with the greatest tact and delicacy, to spare their feelings (not to have done so would have been bad for business) he realized what a mug he had been. And a mug was the last thing he wanted to be or to be called: it was the ultimate degradation.

True, there was no one to call him a mug except Lady Franklin: there was no other witness of his discomfiture, he had seen to that. But would she keep it to herself? Would any woman? No, she would tell all her friends that he was a man unsafe to go out with and he would get a black mark and lose half his customers.

But again, would he? His cynicism, struggling to regain its hold, told him that some women would employ him all the more readily: and they should get what was coming to them, by God they should, the bitches! All women were bitches and Lady Franklin was the biggest bitch of all. He hated them in every part of their persons. Most women were so short in the leg that when they stepped off the pavement their bottoms bumped the kerb-stone. As for Lady Franklin she was like a pregnant salmon, a pregnant salmon, he repeated to himself, pleased with the comparison, for Lady Franklin's figure was her weakest point.

Memories of red-light districts came back to him, and the patter of solicitation. 'Come in quick, you, Lofty! You, you short, low fellow! You, Ginger! You with the two warts under your chin – I know you! You haven't any money – get away!'

For the first time since his adolescence he was haunted by images of obscenity: the mere thought of Lady Franklin, and she was seldom out of his thoughts, was enough to call them up. Army songs, songs he remembered himself, songs he had picked up from his father, made a ready outlet for his feelings. Once he had sung them with a grown man's smile of indulgence for their innocent indecency: but now, coupled with the image of Lady Franklin, he sang them with savage relish.

'I think of everything that I possess
The lavatory is the best
To sit in gentle bliss –'

What do you think of that, my lady? Oh, Stephen, wouldn't you rather we talked about cathedrals? But he wasn't Stephen any longer to her, he was Leadbitter.

He didn't blame himself in the least for what had happened, except as one blames oneself for having been a fool. When he remembered that he had started out that very day half meaning to make a pass at her, it didn't change his view of the situation; indeed it made him feel all the more a mug, to think how the tables had been turned on him. Happiness! Happiness! That word had been for ever on her tongue. 'You have made me happy, Leadbitter.' And what had she made him?

It happened that for a day or two after the episode business was rather slack: fewer calls came to him, fewer calls came to his clerk, and some of those that came were cancellations. Lady Franklin, of course! She had been broadcasting his offence: she had been warning all her friends to steer clear of him. When he took up the receiver he could hardly keep the anxiety out of his voice; he adopted a placating, almost servile tone; when he booked an order he felt that it was the first he had ever received, and the last he ever would receive. He would have to go out of car-hire, he decided, and try to get a partnership in a garage. Thanks, Lady Franklin, thanks a lot. He warbled to the tune of Clementine:

'Fetch the night-pan
Fetch the night-pan
Poor Pa is feeling queer;
Fetch the night-pan
Fetch the night-pan,
His end is very near.'

What do you think of that, my lady? I don't like it at all, Steve; I think it's very vulgar and disgusting. I would much rather talk about the great cathedrals of France. Only he wasn't Steve, he was Leadbitter. 'That will be all, Leadbitter.'

And it would be all: the last he would hear of her. For of

course she wouldn't pay her latest monthly account. She would snatch at the opportunity not to – what woman wouldn't? – and how could he write and ask her to pay, still less sue her for it?

'This man, my lord, made an indecent assault upon me in his car – *his* car! – my car, since I paid for it.' (This was the first time since the incident that Leadbitter remembered Lady Franklin's benefaction.) 'And now he has the impertinence to suggest that I should pay his bill! I absolutely refuse to, and I hope every decent-minded man or woman who is unlucky enough to be his customer will do the same.'

Leadbitter persuaded himself that Lady Franklin would refuse to pay his bill, and was as angry with her as if she had already refused. He almost persuaded himself that her entire behaviour, from the moment when she first engaged him, had been framed and directed towards one end: to trap him into making love to her so that she might turn him down. He had never tried to stifle his hostile feelings towards anyone and would have thought it wrong to, except for prudential reasons, and he didn't realize that he was making himself miserable by hating Lady Franklin, and if he had realized he wouldn't have known why. He was not the first man, or woman, to have mistaken gratitude for love.

> 'It was Christmas Day in the workhouse
> And the eunuchs all were there
> Watching the Emperor's maidens
> Combing their pubic hair.'

Isn't that a nice song, my lady? No, Steve, it isn't at all a nice song, and I would much rather we talked about the cult of the Virgin Mary. Only of course he wasn't Steve, he was Leadbitter....

Well, the question of the account would soon be settled one way or the other. March was nearly over. On 1 April (April Fool's Day, as he grimly reminded himself), his secretary sent out Lady Franklin's bill. She had made little use of Leadbitter's services in March, very little use, and the bill was a small one, except for the last item: To Winchester, wait and return £8 10s. 6d. It was the exact fare: he had not added on anything for the insult. He hadn't forgotten it, though.

> 'And the oars were shining brightly
>   On the flashing stream,
> And the whores were scrapping nightly –'

'Don't you want me to go on, my lady?'

'No, thank you, Leadbitter, I've heard quite enough.'

Two days later arrived an envelope, among the many envelopes, addressed in a handwriting that was strange to him. There was nothing surprising in this: what did surprise him was that the missive came from Lady Franklin, whose previous communications had all been typewritten, presumably by her secretary. In this instance she had, he supposed, addressed the envelope herself. And the cheque was signed not with the initial E, as her habit was, but with her full name, Ernestine Franklin. Comparing the handwriting on the envelope with the handwriting on the cheque, he saw they were the same.

Leadbitter's first sensation was one of violent relief: he had not lost his money after all. The second was of relief, too, but was more complex. Had her secretary been away? She might have been; he couldn't tell. But taking the two things together, the envelope and the signature, it didn't seem like a coincidence. It seemed as if ... as if she meant something by it, as if she was trying to tell him something. If so, it could only mean that she didn't have hard feelings for him.

She had paid, paid on the nail as she always did; and done it graciously. For the first time his feeling about her was softened by regret. Not only was it regret for a lost customer, one of his best, and one that he could ill afford to lose. He could have kicked himself for making that stupid mistake. It wasn't like him to take such a risk. Had it come off, had she yielded to his embraces, he might have been – who knows? – set up in life. Lady Franklin and her money were soon parted. But she was too inexperienced, as he might have known. The step was too big for her to take. Well, he had staked and lost. Playing for the thousands of her love, he had lost the hundreds of her custom.

Ernestine ... Ernestine ... He said the name over to himself, first parrot-wise, then with expression, almost as if he was calling her to him. It was an uncommon name, yet he had heard it before, heard it in a conversation between customers in his car. But he had heard so many conversations without paying much attention to them.

'That will be all,' Lady Franklin had said. It hadn't been quite all: here was the cheque. But as he endorsed it, stamping it with the firm's stamp, he felt the unmistakable sharp click of finality: it *was* all, now, and what a fool he had been. Women, you couldn't trust them; they didn't know what they wanted themselves. Steer clear of any entanglement with them, that was the first rule; and forget about them, that was the second. Leadbitter set about forgetting Lady Franklin. It would be easier to forget her now that he was no longer so angry with her – in fact hardly angry at all.

Chapter 15

'DARLING, it's a lovely plan of course; but why this second extravagance? Have you had a legacy? You didn't seem noticeably richer at the Lame Duck the other evening.'

'Meaning I didn't pay my whack?'

'Of course not. But what a bad conscience you have.'

'It isn't my fault if people treat me . . . But something has happened since then.'

'I thought it must have, Hughie. Tell me.'

Hughie was silent a moment.

'I'm not sure that I shall, Constance. I'm not sure you would approve.'

'I approve of anything that brings in money.'

'You say that, but you don't really.'

'Have I ever disapproved when you turned an honest penny, or even a dishonest one, for that matter?'

'Yes, you have.'

'When?'

'Well, for one thing, you don't approve of my painting, which is after all my staff of life.'

'I may not approve of your painting, as such,' Constance said. 'But I don't object to your being paid for it.'

'Some people like my painting,' said Hughie a little sulkily.

'You're telling me, and I'm so glad they do. But has it become a gold mine?'

'Well, it's produced another nugget.'

'May I know who from?'

'You may. From Ernestine.'

Leadbitter, who was driving them out to Richmond for dinner, didn't move. But when he heard the name he was all ears.

'Why, has she given you another commission?' Constance asked, lightly, as who should say, 'Did you enjoy your dinner yesterday?'

'Yes, she has. She liked my portrait of her husband very much.'

'But has she more than one dead husband?'

'No,' said Hughie.

'I believe she has an affectionate nature, and we know she lives a great deal in the past – or did. Is it some very dear aunt she wants you to commemorate?'

'No,' said Hughie, aware of Constance's curiosity, but not disposed to satisfy it at once. 'This time she has asked me to paint the living.'

'How very rash of her. No, Hughie, I didn't mean that. I can't wait to know who it is.'

'I'll give you three guesses.'

'Now, Hughie, don't be tiresome. I'm not in a mood for guessing, and I don't know who her friends are, though I know she has a lot, as all rich women have.'

'It isn't a friend of hers.'

'Isn't? Then why this act of altruism – I was going to say misguided altruism, but I won't.'

'I don't think she's being altruistic,' Hughie said.

'Not? If it isn't a friend? Is she going to present the portrait of a distinguished person to a public gallery?'

'I don't think you could say it was a friend,' said Hughie. ignoring Constance's last question. 'I don't think you could say she was a friend of Ernestine's.'

'Oh, it's a woman, then. Hughie, you must tell me.'

'It's Ernestine herself.'

There was a pause in which Constance tried to sort her thoughts out, as did Leadbitter.

'How slow of me not to guess,' she said. 'Perhaps it was because I didn't want to. Darling, I do congratulate you. It's splendid, isn't it? It may be the making of you, in more ways than one. I am so pleased.' She turned to him, and they embraced, as Leadbitter thought they would.

'But of course I *am* a little jealous,' said Constance, when the embrace was over.

'Of whom?' asked Hughie.

'Oh, of nobody – just of your painting her.'

'You've no right to be,' said Hughie, pleased at having kept his end up in a conversation with Constance for so long. 'You will never let me paint you.'

'No, that's true,' said Constance. 'I won't, because I love you and I don't want to love you less.'

'Thank you,' said Hughie, 'thank you. But then why be jealous? Perhaps Ernestine *does* want to love me less.'

'Do you call her Ernestine?' asked Constance.

'I told you I did.'

'I'm not really jealous,' said Constance, 'because she's not that kind of woman – I mean the kind of woman who falls in love.'

'What makes you think so?'

'Well, didn't we agree she wasn't? Once she lived in a dream of the past, and now she lives in a dream of the present.'

'I'm not so sure. She's changed in the last few days.'

'Oh, have you changed her?'

'No, but something has.'

'Or someone?'

'She said she'd had a shock.'

'What kind of shock? A pleasant one?'

'She didn't say.'

'She doesn't tell you everything, then.'

'No, but she tells me more about herself than she used to. She seems to have realized herself, become a person in her own right. Before, she was all ideas and theories, with her head in the clouds. Now she seems to have got her feet on the ground.'

'Is that how you're painting her?'

'No, with her feet up on a sofa.'

'Mme Récamier?'

'I thought you'd say that. Of course, it's much less tiring for her.'

'How considerate you are, Hughie. And if she's suffering from shock ... she should lie down. I wonder what it was. Do you think somebody said "Bo" to her?'

'She said it was the result of an experiment, and largely her fault.'

'Shocks generally are one's own fault,' Constance said. 'She didn't tell you what kind of experiment it was, or with whom?'

'Darling, you *will* see the personal in everything.' (Constance winced at this.) 'She didn't say it was with anyone. I was finishing her husband's portrait, and she came in in rather a flutter, and was restless and couldn't sit down – she was quite unlike herself – and then she said, excusing herself, that she'd had a shock the day before and hadn't quite got over it, but it was a good deal her fault. I said I hoped no bones were broken, or something like that, and she said, Oh no, it wasn't that kind of shock, it was the result of an experiment which had done her a lot of good – to her nerves I gathered – but it had upset her because she wasn't expecting it.'

'It wouldn't have been a shock if she had been expecting it,' said Constance.

'And she said she hadn't behaved very well and was sorry about it. Guilt is one of her things, you know. I tell her she must learn to forgive herself.'

'You could teach her – you're an expert at it.'

'Oh, I don't know. I try to see myself in a favourable light, and Ernestine has helped me. She thanks me over and over again. Gratitude is another of her things – it's a compulsive neurosis.'

'I hope you won't catch it from her.'

'Why?'

'Because I like you to be yourself.'

'*Le bel homme sans merci?* Thank you, Constance, thank you.'

'But what has Ernestine to thank you for?'

'Oh, just for being. And then she said how much she liked my portrait of her husband, and how it was just the way he used to look at her, and now not only did he look at her, but she could look back at him as if he was really there; she said she didn't mind thinking about him any more, she liked to think about him, because though she still grieved for him at times, it wasn't an obsession any longer. And then she hesitated a little, and said would I paint her portrait.'

'She hesitated and was lost,' said Constance. 'Whose idea was it that she should lie down?'

'Mine really,' Hughie said. 'I said, "Hadn't you better lie down?" – and to my great surprise she did, like an obedient child. She wouldn't have, and I shouldn't have dared to ask her a week ago.'

'Do women never lie down in your presence?' Constance asked.

'Well, models do, but other women don't, I mean unless –'

'Unless they're ill. Well, to your surprise, Ernestine lay down and then –'

'And then I saw it suited her and that there was a picture in it, and I said: "Stay like that and I'll begin now."'

'What, had you another canvas with you? Had you foreseen that this would happen?'

'No, I took a sheet of writing-paper and made a sketch. There's more light in the room now that she has had the curtains taken away.'

'Oh, she's had the curtains taken away?'

'Yes, the net curtains, I don't mean the heavy brocade ones. She had it done after her cure, or whatever it was. She said, "I want to look out and I don't mind if people look in."'

'Even when she's lying down?'

'You can't really see into a room, Constance, unless the lights are on, any more than you can see into a car.'

'I suppose that's just as well.'

'I'm painting her with her hands clasped behind her head like the *Maja Vestida* –'

'But Ernestine isn't in the least like that bold, provocative female.'

'No, but she's a little more like her than she used to be.'

'Wasn't the Duchess of Alba Goya's mistress?'

'I think she was, I hope she was. But surely, Constance, you're not jealous of Ernestine?'

'No, darling, of course not, but I'm not altogether happy to think of you cooped up with this rich, un-merry widow even if she hasn't been awakened. Couldn't you paint her as the Sleeping Beauty?'

'She's not exactly beautiful. Her eyes are too large for her face.'

'I know. But you could easily prettify her, it wouldn't be the first time you have done that. And if she was asleep her eyes wouldn't show. Besides, I should feel safer if she was asleep, and she would recover from the shock quicker. How do you keep her awake, by the way?'

'I talk to her,' said Hughie.

'And does she talk to you? Isn't it rather awkward, painting a moving mouth? You must need a cine-camera.'

'It's better for them to talk a bit, it keeps their faces from going dead.'

'"Their" faces? Darling, how promiscuous you sound. Still, I'm glad you think of her as them. What does she talk about?'

'Me, to some extent.'

'I thought she only talked about herself.'

'Oh no. That was when she was trying to cure herself. Someone told her not to keep it bottled up. She said she cured herself by talking to someone.'

'I wonder who.'

Leadbitter was listening intently.

'She said it was someone very patient and understanding, who couldn't get away. But for some time after that she always talked about a subject – art, you know, or the state of the world. She was tired of the sight and sound of herself – the whole idea of herself – it was sheer happiness, she said, to be able to think of anything she wanted to, without reference to herself – to have complete freedom of thought. She could be a cloud or a tree, or just an idea. She liked to identify herself with things that were going well – well for her, well for everybody, happy centuries, happy families, and so on –'

'It sounds like a child's game,' said Constance.

'I suppose it was. Anyhow, she shrank from the idea of personality, especially her own, you couldn't get near her as a person, any more than you can get near a preacher or a lecturer –'

'My dear Hughie – *what* you must have been through –'

'Well, she was like that, a shape in sunlight, until –'

'Until what?'

'Until she had this shock.'

'And is she more paintable now?' asked Constance.

'Oh yes, much more. You see, now she has an expression, her own face, whereas before she had a look of impersonal sweetness and happiness, like a nun's.'

'You certainly couldn't paint a nun lying on a sofa with her hands clasped behind her head,' said Constance. 'I wonder what you'll make of her. But you mustn't make her look like a tart, either. The effects of the shock may wear off: people don't change fundamentally as quickly as that, in my experience. She may go back to being a preacher or a lecturer, or even an ego-maniac. Do you enjoy her company, Hughie?'

'Well, I rather like being on my best behaviour.'

'I shouldn't know what that was,' said Constance. 'Mind you keep on it, Hughie, mind you keep on it. But be warned: I don't think she's for you, even in paint. She isn't quite there, if you know what I mean. She exists in our imagination of her. You might come in one morning, and find the canvas blank. Then *you'd* get a shock. Can you imagine her in this car, sitting beside the driver?'

'No, I can't. But it's thanks to her we're sitting here.'

'She's paid up again?'

'She has.'

'I don't like all this paying in advance. It's corrupting. She's paying for her idea, not for what she gets. Paying for paying's sake, that's what it comes to. She's relieving her feelings on you.'

'What a horrid way of putting it.'

'Well, she is. You are her – I won't say what. And there's something else she's doing.'

'What is that, Cassandra?'

'She's laying on you the burden of a lifetime's gratitude.'

Hughie thought a moment, but did not look too seriously dismayed.

'Oh well, she's taught me to say "thank you".'

'Suppose she doesn't like the portrait?'

'Oh, but she will.'

'Because she likes you, you mean.'

'I didn't mean that.'

'You did, and I dare say you're right. Who was it got a shock, and then fell in love with the first thing they saw?'

'No one I ever heard of, and don't call me a thing.'

'A poor thing but mine own. You are mine, aren't you, Hughie?'

'I'm less poor than I was, but yes, Constance, I'm yours.

'Not Ernestine's?'

'Oh no.'

For once Leadbitter was wrong: they didn't kiss. How could they, when Lady Franklin, Ernestine, was sitting on the seat beside him, far more real than they were?

Chapter 16

THE image of Lady Franklin, that vanished benefactress, returned to plague the inventor. The inventor: for she did not return as Lady Franklin, she returned as Mrs Leadbitter, his own invention, and he was realist enough not to confuse the two.

Leadbitter had almost succeeded in writing Lady Franklin off as a bad debt. For potentially, in the future, she was a debt. She had been one of his best customers, he had lost her custom, and the money he had counted on from her in the future would never now be paid. Even though, thanks to her handwriting on the envelope and her signature on the cheque, he had forgiven her, washed out the social slight, and almost forgiven her the worse injury to his masculine pride, his pride was still wounded at having lost a customer. He worked it out: taking an average of Lady Franklin's monthly accounts, in six years he would have received from her as much as she had paid him in that one lump sum. But that had been a gift, and free from Income Tax. To get the real equivalent, he would have had to serve her for ten years. Ten years of steady bookings coming in! One thing he did not let his mind dwell on if he could help it: the capital gain, the enormous capital gain, if his tactical manoeuvre on the road from Winchester had succeeded.

Why had he done it, he sometimes asked himself, for he was not naturally a gambler. He didn't bet, not even on the football pools. Gambling was a mug's game, he thought. He didn't need that kind of stimulus, any more than he needed, beyond a carefully prescribed amount, the stimulus of alcohol. Apart from work, he didn't need an outside stimulus, except that curious one of picking a quarrel. It was in hostility that his being fulfilled itself. As a soldier should be, he was sudden and fierce in quarrel. In a way it had been a deprivation to him to forgive Lady Franklin: he lived at a lower rate, a slower pace, since he had stopped hating her. But those moments of escape from discipline he had under control: he would never have let them injure his pocket, never let a customer see the demon that lurked in him. Unless rude or drunk or both, the customer was always right 'They', the customers, did not impinge on his emotions; he hardly liked one better than another, they were like patients to a doctor, subjects for his professional skill.

Why then had he made a pass at Lady Franklin? He didn't know, it was just one of those things.

They hadn't talked about her any more, they had talked about each other and about people he didn't know. He listened with half an ear. Why weren't they married? Because there wasn't enough money, apparently. Constance was some kind of secretary, he gathered, as so many unmarried women were, and married women too, though not the women who employed him; not Lady Franklin, for instance, who was really paying for this jaunt, paying for their dinner, paying for the car. In a wry way the idea that, at one remove, he was still in her employ, amused him, for he could not think of her, or anyone else, out of a business context.

It was when he got home, soon after midnight, that the phenomenon happened. He had been up at half past five to take a party to the airport, and he was very tired. He wouldn't have admitted this to himself but he knew it, because instinctively he avoided looking at himself in the glass, so as not to see the circles under his eyes. Going from the bathroom into his bed-sitting-room, where by day his secretary sat and where, on the rare occasions when he was at home, his landlady served him with his meals, he switched the light on and saw, only for a second but quite distinctly, the outlines of a scattered group – a woman and three children; the woman was a bit like Lady Franklin, yet not like her. What are they doing here? he wondered, and then the vision dissolved, and he was alone, very much alone in the room with its bright centre light and two armchairs, pale brown in colour, patterned with overlapping rectangles of darker brown. He sat down in one of them and almost before his head had touched it fell asleep. He dreamed, and in his dream his family came back and bustled round him. His wife knew that he was tired and warned the children to be quiet: they tiptoed about, with set expressions as though their very faces might make a noise. Gradually he relaxed and his wife began to recount the day's events and he listened attentively, for here was something to tell Lady Franklin. But what vexed him was that he couldn't quite take in what his wife was saying. 'Say that all over again,' he said, for he didn't stand on ceremony with his wife – but still the sense of what she was saying eluded his tired mind, until he was on the point of quarrelling with her. Frustrated and distressed he breasted the ripples on the shores of sleep, and woke, still warm and glowing with the unfulfilled promise of his dream. Then came the chill of reality, and the bitter awareness of being cheated. It was half past two and he still had to undress; but was it worth while going to bed when he had to be up again at five? A bleak decision to take – and bleaker taken alone. It was nearly three before he set the alarm-clock and stretched out his long limbs between the sheets.

Thereafter he was haunted by his fantasy and led what was to become a double life, like a novelist who has one existence in the outside world and another in his book. It began, as many fantasies do, in deliberate day-dreaming, in bouts of wishful-thinking which he could start and stop at will; but soon, like other forms of self-indulgence, it got a hold of him; it came before he called it and would not go away when he dismissed it. The times when he was a single man, the most single of single men, absorbed in making money for himself, grew fewer; more and more frequent the times when he was breadwinner to a wife and family whose lives enriched his own, and whose personalities were as clear to him as if he had known them in the flesh.

He wanted to go on with the story, to bring it up to date, but he couldn't, lacking Lady Franklin's presence. He knew by heart the history of the Leadbitters down to Don and Pat's escape from chicken-pox; but there it stuck, the day at Winchester had beheaded it. He could not add to or develop it for only Lady Franklin knew about it, only she wanted to hear it, only she could draw it out of him. It was something shared between them. Imaginatively he lived in a perpetual past that was both intoxicating and frustrating. If only he could see her, and take up his tale again! Or just meet her and say something to her, however trivial. 'Good morning, my lady!' But that was out of the question: there could be no communication between them. She had gone out of his life, leaving him a great deal better off, he had to admit, but taking something from him, his flawless independence. Before, he had never been aware of being lonely; now, between his doses of the drug, he was often acutely lonely, so lonely that he didn't like to go home at night. Even his best pal, the telephone, began to fail him, not as an instrument or a money-getter, for bookings did not fall off, rather the opposite, but as a companion; as a means of keeping up his interest in himself, it was no help at all. And sometimes the drug of which he had become an addict failed him too; the same scenes repeated lost their power to beguile him; the mirage of domestic happiness grew thin and through it he could see the desert of loneliness, barren and featureless.

If only he could see Lady Franklin, if only he could tell her –

One day he thought, 'Why not get married?' He had a good laugh over this, but the thought came back and in the end it did not seem a laughing matter.

They, he and the woman he had lived with, whose photograph had once adorned the silver frame which now enshrined his list of the week's bookings, had had many scenes before the final one. He hadn't really meant it to be final when he said, 'Well, so long, Clarice.'

'It has been long, hasn't it?' she answered. 'A lot too long for me, at any rate.' 'You took the words out of my mouth,' he said. 'I'm surprised – I thought you'd taken everything you could take.' 'And me?' she countered. 'I suppose you've given me everything you could give? You wanted me for bed and breakfast. Bed when you felt like it and when you didn't, well, what? What is it that a woman wants? Your face to look at? It's not a bad face, I admit, it's the best part of you or nearly. But what's behind it? Nothing that is any good to me. You're hard all through – I liked that once, but I don't like it now. If it's true that I have taken things from you, it's because you wouldn't give me anything, you're a skinflint, all that comes off you scrape off like the stubble when you're shaving, and that you do yourself, and for yourself.' 'That's what I mean,' he said, 'I can't do right. The angel Gabriel himself couldn't do right. You wouldn't like me if I didn't shave, would you? You'd nag at me, you have nagged at me when I haven't had time to shave. You want me to be different to what I am, you want to mould me. You want to make it so that I'm not happy unless I'm doing something for you, and when I do it's never the right thing, because you don't know what you want yourself.' 'I do know now,' she said, 'I've known a long time. I know when I'm fed up – and not from eating, mind you, for you'd let me starve.' 'Starve?' repeated Leadbitter, looking down at the ample figure whose curves, three years ago, had so enchanted him; 'I don't know who has let you starve, but I haven't. You're remarkably well covered for a starveling. Once round you is twice round the gas-works, as they say.' Clarice moved her golden head about impatiently. 'There's other ways of starving besides one,' she said. 'You wouldn't know, because you feed off yourself, like a camel. In the Army, you cleaned your boots and buttons till they shone, and burnished your bayonet with a knitting needle, or so you told me, to be the smartest soldier in the regiment, but did you ever do it for anyone else? Not likely.'

'You're wrong for once,' said Leadbitter. 'I done it for a score of chaps, and mark you, they said, "Ta, thanking you," but they didn't say, "You might have smiled at me as well," or "You didn't tell me how I looked this morning on parade" – meaning, "You ought always to be thinking of me."' 'Your boy-friends knew you better, I suppose,' sneered Clarice. 'I'm not a soldier, worse luck, I'm just a woman that took up with you and now wishes she hadn't.' 'Well, that's O.K. by me,' said Leadbitter. 'Let's call it a day.' 'Is that all you have to say?' asked Clarice, after a moment. 'Well, isn't it what you wanted me to say, or do you want me to make a scene?' She didn't answer this but said, 'Who's going to look after you?' 'Oh, please don't worry about me,' he said, 'I think I'll try a spell of living on my own. I shall rather look forward to strolling about spare.' 'You always have,' she said, 'that's just what I complain of, and if you didn't, there'd be some woman I should feel sorry for, God help her. But still –' 'Well, what?' he said impatiently. 'Who's going to darn your socks?' she asked. 'Oh, I can do that myself,' said Leadbitter lightly. 'And do it a darned sight better than some people I know of.' He chuckled at the joke, but Clarice didn't smile. 'You're so sharp,' she said, 'one day you'll cut yourself, unless your skin's so hard it'll turn the blade.' The notion of his toughness seemed to soften her, for suddenly her eyes filled with tears. 'Oh well,' she said, 'I shan't let myself hate you, you're not worth it.' The tears overflowed and sat, fat globules, on the supporting contours of her cheeks; swelling, they burst and trickled down the sides of her nose towards the corners of her mouth. Blackmail! How women always tried it on! 'If hating me makes you feel any better,' he said, 'go ahead. I shan't notice the difference.' And when she flashed at him her glistening tear-bright fury, 'Bye-bye for now,' he said and turned and went.

That was three years ago. Perhaps Clarice wasn't such a bad sort after all. One day he might look her up.

Meanwhile, if he happened to pass through South Halkin Street, he slowed down when he came to Lady Franklin's house, and looked in through the windows. A chandelier, a standard lamp, a mirror stood out in the rich dusky interior; there must also be a sofa with Lady Franklin lying on it, her hands clasped behind her head; but he could not see it or the painter, who would have his back to the light and his eyes fastened on the figure on the sofa. Why not stop, why not peer in? There were no curtains now. But suppose she came to the window for a rest, and saw him? What nonsense! She wouldn't want a rest when she was lying down, besides she might not recognize him, she might have forgotten what he looked like. But she might come to the door; she might be going out in another car, with another driver. He felt as if the house had fallen on his spirit and crushed it, and hastened past its shadow into the bright pale spaciousness of Belgrave Square.

Yet even in that least changing of London squares, he did not recover the self that he was used to, the hard impersonal self that the war and Army life had polished into a shell. There was a chink in his armour and under it a self-inflicted wound. Yes, unknowingly he had stabbed himself and with a weapon soft as thistledown – a dream.

Often after that, even if South Halkin Street wasn't on his route, he would make a detour to go through it, and sometimes look in through the windows, and sometimes drive on without looking.

Chapter 17

CALL at the studio in Chelsea first, and then pick up the girl-friend on Campden Hill – that used to be the form. But this time, the third time Leadbitter had taken out the couple, it was to be the other way round. As always he was punctual, but Constance was already on the doorstep.

'Good evening,' she said. She did not know his name.

'Good evening, madam,' said Leadbitter.

'What a lovely evening,' Constance said. It wasn't really a lovely evening but her happiness made it seem so.

'The wireless said rain later,' said Leadbitter, who had been listening in.

'Oh, but they're always wrong!'

Again the happy note, as if everything she wished for must come true.

'They do sometimes make mistakes,' agreed Leadbitter, who seldom contradicted a customer.

She sat down on the back seat and Leadbitter drove off.

At the studio he pressed the door-bell, but no one came.

'He isn't often late,' said Constance, 'something must have kept him. He'll be here in a minute.'

She tried to settle down to wait, squeezing herself further and further into the corner of the car, as though the pressure of its upholstery could restrain her impatience; but after a few minutes impatience got the better of her, and she reached for the door-handle, mistaking it, however, for the handle that regulated the window. Muddled, she tried both in vain. Leadbitter came to her rescue and opened the door for her. She stood on the pavement looking down the street.

'This is the way he would come, I think,' she said, more to herself than to Leadbitter. 'You don't think anything can have happened to him?'

Leadbitter's eyes followed hers. He was not fond of Hughie, anything but. Hughie was a heel or a gink or anything you liked to call him. And he had no great regard for Constance, except in so far as she sometimes took the mickey out of Hughie. Moreover he was paid for waiting and it didn't matter to him how late Hughie was. Once he would not have understood how one human being could set so much store on seeing another, especially when that other was Hughie; but today he found himself sharing Constance's anxiety, and said as sympathetically as he could:

'The time always goes slowly when you're waiting, madam. The watched pot never boils.'

'You're quite right,' she said, 'but it isn't like him to be late. I don't usually worry when people don't turn up: there's nearly always some simple explanation.'

She strained her eyes as though the intensity of her gaze could draw him to her.

'He'll probably take a taxi,' Leadbitter said.

'He doesn't take taxis much – at least he usen't to. It's silly of me, but I can't help feeling anxious.'

The street seemed empty of everything except her longing for him. She drew herself up and leaned back, to get a better view.

'I think you'd be more comfortable inside the car, madam,' said Leadbitter. 'I'll keep an eye open for him and tell you when he comes.'

Obediently she got back into the car, leaving Leadbitter standing sentinel beside it. The keen edge of her anxiety was wearing off and she was giving herself up to the impersonal process of waiting, when unseen by both of them a taxi drew up at their rear and Hughie stood before her, long before her thoughts were ready for him.

'Well,' she said, trying to conceal her joy. 'This is a nice way to treat a lady.'

'Another lady was to blame,' he said, and kissed her rather perfunctorily.

'I guessed as much,' said Constance. 'May I know which lady?'

'Yes,' said Hughie, 'but first we must decide where we are going to dine.'

They fixed on the hotel at Richmond.

'And now tell me who the siren was,' said Constance.

'Can't you guess?'

'I'm not very well up in your private life.'

'It was Ernestine.'

'Oh, Ernestine.' Constance's voice trailed into indifference at the name. 'Are you still painting her?'

'I've almost finished.'

'But you couldn't have been painting her till now,' objected Constance. 'It's nearly dark.'

'I stayed to have a drink.'

'Oh, did you? Does Ernestine make a good Martini?'

'Not quite dry enough for my taste.'

'Not strong enough, you mean.'

'Perhaps I do.'

'Is the portrait being a success?' asked Constance, conversationally.

'Oh yes, I think so.'

'You don't sound too sure. Should I like it?'

'I expect you'd say it flattered her.'

'I know I should. ... Does she like it – Ernestine?'

'She dotes on it.'

'Oh dear, oh dear, these nice women. She is a nice woman, of course, though she's a goose.'

'Yes, but aren't all nice people geese?'

'Cheap cynics might say so.'

'At any rate she lays golden eggs.'

'And dotes on you, as well as on the portrait?'

'Well, yes, I think she does.'

'Misguided creature. It's hard to find a silly woman nowadays, but she is one. What have you done about it?'

'Nothing to speak of – that is, well, nothing.'

'I keep seeing her stretched out on that day-bed,' said Constance. 'It seems so incongruous, somehow. She should be upright, shouldn't she? How long is it since you started painting her?'

'Oh, two or three weeks.'

'And now the idyll's coming to an end?'

'She doesn't want it to,' said Hughie.

'Doesn't want it to?'

'No, she wants to marry me.'

There was a silence, during which Leadbitter became aware of a rattle in the car which he could not account for.

'You mean,' said Constance at last, 'that she has asked you to marry her?'

'We were talking about money,' Hughie said, 'and the way it keeps people apart – keeps them at arm's length, I mean.'

'I've never known it do that,' Constance said.

'Oh, I have. . . . She said it made a barrier between people who were fond of each other. She'd known an instance in her own experience. She didn't say what it was but someone had been made to suffer, through this very thing. "And I shouldn't like it to happen again," she said.'

'And what did you say?'

'I said, "Neither should I. But who would suffer?" and she said, "In this case I should." '

'And what did you say?'

'I didn't quite know what she meant, and yet I did, if you understand me. I didn't like to ask her, and yet I couldn't not ask her. It wasn't any use trying to go on painting her, because she'd broken the pose and was standing up. So I got off my stool and stood up, too.'

'And then, when you were both perpendicular –?'

'Then I saw that it was crucial for her, whatever it was, and I moved towards her. But she backed away, and I said, "Don't you want me to paint you any more?" – I suppose it was a silly thing to say.'

'Well, it gave her an opening.'

'Yes. And then she said, "Yes please, but not just now." I saw that she was trembling, so I went to the tray and poured out something for her – brandy, I think it was. It caught her throat and made her cough. But she tried to get it down and then she looked at me and said, "But you have nothing to drink." I was touched by that and mixed myself a Martini – I could tell she didn't want me to look at her. But I couldn't drink it just ignoring her – after all she was my hostess. So I waited a moment and said, "Whom shall I drink to?" – I wanted to say something – and she said, "To love." '

'And then you kissed her?' Constance said.

'Well, no, I meant to, but she didn't put her glass down, and said, "If we were married, would you still want to paint me?" '

'And you said, "I must have notice of that question"?'

'I didn't know what to say. And then she said, "What I meant was, would you still want to paint? I shouldn't be taking away your occupation?"

' "Oh no," I said.

' "I'm not an occupation to anyone," she said, "but I could be a background. . . . the background you know so well" – and she looked round the room without looking at me. "Now if I've said something I shouldn't have said, and asked a question I ought not to have asked, it's because of what we were just saying. It isn't my fault that I'm rich, rich enough to frighten some people off, so why should I suffer for it? But I shouldn't want you to suffer for it either, beyond the embarrassment of saying no. And anyway it's leap year – I have that excuse." '

'She must have thought it all out,' Constance said. 'If she hadn't had the delicacy to ask you first, would you have asked her, Hughie?'

'No.'

'Because of her money?'

'Well, that was one reason.'

'What was the other?'

'I'm not in love with her.'

'But you did in fact say yes? What else could a gentleman do?'

Hughie's silence gave consent.

'So that was why you were late. Well, good luck to you, my dear,' said Constance. 'Good luck to you. Good luck,' she repeated.

After a minute or two she said, 'Do you know, I don't think I'll go out to dinner after all. Should you mind very much? I somehow don't feel in the mood for it.'

Hughie said miserably, 'Oh, but you must dine somewhere.'

'No, I don't think I need. If I feel like eating, I'll get myself something on a tray, like women do. Please, Hughie, tell our kind driver to turn back.'

'Oh, but we can't do that, it's all arranged.'

'Yes, but all the same I'd rather. I oughtn't to have come out this evening anyhow, I've got a lot of homework. You forget I'm a working woman.'

'Oh, just this once,' pleaded Hughie.

'No, not this once. I'm not really in form. I know you won't believe me, but I've got a bit of a headache.'

'Then we'll go back,' said Hughie. 'Leadbitter,' he said, clearing his throat, 'would you turn round? My friend wants to go home.'

'Very good, sir.'

The car stopped. It was not quite easy to turn round. An unbroken stream of traffic conspired to keep them stationary. But Leadbitter was a driver as patient as he was vigilant, and at last with a sharp inward movement which flung the two on the back seat against each other, but not into each other's arms, they started on their homeward way.

Chapter 18

Leadbitter listened to their silence as intently as he had listened to their speech. Would they never speak again?

Whatever else happens, he thought, I have lost a customer. Hughie won't employ me again to take his girl friend out; he won't take her out again. And when Lady Franklin becomes Mrs Hughie, and wears the pants as no doubt she will, she won't give any work to Leadbitter's Garages Ltd.

Well, it was just too bad and he had only himself to blame. He couldn't swear, but it seemed pretty clear from what they said that the one taste of love-making he had given Lady Franklin had whetted her appetite for more: he had given her the shock, the liberating shock, and Hughie had reaped the benefit.

He had been had for a mug.

Hughie said he had made no advances, or nearly none, to Lady Franklin, but was it likely? Was it likely, with her stretched out on the couch, day after day, with her hands clasped behind her head, lifting her breasts in a way that he didn't have to imagine because he could see them before his eyes – he couldn't help seeing them. Day after day Hughie's paint-brush lovingly portrayed those curves; and was it likely that his hand was satisfied with putting them on the canvas?

For the first time Leadbitter knew what jealousy was: its poison paralysed his being; if he had been spoken to he could not have answered, so completely were his faculties turned inwards. Of love, the cause of jealousy, he was unaware; his hostility to Hughie seemed to include Lady Franklin, too. The pair of them! And it included Constance, whose sudden change of heart and mind, cutting the evening short, would rob him of a pound, at least. Customers could cancel to their heart's content; it wasn't policy to charge them for their defections, but woe betide him if he failed to keep an appointment! The customer would go elsewhere.

But his hearing did not share the turmoil of his spirit. Constance's voice was breaking the long silence.

'I'm sorry, Hughie,' she said, 'to be such bad company. I said I wished you luck, and so I do. Only I can't quite realize yet the change it's going to make to us – to me, I should say.'

'And to me,' said Hughie.

'And to you, of course. Only for you it will be a change for the better, won't it? Materially, I mean, and in most other ways. Whereas for me –'

'Darling,' said Hughie, 'what good have I been to you? I've been an encumbrance, really. All these years –'

'The best years of a woman's life,' put in Constance, mimicking a voice.

'Well, you've been tied to me. You could have married.'

'I could have married,' Constance said. 'But did I want to? Once, perhaps – but no. I can't pretend you've robbed me of the joys of marriage. No, instead you've given me a great deal, Hughie; you may not have meant to but you did. I shouldn't have stuck to you if you hadn't. I'm a bit of a clinger, aren't I? I've thought that more than once. And what have I given you in exchange? A good deal of discouragement –'

'Oh, I don't know,' said Hughie, listlessly. 'You kept me up to the mark. I shouldn't have gone on painting if you hadn't kept telling me how bad it was. I'm made like that.'

'Ernestine won't tell you it's bad.'

'No, she thinks I'm smashing. ... You could give her a wrinkle or two about me.'

'I could,' said Constance, 'but it wouldn't be very seemly,

would it? I shall have to fade out. I feel I'm fading out already. Am I here, do you think?'

'Yes, you're here.'

'I wasn't sure. I feel like a stranger. In a minute I shall be making conversation. What do you talk to Ernestine about?'

'I told you. About myself, and about herself, and coming back to life. Everything's new and exciting to her.'

'God, you make me feel old. But I don't suppose I'm much older than she is.'

'I shouldn't think there was a lot in it. She's twenty-seven.'

'Then we're both cradle-snatchers. Her first husband was a good deal older than she. She worshipped him, didn't she? He was like a father to her. I fancy she would worship any husband. How will you like being worshipped?'

'Well, it would be a change.'

'You don't sound as greedy for incense as an idol should. But I see I made a mistake. I ought to have worshipped you.'

'Well, you were rather tough with me sometimes. Sarcastic, you know.'

'Yes, and I regret it. You won't remember it against me, will you? I should like to be a pleasant memory – that is, if you remember me at all.'

'I shan't forget you,' Hughie said.

'Well, that's something. You'll have a lot of new friends, Ernestine's friends with Bentleys and Rolls Royces. An unending round of gaiety – you know what serious-minded people are when they take to social life! It quite goes to their heads, they make a religion of it. Goodness and worldliness are terrifying together. And Ernestine was very *mondaine* once – in the nicest way, of course. She'll organize you. No more corduroy trousers, no more open shirts, and perhaps no beard. You'll have to paint her as Delilah next – she would be a very thorough one – conscientious, you know, even with the shears. I shouldn't be surprised if there's quite a streak of determination in her, in spite of all her vagueness. As her consort you'll have to toe the line. What's done in Chelsea won't do in South Halkin Street.'

'She seems to like Bohemians,' said Hughie.

'Yes, in the same way that visitors to the Zoo like lions. I expect she is a lion-huntress, it's part of her idealism. But she likes them in a cage. Yours will be a gilded cage, poor Hughie.'

'I don't think you're being very fair to her,' said Hughie.

'No, I'm not. Why am I talking like this? Why am I talking at all? I wish to God we were home. Dear, dear, Hughie, please tell our driver to step on the gas. Tell him I don't a bit mind arriving dead – in fact I'd rather.'

Hughie spoke to Leadbitter, and the car moved faster.

'You'll let me come in with you, won't you?' Hughie said.

'No, darling, I'd much rather not, if you don't mind. I really couldn't bear it. I want to be alone – alone with the difference.'

'Why need there be a difference?' Hughie asked, and his voice changed so much it might have been another person's. 'Why need there be a difference?' he repeated.

'What do you mean, Hughie? I don't understand.'

'I mean there needn't be a difference,' Hughie said.

'Not a difference, and you married to Ernestine?'

'It needn't make a difference to *us*,' said Hughie.

There was a pause, and Leadbitter could hear Constance catching her breath.

'Oh no, Hughie,' she said at last. 'I think there *must* be a difference. It was sweet of you to say there needn't be. But no, no, no, there must be.'

'Why can't we go on as we are?' said Hughie, his voice driving home the words like a soft hammer. 'Why can't we go on as we are, Constance? I mean, what's to prevent us?'

'What's to prevent us?' Constance repeated dully. 'What's

to prevent us? Do you really want me to try to answer that?'

'If you can,' Hughie said.

'I can't in any way that would convince you. Please, Hughie, please, let me go home – we can't be far from home now.'

'Will it be home without me?' Hughie asked.

'It might be, I can't tell.'

'Do you want it to be?'

'I don't know what I want. You've upset me, as the gardener said.'

'What gardener?'

'Oh, it's an old story that my father used to tell. The gardener was upset, so he gave in his notice.'

'Is that what you are going to do?' asked Hughie.

'I rather thought you'd given *me* notice,' Constance said.

'I'm getting mixed,' said Hughie, 'with all this gardener stuff. Couldn't a mistress have two gardeners, or a gardener have two mistresses?'

'I don't know what you mean by mistress.'

'Well, try to think.'

'A little while ago,' Constance said, 'you told me I was being unfair to Ernestine. Now I think you are being unfair to her, that's all.'

'It doesn't matter so much about Ernestine. Am I being unfair to *you*? That's the question.'

'Yes, no. . . Of course you have a perfect right to marry.'

'And haven't I a right –?'

'No, I don't think you have.'

'Not even the right to make you happy?' Hughie asked.

'Why do you think it would make me happy to share you with another woman?'

'You've shared me with another woman before.'

'I know. I know you sometimes strayed. But that was different.'

'Why was it different?'

'Oh, Hughie, you're like a child, always asking questions. If you can't see it's different, you're not fit to be a married man. Now don't say any more till I get home.'

'Why are you so cruel to me, Constance?' said Hughie, his voice roughening. 'Why do you want to punish me? You said you wish me luck: well, what luck should I have without you? You are my luck. I'm not in love with Ernestine and never should be! I'm in love with you. Darling, please, please be reasonable. Don't deprive us both of what we both want. Or even if you no longer want it, don't deprive me.'

Constance didn't answer for a moment, then she said, in another voice, and as if she was changing the subject:

'I don't know Ernestine well, she's really only an acquaintance. I knew her before she was married and got rich, and she kept up with me a little until ... until she had her breakdown and saw no one. She's always been a little unreal to me: I told you that. I don't know how she thinks and feels; she's carried away by her enthusiasms; you're the latest, Hughie. Perhaps she doesn't feel much, in a direct human way of feeling; you wouldn't know that. But I don't suppose she ever thinks about me, unless she's sending out a card. She's not like us – she can have all the friends she wants, a whole new set tomorrow. She's privileged and protected like a minor royalty. She has so much it doesn't seem quite fair – but that's no reason. The reason is, the reason is, that I can't do without you. Oh, Hughie –'

'Look, Constance!'

'No, I mustn't look, don't let me look, and don't look at me. I can't bear to be looked at.'

'Well, then.'

The kiss brought down on each its cloak of invisibility. They did not see, nor were they seen, save by Leadbitter, when a street-lamp or a passing car shone on his mirror. Nor did they emerge into the light of each other's eyes: they shrank from such awareness; only their hands still kept in touch.

'Where are we?' asked Constance. 'Do you know where we are, Hughie? I haven't the least idea – we might be anywhere.'

Hughie didn't answer, but Leadbitter said:

'About five minutes from Campden Hill now, madam.'

'Good heavens! Campden Hill!' said Hughie. 'Why are we going there? You don't want to go there, do you, Constance?'

'Not specially,' said Constance.

'Well, what about going back, going back to Richmond?'

'I've nothing against it.'

'But of course. Leadbitter, we have changed our minds. My friend doesn't want to go home, after all. Will you go back to Richmond?'

'Very good, sir.'

'I am so terribly hungry,' Hughie said.

'Yes, so am I,' said Constance. 'Ravenous.'

Slowly their spirits rose: the hotel when at last they reached it, seemed a paradise: a paradise regained. All that they thought they had lost was given back to them. Their eyes regained their boldness; they feasted on each other, lingeringly, unashamedly, while they were waiting for their further feast. It was as if they had not seen each other for years – for years, or never before.

Half-way through dinner the porter came to their table and said to Hughie:

'Are you Mr Cantrip?'

'Yes, I am,' said Hughie, proudly, as if to be Mr Cantrip was the greatest distinction in the world.

'Your chauffeur would like to speak to you.'

Hughie got up and went out. When he came back he said:

'It's nothing serious. He's had to go home, his wife's not well.'

They laughed immoderately at this, not out of heartlessness or because the mere idea of a sick wife was funny, but because they were in a mood to laugh at anything.

'But how are *we* to get home?' asked Constance.

'He's arranged to send another car.'

'Well, that was good staff-work.' Making an effort, she jerked her mind to someone else's problems: they seemed unreal and very distant from her.

'How did he know his wife was ill?'

'He always telephones to her, apparently, when he's out on a job for any length of time.'

'What an ideal husband! I hope you'll be as devoted as he is, Hughie.'

'You bet I shall be.'

Chapter 19

LADY FRANKLIN,
Madam,
It has reached the ears of a well-wisher that the man you intend to marry is unworthy of you. He already has a woman in tow and he intends to go on living with her after he is married to you. I thought you would like to know this.

Leadbitter stared at the letter. Like many, perhaps most, anonymous letters, it wasn't the first draft; quite a number of earlier attempts had found their way down the w.c. It was laborious and frustrating, printing the message out in capital letters, always hoping it would be the final version, the fair copy, and finding that it wasn't. He wasn't satisfied with this one either, substituted 'I thought you ought to know' for 'I thought you would like to know' and wrote it all out again. She wouldn't like to know perhaps, but she ought to know, of that he was sure.

Or was he?

Since that evening, not many evenings back, when he had surprised himself by leaving the loving couple guzzling at their hotel in Richmond, thereby costing himself two quid at least for the other car, he had undergone so many changes of feeling that he hardly recognized himself. He hadn't forgotten Lady Franklin of course, though he had tried to. She was like one of those items on a balance sheet, which can appear as a profit, or a loss, according to the taste and fancy of the accountant. In the past, she had been a profit, certainly; incomparably the largest single profit he had known. Yet he couldn't think of her as a profit: he thought of her as a lost customer who, but for his mishandling, would have been worth far more in the future than she had been in the past. As such he had succeeded in keeping her separate from Frances, his wife who was her substitute; Frances was all profit, she was what Lady Franklin might have been had all gone well; she was Lady Franklin shorn of Lady Franklin's shortcomings: his fantasy of Frances had helped to keep at bay the real Lady Franklin.

But the conversation in the car broke down that frail distinction, and long before Hughie and Constance had had their talk out the two women had united in one image. In vain he tried to recover his old cynicism by remembering the snub she had given him. Serve her right, serve her right, he had told himself; she asked for it. She led me on, she played with fire, but she wouldn't have me, because I'm not her class. But at any rate I hadn't got another woman tucked away on the back seat; I wasn't going to use her money to keep a mistress with. She would have had me to herself, such as I am.

At that a wave of tenderness broke over him, almost as painful physically as if it had been tears, so many adhesions were washed away by it. As though awakening from an anaesthetic, he could not remember how he had felt before or find his way back to his old self. Discipline had prevented him from telling the couple what he thought of them, discipline made him drive them back to Richmond; but then it failed him. He could not face the thought of listening to what they would say on the way home; he could not trust himself to listen to it.

Driving home alone he let his fancy loose on Lady Franklin. For the first time he thought of her out of a business context, and remote from actuality: she was his in any way he liked to think of her, nothing could come between them. Their freedom was not earth-bound. But since fantasy requires a scene, a local habitation, and a kind of verisimilitude, he began to recall the places where they had been together. At first it was a vision of a door, the door of his car, opening and closing as she crossed and recrossed the threshold of his presence; and always there had been in him a pocket of resistance to her effect on him; it was something which he felt he must not yield to, it challenged his attitude to life. Why had he armed himself against her, why had he felt that like all women she was threatening him, encroaching on his freedom? Now, in his fantasy, this resistance melted; he acknowledged her kindness to him, which before he would not admit, attributing it to many other causes – caprice, ostentation, sexual attraction, never to what it was – a generalized benevolence which had found its outlet in him. He would not have welcomed this explanation, perhaps no one would have; he thought that her benevolence was for him alone, for something she had seen in him that others could not see. He had glimpses of it in his fantasies of family life; but obsessive though they were he knew that they were make-believe, variations on a theme while this was the theme itself. Lady Franklin was a real person; Frances and Don and Pat and Sue were figments.

He did not analyse how it had come about that his thoughts of Lady Franklin were now full of sweetness. Like a traveller benighted in a wood, who comes out at dawn into the sunlight and is filled with a sense of thankfulness and blessing, he dismissed from his mind the mazy wanderings of the night, not realizing that they had brought him to his goal. But if the stranger, love, now occupied his heart, there was another, older tenant who, strange to say, agreed with the newcomer. Hostility was natural to Leadbitter; his being thrived on it. It did not thrive on hatred, for hatred was too personal an emotion; he would not flatter anyone by hating him. In war he did not hate the enemy, but his hostility never wavered, just as his loyalty to his own side never wavered. He did not love his own side; quite often he was far from loving it, but he was loyal to it. In the civilian world his trouble was that he had no side to be loyal to. Now he had one. Lady Franklin was threatened and he must save her.

In war, beyond a certain point you did not count the cost. You had to be prepared for losses or you could not hope to win. You might have to proceed regardless. You must take risks for yourself; you must take risks for your side and without consulting them. The men understood that you did not always tell them what the risks were when such and such a position had to be taken; you took the risk on their behalf and yours. If there were casualties it was just too bad, but they did not matter if the operation was successful.

Lady Franklin would be upset when she got the letter; she would be very upset, she would cry, perhaps. In war soldiers themselves sometimes cried, and their relations cried quite often. You can't make an omelette without breaking eggs. It was better to have a good cry than to marry a man who was keeping another woman with your money. That was as clear as clear. And if Lady Franklin ever came to know whose hand had struck the blow that freed her, she would thank him.

There was a risk, of course, that she would find out, but it was a small risk and a risk that had to be taken. Leadbitter had been brought up in a world where tale-bearing was not unknown but where no one ever asked 'Who told you?' – for it wouldn't have been etiquette. Lady Franklin would never trace the letter to him; he did not think she would mention it to Hughie. The poison would work in secret. And if she taxed Hughie with its message, what then? Would Hughie guess who had sent it? No, because he had no idea that Leadbitter knew Lady Franklin.

If Hughie did seek him out and cut up rough, well that would just suit Leadbitter, who would only be too glad to show him where he got off.

Why then did he hesitate to send the letter?

Because somehow, in his total vision of Lady Franklin, the letter was out of place. It didn't fit in. This matter of her marrying or not marrying Hughie was only one aspect of what she meant to Leadbitter; an ugly aspect, and therefore foreign to her. He could not associate her with an anonymous letter. It was an anomaly, like a gasometer built on to a cathedral. She was much more than someone who is to be the victim of skulduggery; it didn't touch her, somehow.

Of all the images he associated with Lady Franklin, a cathedral was the one that occurred to him most often. There it rose – a monument to something. To what? Perhaps to the Virgin Mary; perhaps like the French cathedrals she had talked about, it was a product of the cult for her. A great deal of money had gone to building it, it was impersonal, no one's property, and yet it was his because she had shown it to him, he saw it through her eyes. It couldn't be seen as a whole because there were too many viewpoints, too many ways of looking at it; he himself added a new one every day. Yet it had an entity, a self, and that self was his: to admire, to adore, to add to at his pleasure. At times she filled his mind so completely that he couldn't remember what she looked like. If he tried a more familiar, and a more tormenting approach, and imagined her on the couch, the day-bed as they called it, with her hands clasped behind her head, he couldn't see her face, it was a blur. But as a cathedral, though the qualities he looked for on the bed were absent, she satisfied his spiritual needs. For he had them, more urgently perhaps than physical needs, of which he took a hygienic, narrow and belittling view. They were the complement of what his mirror showed him, the necessary counterpart to his self-admiration, whereas in the cathedral he could lose himself.

And if he did not associate Lady Franklin with an anonymous letter, neither did he associate himself. Anonymous letters were against his code.

Leadbitter was a stranger to moral problems, but not to moral habits, he lived by his code. Roughly it was the code that was recognized in the Army, but it was stricter than that: it didn't allow scrounging, for instance. It couldn't, for as a warrant officer he had to be looked up to. Anybody's property was safe with Leadbitter, and not only because it would have been bad business to take it. Customers often left things in his car; sometimes they rang him up about them, sometimes they didn't. Sometimes when they did ring up it was just to make an inquiry: did he remember if they had left anything? It would have been easy to say no, without the slightest fear of being found out: Leadbitter could have made a good thing of a private lost-property office. But he never tried to, because he didn't see himself as that sort of man. It wasn't so much that he disapproved of stealing as that he despised the kind of man who stole. If he had stolen he would have had to despise himself, and that he couldn't do. A habit is harder to break than a resolution; Leadbitter was much more moral, according to his lights, than many men who search their consciences. So cut-and-dried was his code that he was as immune from temptation, in the moral sphere, as on the barrack-square; he could as soon have come on to parade looking like a pox-doctor's clerk (in army parlance) as have transgressed his own ideas of what was fitting.

It wasn't fitting to write an anonymous letter, he would have despised the man who did it.

But Lady Franklin had revived in him the faculty of loyalty – loyalty which since he left the Army he had owed to nothing and to no one but himself. Loyalty had been the ruling principle of his nature; loyalty to his side, his regiment, his country, and loyalty demanded he should send the letter.

Leadbitter had no one to confide in; his thoughts went on inside him and his deepest thoughts were secret from himself. In a good mood he was anything but taciturn: he talked a lot and made his hearers laugh. But his conversation was decorative, if not always decorous; it was a game, an exercise in irony. Banter and insult and leg-pulling were the ingredients. Everything must be handled with a light touch. He seldom meant what he said, though he sometimes meant the opposite of what he said. In business talks he listened not so much to the words, which were often misleading, as to the sense behind them, which was usually more apparent in what was not said than in what was said – he listened to hear if the deal was going his way, and his replies were framed accordingly. He seldom spoke his thoughts and still more rarely, and then only in anger, did he speak his feelings, because to expose them made him feel naked, and worse than naked – flayed.

Feelings with Leadbitter were something to keep hidden, something of which, if people knew, they would take advantage, and the deeper the feeling, the more closely he guarded it. If he had been accused of murder, he might almost, from a kind of pride, have withheld the one fact that would have cleared him.

So the conflict between his loyalty and his code was conducted without words and almost without thoughts; guns went off, the battle swayed this way and that, but of rational, articulate argument there was as little as there is on any battlefield. But loyalty held the heavier guns, for Leadbitter knew that discipline – the code – was but a means to loyalty. If circumstances called for an act of indiscipline, as in war they sometimes did, for the greater good of the side, then discipline must go and codes that ruled anonymous letters out must also go. The issues were quite clear: if Lady Franklin married Hughie, she would be making the biggest mistake of her life. Her welfare was at stake; her welfare consisted in knowing Hughie for what he was, and in not marrying him. ... Nothing else came into it; facts, not feelings, counted. Lady Franklin must send Hughie packing, and then, and then – Well, then the battle would be over, and with it Leadbitter's responsibility. Lady Franklin would be free, free as a conquering country, free to think again, and free to choose again.

She would not think of him, of course. Among the forces fighting for loyalty was one that Leadbitter had no idea of – jealousy.

Yet the code did not easily admit defeat, it fought a long rearguard action, the first such action that had ever taken place in Leadbitter's mind, and it was still struggling feebly, still blackmailing him with the threat that now he would have to think of himself as the kind of man who wrote anonymous letters, when Hughie rang him up. Could Leadbitter call for him at his studio, at seven o'clock in the evening, three days hence? 'I'm taking a friend out to dinner,' said Hughie, carelessly. 'Will you be free, say, till eleven o'clock? And by the way,' he added, before Leadbitter had had time to answer, 'I hope that wife of yours is better?'

'Oh yes, sir,' Leadbitter replied, 'she's quite all right now.'

'And how are you yourself?' asked Hughie with his easy charm.

'Oh, I'm fine, sir. . . . But I'm not sure about Thursday – I've got a tentative booking for then. Can I find out whether it's on or not, and ring you back?'

'Yes, certainly,' said Hughie, and Leadbitter resented the happiness in his voice.

'I could send another man in my place,' he said.

'Just as you like, but I'd rather it was you, so come if you can.'

'Very good, sir,' and Leadbitter rang off.

The tentative booking was fictitious, a ruse for gaining time. Somehow it had never crossed his mind that Hughie would require his services again. He had taken such a strong dislike to Hughie that instinctively he felt it must be returned. Yet how could Hughie know what he felt? And if he did know, why should he worry? To 'them' Leadbitter was just part of the car's furniture, with as little personal feeling as the car had, perhaps less, for the car had its moods and might break down, whereas Leadbitter had no moods, or was supposed to have none, and couldn't break down, he couldn't afford to. For at least half his customers, Leadbitter didn't exist as a man.

But for Hughie, surprisingly, he did. Hughie had asked him, contemptuously no doubt, about his wife – 'that wife of yours'. Leadbitter had no wife, but if he had had, he would have been gratified to hear her asked about. He had asked about him, Leadbitter, as well. It was rather decent of Hughie: decent of him too, to say he wanted Leadbitter in preference to someone else. Was he such a bad chap after all?

Suppose he put the job out? There was always the risk, if you sent a substitute, that the substitute would steal the customer; they very often tried to. 'If ever you want me again, sir, here's my card. Leadbitter's often pretty busy, sir, perhaps I can help you out when he can't come.'

Certainly Leadbitter had never wanted to see Hughie and his girl friend again. But was it wise to let his personal feelings get in the way of business? Wouldn't he be a Billy Muggins to sacrifice a job worth several pounds? He wouldn't be helping Lady Franklin; on the contrary he would be deserting her, deserting her and the post from which he could best watch her advantage.

'How's that wife of yours?'

Most of his customers neither knew nor asked nor cared whether Leadbitter had a wife or not. Leadbitter had no wife; but there was someone, Frances, who had been like a wife to him – all bull, of course, all ballyhoo – and Hughie had asked after her. Few of his customers asked after his health, but Hughie had. Hughie had never done him any harm, indeed he had put money in his way – not his own money, but good money all the same.

A kind word or act from someone you dislike often carries more weight than the same kindness from a friend. And so it was with Leadbitter. He still didn't like Hughie – Hughie was a clot – but he couldn't think of him as hardly as he had. He would have to send the letter, of course, but not just now, not for a few days at any rate. Meanwhile – and it was more of a relief than he would have admitted – he needn't think of himself as the sort of man who wrote anonymous letters.

So out of the very shadow of defeat the code had snatched a momentary victory.

Leadbitter rang Hughie up and said the booking was O.K.

Chapter 20

'WILL you drive to 39 South Halkin Street?' said Hughie. 'I want to pick up someone there.'

Leadbitter's heart turned over.

'South Halkin Street?' he repeated.

'Yes, you know, a turning out of Belgrave Square.'

Leadbitter drove off slowly. It had never come into his calculations that Lady Franklin might be the other passenger, and his mind refused to accept the actuality of it. He who had stood up to so many situations involving life and death, felt he couldn't stand up to this one. Yet how could he get out of it? Deliberately he took a wrong turning and began to drive at right angles to his destination.

'This isn't the nearest way,' said Hughie, irritably. 'The nearest way's through Walton Street and Pont Street.'

'I know,' said Leadbitter, who even at this crisis resented being told the way. 'But Walton Street is up. You can't get through there.' It wasn't true but any excuse was good enough.

They crawled up Gloucester Road towards the Post Office, and suddenly Leadbitter had an idea.

'Do you mind, sir,' he said as casually as he could, 'if I stop here and do a telephone call? My wife's not well and I want to ask how she is.'

'Oh, look here,' said Hughie, 'your wife's always falling ill.'

'She's in the family way,' said Leadbitter briefly.

'Oh, is she? Well, I don't know whether to congratulate you or not. But don't be long: I'm a bit late already.'

Slowly, and almost for the first time in his life with a

bent head, Leadbitter entered the Post Office. Passing the telephone box with scarcely a look he asked for the London Trades Directory and taking it to a window began to turn the pages, to give himself a pretext for delay.

Was he so yellow that he couldn't face seeing Lady Franklin again?

The imputation of cowardice, even self-inflicted, put him on his mettle. And was he to go throwing away jobs like this? Hughie wasn't a good man, maybe, but he was quite a good customer. What business was it of Leadbitter's how Hughie behaved? And at this eleventh hour he couldn't find another driver. For a moment his business self, on the side of courage, got the upper hand. He gave the Directory back to the girl at the counter, and started for the door. Of course he would go through with it.

But no, he couldn't. How easy it had been, with only himself to think about, to make up his mind! But Lady Franklin – how would *she* take it? How would she like meeting him? Not very much, not very much, he told himself. She was nervous; she might tremble, she might even faint. She had spoken kindly of him, that he knew; but at heart she must regard him as a renegade. A vision of what he must mean to her pricked him with self-loathing. No, he couldn't expose her to his second shock: Hughie must find another means of transport.

Braced to say this, he pushed open the door. But on the threshold another thought attacked him – attacked him so violently that it drove all other thoughts like chaff from his mind.

He wanted to see her again, didn't he? Wasn't it what he wanted most, to see her again? Wasn't there something he wanted to say to her? And how could he hope ever to see her, except this way? He thanked his stars he hadn't sent the letter. If she couldn't face him that was her look-out; he could and would face her.

'My wife's all right, sir,' he told Hughie, and had an odd feeling that he was speaking of Lady Franklin.

'I'm glad to hear it,' Hughie said perfunctorily. 'Well now, let's get on.'

This time Leadbitter took the nearest route and drove at his usual pace. That clot in front was doing some fierce braking. ... In the mirror he could see Hughie fidgeting on the back seat. He's nervous, thought Leadbitter: he's as nervous as a kitten, he's more nervous than I am. And just as though he had been going into battle he tried to clear his mind of hopes and fears, of any preconception of what might be going to happen, so that he would be free to deal with the situation as it developed. It was laughable to be taking these precautions; could any enemy be less dangerous than Lady Franklin, the mildest creature in the world? And yet excitement stirred his blood and try as he would to unify his faculties he was divided between the hope and fear of seeing her.

The car swung into the octagon of Belgrave Square. Only a minute or two now to zero hour. He stiffened his face and pressed his shoulders against the back of the seat, while behind him Hughie bounced about as though he was on springs.

How strange yet how familiar it was to be pulling up at her door, the door he had passed so many times, but had never expected to stop at again. How long ago was it, the last time he had called for her? Over a month; but not so long ago as the last time he had brought her back. What had happened to her on the road from Winchester? Did she have far to walk before she got a lift? Did she thumb a lorry? Sometimes he had pictured her trudging for miles, carrying her heavy bag – pictured her at first with glee, then with mixed feelings, and lastly with remorse. She must have got home somehow; how, he would never know, unless –

'That will be all, Leadbitter.' But it wasn't going to be all; he was to take her out this evening, unless –

Unless she refused to let him drive her.

He pressed the bell, and after some delay the door opened.

'It's a long time since we saw you,' said the butler. 'Never since the day of the accident.'

'What accident?' said Leadbitter. 'I've never had an accident.'

'You've a short memory then,' the butler said. 'The last time you took her ladyship out, you had an accident, and her ladyship came back in a taxi. Properly frightened she was, all trembling. It upset her ladyship for days. And yet you say "No accident".'

'Oh that,' said Leadbitter. 'Yes, I'd forgotten that – that little spot of bother that we had.'

'Her ladyship hasn't forgotten it,' said the butler. 'That's why she didn't want to trust herself to you again.'

'Gangway, please,' said a voice behind and below them, and Hughie strode impatiently up the steps.

'Oh, good evening, sir,' said the butler, with every kind of emphasis in his voice. 'Her ladyship is just coming down.'

He ushered Hughie in and Leadbitter returned to stand beside the car. Facing a firing squad the condemned man has the option of being blindfolded. Leadbitter didn't take this precaution but, to delay the moment of recognition, he pulled his cap down over his eyes. He tried to make his mind a blank, and when that failed, to relieve it by thinking of a sunny day at the sea-side – a mental amulet he sometimes used in times of stress.

So he was in Ramsgate when voices sounded from the doorway.

Lady Franklin and Hughie were coming down the steps. In her eagerness to talk to him she had turned round and was looking up into his face; when he moved his head her eyes followed his. Leadbitter was half out of the car by this time; he hurried round the bonnet and opened the door, standing beside it with a wooden face and looking his own height, as a soldier should. Although he was a head taller than Lady Franklin he could see her face and the change that came over it as it jerked up towards his before she bent her head to enter the car.

Leadbitter felt sick with anti-climax, yet what, he asked himself, had he expected? That she would make some kind of demonstration, some violent show of feeling, either way? Was he so mean a creature that she had forgotten him already?

'Where to, sir?' he asked.

'Oh, I think the Oarsman's Arms at Richmond, it's not a bad place as they go, what do you think, Ernestine?' said Hughie in a voice that alternated between too little and too much self-confidence.

'I've never been there, but I'm sure I should like it,' Lady Franklin answered.

The other one liked it all right, thought Leadbitter, but he might have had more originality than to take this one there. Still it's all the same, her money pays for both.

'I hope you'll be comfortable in this car,' Hughie went on, 'I could have got a bigger one, of course, but this does very well for two. And he's a first-rate driver – I'd trust him anywhere.'

Leadbitter's neck reddened.

'He seems a careful driver,' Lady Franklin said, and said no more.

'Darling, you're rather silent,' Hughie rallied her. 'Nothing gone wrong, I hope? You did want to come out, didn't you? If not, I'll tell him to turn round, and we'll go back to your place. Dear Mrs Darrell would scratch up something for us, I'm sure. I'll break it to her, if you'll let me. She has rather a soft spot for me, you know.'

'Oh no,' said Lady Franklin. 'It's just ... it's just that I am so happy. This is the first time I've been out with you.'

'I know,' said Hughie contritely. 'And it oughtn't to have been the first time, ought it? I did want to ask you before, but I couldn't get the car.'

Couldn't get the car? thought Leadbitter. You never tried.

'I love going out,' said Lady Franklin, 'and it's so romantic and exciting, going to Richmond. Why have I never been before? I expect you often go – to paint, perhaps.'

'Oh yes,' said Hughie, 'I have, by bus, you know. It's more fun like that, in a way. You see so many amusing types of people. But as this was a special occasion – Do you ever go by bus?'

'My dear, of course I do.'

'I can't see you, somehow. I've thought of you in every possible situation, Ernestine, but never in a bus.'

'Oh, but I love buses. The conductors and conductresses are so nice to one. I like being called "dearie" and "ducks", don't you?'

'Would you like it if I did?'

'Yes, of course.'

'Well, ducks – no, it doesn't sound right, it's not you, somehow. I see I shall always have to treat you with respect.'

'Dearest, I couldn't bear it if you did. Cotton-wool isn't good for me. I like being ordered about. Everyone is ordered about now, aren't they? Why should one want to be different? I wasn't happy when I was different. You wouldn't say I was different now, would you?'

'No, dearie, absolutely indistinguishable.'

'I'm so glad. But I should like you to be different.'

'Why?'

'Because men should be different, and painters must be. I want you to be a very great painter.'

'Oh, Ernestine.'

'I shall give you no peace until you are.'

'Perhaps I am already.'

'You are, in my eyes. But I want you to be recognized by *everybody*.'

'Dearie, you have such large ideas,' said Hughie.

'But why not? With your talent and my – I mean, you could be my monument.'

'Why do you want a monument?'

'Well, to exist outside myself and in you. That's possible for a woman, isn't it?'

'Yes, I think so.'

'It wouldn't be unless I believed in you. But I do, absolutely.'

'As a painter,' Hughie asked, 'or as a man?'

'As both. I couldn't partially believe in you – what fun would that be?'

'It might not be such fun,' said Hughie, 'but it might be more realistic.'

'Oh darling, what discouraging things you say.'

'I don't want you to expect too much of me.'

'But that's what you're *for* – to be a beacon for my hopes.'

'And what are you for?'

'I'm just an incense-burner.'

Hughie laughed.

'Well, I *am* rather High Church.'

'But I shall be practical, too,' said Lady Franklin. 'We'll give tremendous parties.'

'How can I paint at parties?'

'In between you can. And have exhibitions.'

'You mean us to lead a very public life,' said Hughie.

'Oh, darling, no, we'll have our private life, that goes without saying. I long for it more than anything. Only you must teach it to me. I'm still a little afraid of private life - I've had too much of it.'

'Too much of being by yourself, you mean.'

'Yes, I suppose so. That's why I have this passion for sharing things. There's nothing one wants to possess in love except an increase in the power of loving, is there? I want to share *everything*.'

'Even me?' asked Hughie.

What's she going to say now? thought Leadbitter, when Lady Franklin didn't answer at once.

'Your work,' she said, 'of course, with all the world. But you, my darling? I hadn't thought of it.'

'I was only putting a hypothetical case,' said Hughie, 'just to try out your sharing theory.'

'Yes, I know, I know. But somehow I still can't picture it. It isn't real to me. Share you? No, I couldn't.'

'Not even your thoughts of me?'

'Those least of all. How should I divide them, without dividing myself? I was divided once; you brought me together, the two me's.... At least –' she stopped.

'I scent a reservation there,' said Hughie. 'What was, who was, this other integrating agent? Out with it, Ernestine.'

All at once Lady Franklin became extremely agitated.

'Haven't I told you – didn't I tell you? I thought I did. It was a gradual process to begin with – then the shock –'

'Oh yes, I remember the shock, the famous shock. What exactly was it? I feel I have a right to know. You ought to have no secrets from me now.'

'It was something – something that happened.'

'Well, of course it happened – at least I suppose it happened – but what *was* it?'

'I told you – a shock, a slight shock, a very slight shock.'

'A shocking shock?'

'Yes . . . no . . . Some time I'll tell you.'

'I demand to know now. How can I marry a woman who has an undeclared shock on her conscience?'

The car swerved.

'Oh, Hughie, please don't tease me. It was nothing much.'

'Well, what was the gradual process? At least you can tell me that.'

'It was a sort of slow awakening, I suppose, from the unhappy trance I'd been in.'

'You *are* being mysterious, Ernestine. I don't think I ought to marry someone who confesses to having had a hidden process. It doesn't sound quite nice.'

'It was rather nice.'

'Yes, I was afraid so. Are you thoroughly awakened now?'

'Of course I am.'

'Should I pinch you?'

'Why?'

'To see whether you're awake or not.'

'Couldn't I pinch myself?'

'Yes, if you'd rather.'

Lady Franklin seemed to consider.

'I used to pinch myself when I was ill,' she said. 'It didn't do much good.'

'Well, then, let me try.'

'I'm not sure I should like it.'

'Not like being awake?'

'Well, not too hard then.'

'Was that too hard?'

Lady Franklin gave a little cry.

'That's what the doctor ordered.'

She didn't sound as if she liked it, Leadbitter thought. She liked my way better. At any rate I didn't hurt her. He drove on faster, his mind a whirl of contradictory feelings. ... Bitterness, frustration, jealousy. But bitterness prevailed. It was like being in an earthquake – the roof of his life came off, the ceilings fell, the fabric tottered. Lady Franklin pinched like a common tart? Could disillusion go further than this? And how was he to drive them back? 'My wife,' he practised it to himself, 'is ill, she's very ill. It's a woman's complaint, and she's taken a turn for the worse. Yes, I know she was all right an hour ago, but these things happen. I must go back. I'll try to get you another car.'

Committing some such phrases to his memory, he drew up at the door of the hotel.

'Oh, are we there?'

'It looks as though we were,' said Hughie.

Leadbitter got out and opened the door, holding the handle as though it dirtied his fingers.

Lady Franklin did not look at him, she stood a few feet

away, waiting for Hughie to join her; then, her arm in his, they went towards the hotel. Half way up the steps she said to him:

'Will you wait a moment? I've left something in the car.'

'Tell me what it is, and I'll fetch it.'

'No, I'll go.'

She did not find the car at once. Leadbitter had driven away to park it with the others, of which there were a number. In the twilight they all looked alike. Then she saw his tall figure bending over it, locking it.

'Steve,' she said. She didn't think she could say it, but out it came.

He straightened himself but didn't come towards her, so she went up to him and held her hand out.

'Steve,' she said, 'I'm sorry.'

'For what, my lady?' he asked forbiddingly, taking her hand and dropping it.

'For everything. You were a good friend to me.'

'My lady –' he began.

'No, don't say anything. I understand now, if I didn't then, and I hope you do.'

'But do you understand?' asked Leadbitter, in his harsh voice.

'Do I understand –?' repeated Lady Franklin.

'Yes, my lady. Do you understand why I –' His utterance nearly strangled him, it was so urgent. Making a great effort he finished the sentence. 'Why I did what I did.'

She didn't answer, but looked up at him with her mouth slightly open.

'It was because ... It was because ... I –' 'love you', he would have said, but this time the words stuck.

'No, please don't tell me,' Lady Franklin said, distressed by his distress. 'Let *me* tell *you*. It was because you are the kindest-hearted man imaginable.'

'No, it wasn't,' said Leadbitter. 'I'm not all that kind-hearted. It was because –' Again he stopped, and his face had the strained look of a stammerer's when he tries to get the words out.

'If it's something you don't *want* to say,' said Lady Franklin earnestly, and mistaking – as well she might – the nature of Leadbitter's confession, 'please don't say it. You'll only regret it if you do. I know you meant to help me, and I don't want to know anything more. We're none of us perfect, I know I'm not, and if what you saw just now –'

'I saw nothing, my lady.'

'– If it hurt and . . . and displeased you, I am truly sorry. But there's one thing I'm not sorry about.'

'What is it?'

'That we met again. . . . Now, I've left something in the car: what can it be?'

Leadbitter opened the door, and turned the light on. His eyes searched the back seat; his hands groped among the cushions.

'There's nothing here, my lady.'

'Oh, but there must be. I said there was.'

She had a superstitious wish to have her word confirmed by the event.

'I must have left something,' she muttered. 'I told him I had, and oddly enough, I *felt* I had left something. Could you give me something? I'll give it back to you.'

He looked down at her helplessly.

'What can I give you?'

'Oh, give me a shilling.'

He felt in his pocket and handed her the coin.

'Thank you so much. If I forget, remind me. And oh, your wife – how is she?'

'Better today, my lady.'

'Oh, has she been ill?'

'She goes up and down.'

'And the children?'

'They're fine.'

'And business?'

'Just ticking over. Mustn't grumble.'

'I'm glad. I'm glad that things are going well. I always hope they will, but sometimes they don't, where I'm concerned – I don't mean only for me. But now they are going well for me, too.'

Lady Franklin waited for Leadbitter to make a comment, and when he didn't, she said:

'Will you congratulate me? I'm engaged to be married. I'm so happy.'

A strange look of intensity came into his face; his features faded from it, it was all expression. But still he said nothing.

'I'm so happy,' Lady Franklin repeated. 'Won't you wish me luck?'

'I wish you luck, my lady,' Leadbetter said, and try as he would he couldn't keep an ironical inflexion out of his voice. 'Yes, I wish you luck.'

'You sound as if you thought that I might need it!' Lady Franklin exclaimed, delighted but incredulous. 'But I assure you, Steve, I don't. I'm just going into the world, it's my new début, my second coming-out! I don't mean the world of parties and so on,' she added hastily, 'but the real world of normal feelings and experiences that you have known so long – indeed I lived in your world before I began to live in mine. Yours was my stepping-stone, my half-way house! From you I learnt' – she hesitated – 'oh, so many things! That I could be real to someone else was one. I'm real to him, I know I am, and he is real to me. Perhaps it is what one wants – to be real to somebody! How strange that you should have been driving him! Don't you think he's charming?'

'I've only driven him once or twice before,' said Leadbitter.

'That makes it all the odder! But I'm sure you'll like him when you get to know him – and he's so *talented*! I've never known a genius before – I'm sure he is one! I've no secrets from him, naturally; but shall we keep to ourselves –?' she stopped.

'I never talk, my lady,' Leadbitter said.

'Well, you do, about your family! At least, I forced you to. But this, this fact of our having known each other, perhaps it's best –'

'I never talk, my lady,' Leadbitter repeated.

'He might misunderstand, and he's so dear to me, I couldn't bear the smallest cloud –'

She got no further, for at that moment a voice sharp with impatience, resonant with command, and yet not quite sure of itself, rang out from the hotel doorway:

'Ernestine!'

'My lady,' Leadbitter began.

'I must go,' said Lady Franklin, hastily. 'Good-bye, for the moment, and don't forget to get yourself a good dinner.'

She hurried off, leaving Leadbitter motionless, still holding the long breath he had taken, until it expired in a sigh.

'What a long time you have been,' grumbled Hughie. 'I thought you must be buying the car. Did you find what you were looking for?'

'Yes,' said Ernestine.

'What was it?' Hughie said. 'You don't seem to be carrying anything extra.'

'It's in my bag.'

'How secretive you are! What was it?'

'A shilling,' Ernestine confessed.

'A shilling! You went back for a shilling! I've got plenty of shillings.'

'But I mustn't sponge on you,' said Lady Franklin gaily.

Chapter 21

'My wife she is dying, hurray!
My wife she is dying, hurray!
My wife she is dying
I laugh till I'm crying –'

LEADBITTER broke off. He didn't feel like laughing, and he didn't want to be single – he had had quite enough of being single even if his pockets jingled from it.

His pockets did indeed jingle. Business had been increasing steadily and prosperity, which had once seemed such a distant prospect, now seemed within his grasp. At odd times he was still slack; but on some days he had three or four men working for him. Success, as Lady Franklin had foretold, brought its own troubles. He could never quite rely on the men doing the jobs they had promised to do. If the offer of a better job came along they would throw his over. He was prepared for this, and almost counted on it, but it made him constantly anxious. As far as he could he served his most regular and cherished customers himself. They greatly preferred this and would sometimes make a fuss if he sent another man in his place, though it was nothing to the fuss they made if the man failed to turn up. Unreasonable b—s they were, most of them; they didn't mind how long they kept him waiting, but they raised bloody hell if he kept them waiting. The women were the worst; when they wanted to keep him longer than the prescribed time they couldn't or wouldn't understand that he had another job on hand, and if they understood they didn't care.

This was all part of the day's work; he was used to it and he accepted it. At least, he had. But increasing prosperity had brought increasing fatigue. He drove himself as unremittingly as he drove his car, and much more relentlessly, for to the car he showed every consideration while to himself he showed none. After every five thousand miles he took the car to be overhauled but he never took himself. He had increased his average daily mileage from ninety miles a day to over a hundred and twenty. He was out at all hours; he never gave himself an evening off and apart from casual encounters his only contact with the outside world – his only unprofessional activity – was listening to the wireless. He took his meals when and where he could; more and more rarely did he eat at home. He couldn't help knowing that he was tired, for he had the evidence of kind-hearted if misguided customers, who told him. But his general health was so triumphant that he didn't feel ill, and fatigue was a weakness which he wouldn't acknowledge. To have done so would have contradicted his conception of himself as tireless and lowered him in his own esteem. He didn't realize the toll fatigue was taking of his nervous energy or the subterfuges he was adopting in his efforts to ignore it. When he shaved he contrived not to look himself in the face, to be spared the sight of the dark tell-tale circles round his eyes; he concentrated on the rest of him, which still bore out his idea of himself as a fine animal. As for his habit of falling asleep at odd times, he prided himself on it; it was a compensation for his broken nights. 'I could sleep on a clothes-line,' he said.

His increasing prosperity nourished something in him that went very deep. Business success is what men respect most in each other, and what they are quickest to find out and comment on; Leadbitter saw his reflected on the faces of his acquaintances and heard it on their tongues: 'You must be making a fortune!' And nowhere was its effect more gratifying than in the Bank. Only a few months ago he used to creep into the Bank almost like a criminal; the clerks behind the counter did not raise their heads, or if they did, they showed blank faces. Now all that was changed. He strode in, feeling and looking every inch himself; smiles welcomed him; even the manager, when Leadbitter had occasion to consult him, put on a friendly air – 'Of course, old chap, of course' – and almost bowed him out.

This would have happened in any case, Leadbitter told himself; if any man had earned success, he had. He had sacrificed everything to it, and he had got it.

But he wouldn't have got it for another two years if it hadn't been for Lady Franklin's gift. Lady Franklin's tax-free gift had been worth – well, no matter how much.

Driving kept his thoughts busy; piecing together the jig-saw of his engagements kept them busy too. But during those unaccountable slack periods when he sat alone, or with his secretary facing him across the unlit gas-fire, killing time, watching the telephone and wondering if he would ever get another job, he could not stop thinking about Lady Franklin and he did not try to, for now his thoughts of her were free from bitterness. She had forgiven him, she wished him well; and knowing that, he on his side had forgiven her. In thought their relationship had been re-established at its highest level, the level of the return journey from Winchester before the débacle; higher than that indeed, for being imaginary it was also ideal, untouched by the imperfections, the conflict of wills, that for Leadbitter spoilt every human relationship. Tampering with reality as a day-dreamer must, he pictured her as his wife; sometimes they had children, sometimes not, according as he felt a taste or distaste for a family. The houses in which they were living varied in size, but always the money was his, she was sharing in his mounting prosperity. He had a fleet of six, twelve, twenty cars; he directed it from his offices in the West End; he himself no longer drove, except the Rolls Royce in which he took his wife out. His wife was Lady Franklin now, not Frances. Though his memory for her face was intermittent, it would suddenly flash upon his inner eye more vividly than it ever had in real life, when some veil of diffidence or self-assertion or of the animosity which so quickly started up in him, had come between them.

He had forgiven her and he wished her well; to his conviction that most people would be the better for a small, or perhaps a large dose of misfortune, she was the exception. How then could he destroy her happiness by sending her the letter? Like an unexploded bomb which peace has robbed of usefulness he mentally dismantled it. His happiness now lay in the thought of hers – a state of mind that would not only have been unattainable but incomprehensible to him a few months ago, when hostility still ruled his heart. He understood her character, or thought he did. Since he had seen her with Hughie, distasteful as the spectacle was to him in all ways, and disillusioning as it was in some ways (how could she have allowed the pinching episode, and with that little squirt, too?) he had decided that with Hughie lay her best hope of happiness. She loved the fellow. Incredible as it was, she loved him. Her nature was completely unsuspicious, and in spite of her enormous eyes she couldn't see what was going on under her nose. Had she guessed what he, Leadbitter, felt about her, which any other woman would have guessed? Never for a moment. The chances were that if Hughie was reasonably careful (as his own interest demanded that he should be) she would never find out that he was being unfaithful to her. Where ignorance is bliss – Leadbitter didn't know the quotation, but he believed implicitly in the saving power of appearances, for with his customers his whole life was spent in keeping them up. Let Lady Franklin remain deceived.

For what good would it do to undeceive her? Good in this sense, abstract good as an aim, was not a thing that Leadbitter cared much about. If he had a principle, it was the average Englishman's principle of fairness. Apart from his instinctive dislike of Hughie, which was much more sexual than moral, it hadn't seemed fair that Lady Franklin should be tied to a man who was sharing her with another woman, and using her money to bring off this double event.

It wasn't fair that he should get away with it. But if Lady Franklin *wanted* it that way! – She didn't know, of course, that it was that way; she thought her Hughie was quite true to her; she took his face-tasting at its face value, she liked, no doubt, being tickled by his beard, which even Leadbitter didn't think was false. But even if she did know about his mistress, was it certain she would mind? She had revealed to him, Leadbitter, the most surprising variations of emotional reaction, from her injured and insulted 'That will be all, Leadbitter,' to her declaration of a few nights ago, – 'I owe to you my confidence in life.' She might be quite content, as Eastern wives were, as Mormons were, to share her husband. Hughie had sounded her on that point (the cheek of it!) and she had said No, she couldn't share him; but did she know her own mind?

Leadbitter felt no loyalty towards a past opinion, he was ruled by the emotion of the moment. Be damned to fairness; he only knew that he was happier to think of Lady Franklin happy – and that meant married to Hughie – than unmarried and unhappy, as she would be if he sent the letter.

If he thought of her as unhappy, and through him, his thoughts recoiled from her: he couldn't think of her: his fantasy broke up. But if he thought of her as happy, no matter what the circumstances, she came to his call, and came in any guise he cared to think of – though they were all variations of one role – his wife. If only he could tell her what she meant to him! It was the one fly in his ointment that he couldn't tell her. He had had his chance at Richmond, but the words wouldn't come; and if he got the chance again, they still wouldn't come.

'You were dozing, sir.'

His secretary always called him 'sir'.

'Was I, Bert? I suppose I do drop off sometimes.'

'Yes, and a good job too, or you'd be having a breakdown.'

'Oh, don't start that.'

'I'm only saying what they all say.'

'Look here, Bert, am I running this business or are you?'

'I'm sorry, sir.'

'Well, don't do it again, or if that's too much to ask, don't go on doing it. No one rung up, I suppose?'

'Yes, sir, someone did ring up.'

'Who was it?'

'Lady Franklin, sir.'

'Lady Franklin! What did she want?'

'She wanted you to drive her to her wedding.'

'Her wedding? Why didn't you tell me?'

'I didn't want to wake you, sir.'

'Oh, cut that out. Was she speaking herself?'

'Oh yes, at least it was a lady's voice. I said that you were resting, and she said: "Don't wake him up."'

'I wish to God you had. Did she sound in a hurry?'

'Oh no, sir. She asked how you were, and wished to be remembered to you. She asked after your family, too.'

'My family! What did you say?'

'I said "as well as could be expected", sir. I thought maybe she was mixing you up with someone else. It doesn't do to make a customer feel silly.'

'You're right there. All the same, I wish you'd woken me. There was something I wanted to say to her. . . . Did she say when the wedding was to be?'

'In about a fortnight. She didn't give a date.'

'You must have had quite a long crack with her.'

'Oh yes, and she said she wanted three or four other cars as well as yours.'

'And what did you say?'

'I said you'd do it, sir.'

'Well, I suppose I shall. If only she'd given me a date! You're sure it was Lady Franklin, by the way? Not someone else getting married? Some women make a habit of it.'

'Oh yes, she said so. She's a special customer, isn't she?'

'She was. . . . Now cut along, it's half past six, nearly your bedtime. But thanks for staying, all the same.'

The door closed on his secretary, and Leadbitter was alone.

Between the idea and the fact of Lady Franklin's marriage, what a difference!

His fantasy could ignore the idea, but the fact (albeit without a date assigned), it couldn't. Feeling it wither, perish in his heart, he tried the desperate expedient known to other lovers: He tried to make his single love suffice for two. Surely it would return to him, reflected from her? But it didn't; like traffic in a one-way street it didn't come to meet him.

Nothing is so remote and unrecoverable as a lost fantasy. Deprived of his dream-life, Leadbitter was desolate. His thoughts turned for consolation, as they always did at such moments, to the next best thing, his increasing prosperity. His bank-account at any rate was real; it didn't depend for its existence on a mood. As he contemplated it – a shadowy entity to which his thoughts could give no shape or appearance, only the quality of size – the familiar feeling of warmth stole into his heart. He felt the area of his influence spreading; he was getting somewhere, he was a power in the world. In the past the fact that he had nothing that he could call his own weighed upon him; to see other people's possessions all round daunted and dismayed his spirits. Even the room where he sat had this effect on him, for it belonged to someone else. Thinking of his bank-balance changed all this, for even if he did not own anything except his car, he had the means of owning it. Of any building he chose to look at he could, if he wished, possess a window or a balcony or a chimney stack. When he surveyed the streets his thoughts did not return to him empty; they brought with them spoils from a Promised Land. And if this mental exercise of feeling himself part-owner of what he saw was also a habit-forming drug, it didn't have the reaction that the other had – the fantasy of owning Lady Franklin – for it had truth behind it. To one dream he could give effect, by translating it into action he could make it a reality. But not to the other. Lady Franklin could not be his, she belonged to Hughie.

So he thought about his bank-balance and his heart began to swell with the pride of possession. And then, at the fall of a hat, the warming-up process stopped – stopped almost with a click, like an electric fire when the shilling has done its bit. Surprised, he searched his mind for another shilling; but like a shilling in real life, it wasn't there.

For what was the use, he asked himsef, and asked himself for the first time, what was the use of this increase of personal worth, which the bank-balance so eloquently conveyed, if he couldn't share it with anyone? Everything was the better for being shared, Lady Franklin had said, everything except Hughie. Hitherto Leadbitter had not wanted to share anything with anyone: to share it was to halve it, to decimate it, to lose it: his one idea had been to keep it to himself. But now he felt that something so owned was unfruitful; as unfruitful, as lacking in true delight, as an unconsummated marriage. It was the difference between drinking alone and drinking in company: it was a difference far greater than that. The ambition to know himself and to be known as a rich man seemed all at once utterly unsatisfying; he could not even realize his wealth, he felt, unless he had someone to realize it with him.

His tired eyes roamed round the room where nothing was his to share, nothing, for he had never hoarded reminders of the past; the past was a dead loss, he looked always to the present and the future. In the past, knife, fork, spoon, razor, comb, lather-brush, tooth-brush, button-stick – these had sufficed him; they could be stolen; but they weren't meant for sharing. And even now, apart from his clothes, his only personal possessions were in the bathroom across the passage. The bathroom where he felt most at ease, for it was there that he got rid of the accretions of the flesh – got rid of them almost with passion, for, however tired he might be, he was never too tired to take a bath. Not from any physical need, but from a need to find a more personal setting, somewhere that felt like home, to seek the reassurance of sponge and soap, and tooth-brush, he got up, and as he went towards the door his eyes rested on the telephone, his one faithful friend. The telephone wasn't his, it was hired from the Government. But standing by it *was* something that was his – the photograph-frame which held his list of bookings. Would she have held a torch for him through all these years? He could but see.

Chapter 22

It wasn't easy to find Clarice's address; she had changed her address several times since the day when he walked out on her. She had changed her name, too, he discovered; but that didn't discourage him, for she was already married when they lived together. But he had the car to help him. It wasn't used to traversing such mean streets as those he now frequented. With its sleek black surface, so highly polished that one could see one's reflection in it, and its bars of chromium, so dazzling that one could hardly bear to look at them, it was altogether too resplendent for its surroundings, just as Leadbitter, when he descended from it, looked altogether too distinguished and immaculate. A god and his car! While he went to the door to inquire, little boys collected round it; they gaped at it with awe, they touched and even stroked it, and reverently took down its number. When Leadbitter came back they moved far enough away to be out of reach of possible reprisals, but still kept their eyes glued on it.

The day came when Leadbitter did not reappear at once, like a postman who has left a parcel; he stayed inside, his tall figure framed in the doorway, while the car-intoxicated urchins changed their positions to get a better look. This time he came back with a relaxed face and looking younger than his years.

She was out, he had been told; she would be back in half an hour, if he cared to wait. He couldn't wait, he had to be on a job, but he marked the house in his mind as one that, despite its forbidding exterior, held something precious for him.

For in the last few days he had quite changed his feelings about Clarice. Or rather, he had regained his feelings for her, regained them and others with them that he had not had before. In the past she had been – what? A bedfellow, of course, but what besides? A knife-sharpener, a razor-strop, something to whet his edge on. She had confirmed him in his self-hood, it came to a fine point when she was there. She put his experience into focus; with her, whether in company or alone, he could feel and act with the maximum of self-approval. This often meant doing and saying what she didn't like, for it was in apartness that he felt at his best. Not expansion but contraction of personality was what he sought: and to achieve it he had to be at odds with the world, and her. But there were limitations to his quarrelsomeness; and sometimes when he knew she expected him to be edgy he would be mild as milk, leaving her looking foolish, defences out and weapons drawn when no one was attacking. 'Why, what's the trouble?' he would ask her, innocently, and be amused by the way she hurriedly re-organized her demeanour to meet the change in his. He liked to keep her guessing, and he liked it when she tried to turn the tables on him, as she sometimes did, when near to tears. A stable relationship was irksome to him; with each encounter, he wanted to begin the whole thing over again – to end in love-making if he felt like it, or if he felt like it, a scene. He would have said, had anyone dared to ask him, and had he deigned to reply, that she preferred it that way; she liked a man to be a man and wear the pants. And he was right, up to a point; but the point came sooner than either of them had foreseen.

To measure himself by the respect he could inspire in other men was Leadbitter's first principle; he didn't want the respect of women, few men do. Nor did he want security in the affections, any more than he wanted it in life; he wanted money and prestige, but not security. He did not share the average man of today's longing for material security, and as far as he understood it he despised it. But Clarice did want security in the affections; she was tired of skirmishing, and when Leadbitter threw down his challenge she accepted it. He hadn't expected her to accept it, even after he sent back her photograph; she had been so much in love with him! He didn't believe that women's words were much indication of what they really felt; it would be for him to decide whether to take her back or not. She'll get tired of it quicker than I shall, he had thought, she'll turn up with a face like the back of a bus; and it'll be no skin off my nose if she doesn't. But she didn't tire of it, and any regret he may have felt for her loss, and the blow it gave his pride, was stifled by the resentment that always sprang up in him to meet an injury, fancied or real, and by his recovered sense of independence.

But independence was no longer what he wanted. He wanted something which he didn't name to himself, for fear of being laughed at by another Leadbitter, looking over his shoulder. It was partly nostalgia for his own world that made him want it, the world whose language he spoke and whose behaviour he understood. His own world was all around him, of course, and he was in daily contact with it; but spiritually and emotionally he had been translated to another, whose language he spoke as a foreigner, and whose air he breathed with difficulty. He had been caught up into it and it had meant a lot to him – he didn't deny that. Lady Franklin and her hangers-on had given him a lot to think about, and to feel. Hughie and his girl friend – well, one had to laugh. Lady Franklin, she was different: she was a little mad for one thing, which they were not. He didn't underestimate Lady Franklin's power over his imagination. She might at any moment come back to occupy it, to trouble it with her gleams and flashes, her unpractical ideas which had such practical results. For Hughie and his bit she was money for jam, but not for him, but not for him, not any longer. For him Lady Franklin was 'out'. She had passed out of his life, leaving him sick with longing for something that she couldn't supply. Clarice could supply it, but she couldn't.

'Corrupting', the girl friend had called her, which at the

time had made him laugh. Lady Franklin corrupting! Ernestine corrupting! Yet dimly he now saw what they meant; the pattern of his experience with her confirmed it. She was an indulgence, an obsession, a walking day-dream, who offered for reality a fairy-tale version of life. Her gold was not fairy gold, far from it, but it didn't come through the usual channels, it had to be angled for, not worked for, with many applications of the soft flannel and a lot of blarney on both sides. He would be happier with his own sort, to whom he could speak his mind and with whom he could be himself, not pretending emotions he didn't feel, in language that had to be edited, and polished like his car. On Clarice he depended for the recovery of this lost self and the cynicism that was his cue to life; yes he depended on her for that; only she could give it to him, only she could show him the way back. He didn't think of it as dependence, but it was; he didn't know that he would be offering himself to Clarice instead of taking her, sticking to her like a burr instead of picking her off like a burr, but that was what his new self asked of him.

He called again, and with the same result. Mrs Crowther was out, the woman said who kept the house, looking up at Leadbitter, her eyes wide with curiosity; but she would be back any time now. Would he like to wait? Leadbitter hesitated and said no, he was on a job; but would she leave word that he had called? What name? she asked. Leadbitter told her. It didn't seem to register, but why should it? 'Is her old man anywhere about?' asked Leadbitter casually. 'He used to be a pal of mine.' The woman raised her eyebrows. 'You didn't know?' she said. 'They are living apart.' 'Oh,' said Leadbitter, concealing the relief he felt, 'that's bad luck on someone.' 'Not on her, if I may say so,' said the woman. 'No offence meant if he was a friend of yours, but I think she was well rid of him.' 'I'm not being nosy,' Leadbitter said, 'but what's she doing now?' 'She's in the millinery business,' the woman said. 'She's doing pretty well. If you ask me, she's picking up a packet.' 'Glad to hear it,' Leadbitter said, but for some reason he wasn't. 'Pity about her and her husband, though.' 'Oh, do you think so?' said the woman. 'She doesn't tell me a great deal, naturally, she isn't one to talk about her affairs, but from what I hear he wasn't much good to her.' 'No?' said Leadbitter, and his spirits rose again. 'I shouldn't know about that.' 'No, he wasn't,' said the woman, decisively. 'I won't say any more, since he was a friend of yours.' 'Oh, not all that a friend,' said Leadbitter. 'Pity that she's on her own, though, a nice-looking woman like that.' 'That's what I say to her,' the woman said. 'Mind you, I don't pry into her affairs. But I've said to her more than once, "What you want, dear, is a man to look after you." ' 'And what did she say?' Leadbitter asked, with more interest than he meant to show. Watching him closely the woman answered, 'She said she was through with men.' 'Oh, did she?' said Leadbitter, aware of the woman's scrutiny. 'So now we know,' and he laughed. 'Yes, that's what she said,' the woman repeated. 'She said, "I'm through with men." ' 'A pity,' said Leadbitter for the third time. 'And all because of that husband of hers, I suppose.' 'I'm not saying anything that she has or hasn't told me,' said the woman, ambiguously, 'but I don't think it was on account of her husband, no.' 'Oh, not on his account?' 'No,' said the woman, 'I don't think she ever went much on him. Of course I shouldn't be telling you this if he wasn't a friend of yours. I think it was someone else.' 'Another man?' said Leadbitter. The woman pressed her lips together and nodded. 'Yes. Someone she really liked, but he walked out on her.' 'Too bad,' said Leadbitter. 'Too bad. What would she say if he walked in again?' The woman screwed her eyes up. 'I shouldn't know,' she said, 'I shouldn't know, I'm not in her confidence. But one thing I do know, he'd have to come in another mind than when he went away. He was a real tartar, by all accounts – of course, she hasn't told me.' 'And yet she was fond of him, you say,' said Leadbitter, carelessly. 'Oh yes, what she took from him! Not blows, you know; he never laid a finger on her – she wouldn't have minded that – but a nasty, cruel tongue.' Leadbitter was silent and his face grew wooden. 'Oh well,' he said at last, 'perhaps there were faults on both sides. We don't know, do we? If you don't mind me saying so, women can be the devil. She might find him different, if she saw him again.' 'It's not for me to say,' the woman said, 'but he might try, of course, no harm in trying. If he let her see –' 'Yes?' said Leadbitter. 'Well, that he knew how to treat a woman. ... But why don't you step in, if you're interested, and wait for her? She'll be back any time now.' 'I can't wait,' said Leadbitter, 'I'm due on a job. ... But what did you say this fellow's name was?' 'I didn't say,' the woman said, 'because I don't know; she hardly tells me anything.' 'I've an idea,' said Leadbitter, 'who it might be. He's not a bad sort of fellow, used to get up in the air a bit quick, one time, but he's toned down now. He's strolling about spare, now, but he's done well in business, he's on the job all right, she might do worse. ...' 'Do you want me to tell her this?' the woman said, with sudden intensity. 'Well, what do you think? If she's like you say, wanting somebody –' 'I'm not saying she's wanting *him*,' the woman said. 'I didn't say she wanted anybody. I said she needed someone, like all women do. Now if it was somebody like *you* –' She shot a questioning glance at Leadbitter, making him wonder if his secret had leaked out. He didn't much mind if it had. 'Well, he is a bit like me,' he temporized, 'or was, when I last saw him. Not so good-looking though.' He laughed and the woman laughed, too. 'Supposing you told her –' he stopped. 'Yes?' the woman said. 'Well, something about letting bygones be bygones, because we all make mistakes sometimes, and there's a welcome for her, she knows where – from somebody, she knows who – and it won't be as it used to be, because – oh hell – because the chappie in the case doesn't feel the same way as he did – and if she's got the photo – well, to send it along, and then he'll know that everything's O.K.' 'Stop,' the woman said, 'let me get this straight. She's to send a photo – will she know what photo?' 'Yes, she will,' said Leadbitter impatiently. 'And where to send it?' 'To the same address.' 'She may have forgotten it,' said the woman doubtfully, 'it was a long time ago.' 'Oh, no, she won't have. Tell her he's in a bit of a hurry – no, don't tell her that, tell her to take her time. Tell her he's got something that he wants to give her, something that she'll like – no, don't say that, that sounds corny. Tell her that everything's the same but not the same, if she can understand that Irish. Tell her he'll pick her up and everything she's got – it won't cost her a penny. Tell her not to worry about anything, it's all been taken care of. Tell her I hope she's well. Tell her I'm –'

'So it was you,' the woman said. 'I knew it was you all along, you didn't kid me.... But why not wait and say it all to her?'

Leadbitter seemed a little crestfallen.

'Oh, I dunno,' he said. 'I should feel a bit of a fool, spouting all that stuff. Not that I didn't mean it, but – Oh, hell, you tell her. You know the kind of thing a woman wants to hear. If she saw me she might –'

'Yes,' said a voice behind them, 'she might, and what's more, she would.' They turned to meet Clarice's eyes blazing up at them. 'Now what possessed you, Mrs White,' she stormed, 'to let that man into the house? I tell you one thing: until he clears out, I won't cross the threshold.'

'Oh, Mrs Crowther,' Mrs White said, 'how can you be so hard?'

'Hard?' Clarice repeated. 'Hard? Me hard? I like that. If I was made of flint I shouldn't be hard enough. That man, Mrs White, has done me more harm than –'

'Oh, don't be hasty, dear,' the landlady put in. 'Hear what he has to say. He was speaking about you so nicely just before you came. Don't turn him away without giving him a hearing. You can't expect a man to be a saint: we shouldn't want it, should we? If he's been awkward with you in the past, you should forgive him; we aren't any of us perfect, and I'm sure he's learnt his lesson: look how quietly he stands, and you flaring at him! It isn't many men would be so patient, having their kind words thrown back in their teeth! Now do be sensible, and let him tell you what he's just told me.'

Leadbitter, who had never heard anyone plead for him before, or felt the need of outside support, least of all a woman's, stood sheepishly with all his strength gone out of him, looking hopefully towards his ally, and trying to seem as if he didn't know that Clarice was there. Nor did Clarice, for her part, look at him; she addressed herself to the other woman.

'You wouldn't take his part if you knew what he was like! He hasn't any use for a woman except to suck the juices out of her! Take yourself off, Steve Leadbitter, and never let me hear of you again!'

She burst into tears and under cover of her sobbing, Leadbitter regained his car. Routed, and by a woman too. But for once the self-starter refused to work. Each time he pressed the button it made a noise like someone imitating someone being sick. Finally he dismounted, got out the starting handle, and swung the engine with it. Leaving, he did not look at the two women arguing in the doorway, nor, though automatically avoiding the traffic, did he notice anything very much until at last he looked round with a seeing eye and found himself in Belgrave Square. Yielding to an impulse, he turned into South Halkin Street and slowly drove past Lady Franklin's house.

Chapter 23

FROM that moment Leadbitter took against his car. It had let him down, he almost felt, on purpose, prolonging his humiliation unbearably, and he could hardly wait to get rid of it. All the pride which he had taken in it, when it was first his own, and which returned to him at times, when he was cleaning it or when he saw it among meaner or less well-kept cars, evaporated; the familiarity that endears passed at one stride into the familiarity that breeds contempt. The very things he had most liked about it were now the things he most disliked. Neither emotionally nor physically could he feel at his ease in it; sitting, he developed a pain in his back which he had never had before; he didn't like the feeling or the touch of it; sometimes after a couple of hours' driving he found himself leaning forward, crouched over the wheel, unable to sit back, a symptom of nerves which many chauffeurs knew and dreaded. He couldn't take any pleasure in polishing the car or pride in seeing it bright and shining; he didn't want to handle it at all. He didn't want to provide for its wants or remedy its defects; he grudged every penny he spent on it. The unclouded relationship he had with it – the happiest he had had with any object, animate or inanimate, except the telephone – was suddenly and hopelessly overcast. Towards other cars, cars that were not his own, he had sometimes felt indifference, but never the sour distaste he felt for this one.

He hadn't realized how much it meant to him emotionally, until suddenly it fell into disgrace. The feeling in his nature, which he had always played down and refused to recognize, had now no outlet at all.

But it would have an outlet in a new car, and almost feverishly he set about looking for one. This would be a much grander car than its predecessor, Lady Franklin's present; a car that even she would think twice before buying. When she saw it she would, perhaps, give a little gasp. 'Surely this isn't the car you used to have?' 'Well, no, my lady, it isn't. The old one, well, it wasn't good enough.' 'Not good enough?' 'Not good enough, my lady, for your wedding.'

That would be the tactful thing to say, and Leadbitter, when he rehearsed it and other sentences like it, thought he was being tactful: he smiled to himself, he had the right word for every customer. Yet what had put it into his mind originally, and why, when he started on his quest, did he think of Lady Franklin? She was seldom out of his mind. Did he mean the car to be a kind of offering to her, a sort of wedding present? He had to laugh at the idea, it was so absurd. 'Give me a bite of your apple,' one little boy had begged another. 'No.' 'Then let me smell the core.' All the present that Lady Franklin would get from Leadbitter would be a whiff of the core, a glance, an eyeful, to take away if she could. And yet more and more, as his excitement mounted over the choice and purchase of the car, did the thing he most looked forward to identify itself with the presentation, the formal presentation, the dedication of the car to Lady Franklin. That was to be the high spot of the whole experience.

Hughie wouldn't have a car to give her, not even the smell of one. Hughie's wedding present to her, so Leadbitter suspected, would be paid for by her. She would be giving him many things, no doubt. 'The bride to the bridegroom': Leadbitter tried to think. A fitted dressing case... A cheque ... What else did the blighter want? A mistress! The bride to the bridegroom: a nice, useful mistress.

Forget about Hughie. Somehow, Leadbitter didn't know how, for it was a balance struck in the domain of feeling, imponderable, invisible – the car would square his account with Lady Franklin. Not his material account, he wasn't thinking of that. For a moment, as the owner of that costly adjunct, he would be her equal – well, not her equal, he didn't want to be that, but on the same plane of glory with her. It was a spiritual affinity that he sought: to be spiritually, for a moment, in her class. Leadbitter was a poor man who associated with people richer, sometimes much richer, than himself. In the past, to keep his own end up with them, he had resorted in thought to various compensations: but they were all of a personal kind; his good looks, his punctuality, his efficiency, his tact. Man for man, he was a better specimen than ninety-nine per cent of his customers, yes, better than Hughie for all his face-fungus. In his own sphere he couldn't be beaten. 'They' had to treat him with respect. But it was the sphere of poverty; as a poor man they could one and all look down on him, even Hughie could. But as the owner of this new car he would have something outside himself to impress them with, something that they would have to recognize: the power of money.

He wouldn't actually be the owner, of course. Even by giving his own car in part exchange, and draining his bank balance, he would still have several hundred pounds to find before he could call himself the owner of a new one. He would have to buy the car on the H.P. Except that this would be a much better car, be would be financially back where he was when Lady Franklin came to his help, six weeks ago. He would be an ower, not an owner.

At first the prospect daunted him, then it became part of the intense excitement and exhilaration of the whole transaction – the exhilaration of the quest, the excitement of getting the deal done in time – in time for the wedding, the date of which he didn't know and didn't like to ask.

After so many frustrations, and efforts worse than wasted, it was intoxicating to be whole again, the master of his fate and of himself: to feel all his faculties straining out towards the attainment of a single end. The car! The car would be an answer to all his problems. In it would be manifested, for all to see, the pride he took in himself, the vital principle that had kept him, Leadbitter, going for five-and-thirty chequered years. That gleaming symphony of black and chrome, shaped to elude the wind's embrace, would embody his achievement up till now. It would give him no trouble, or if it did, no trouble that he did not know how to deal with. It would be his friend, his wife, his mistress; he could lavish all his love on it without the fear that it would turn against him.

But though it would mean all this to him in the sphere of the emotions, he knew that he must drive a hard bargain to get it. If he paid a penny too much for it, it would give him a grievance and so lose its spell. Luckily for him, the excitement of the chase sharpened all his faculties, and most of all his business instinct; and though his heart and mind were set on it, he would not hurry over buying it. Many were the cars that he saw, inspected and rejected because their design did not altogether please him. It must be as perfect as his idea of it. He took time off, he even refused jobs, which he had never done when searching for Clarice. A score of times he was baffled, but never did he lose heart or doubt that he would find his ideal in the end.

It came, as such things do, if they ever do, when he was least expecting it: a car the make of which he had always known, of course, but which he hadn't believed could ever be available at such short notice. It seemed to drop into his hand by a miracle; after all the pushing and straining the door appeared to open of itself and show him what he wanted. The moment brought a cessation of effort, a relaxing of all tensions, that was almost unbelievable; Leadbitter tasted the bliss the mystic feels on reaching his objective. He hadn't a second's doubt, he knew, almost before he saw it, that the car was the right one.

But he concealed this from the salesman. With the salesman he put on a critical air, and after he had marked down the object of his desire, he had a look at other cars the salesman had to show.

Perfection is not divisible into parts, it is a whole, and

cannot be analysed. All the same, it is made up of separate desiderata, and one of these in Leadbitter's view – and it was the one which more than any other single requirement made his search difficult – was that the car should be a limousine. Such cars were both expensive and scarce; even more scarce (if the two qualities can be compared) than they were expensive.

A limousine had a dividing wall of glass, a second windscreen. But such glass partitions were of different kinds. Those that could be wound up with a handle, were regulated by the persons sitting on the back seat. It depended on them where the partition should be open or closed: the driver had no say in the matter. But Leadbitter wanted to have a say. Increasingly, the conversation of his customers had got upon his nerves; he didn't want to hear it, or the 'dears' and 'darlings' with which it was only too frequently interlarded, even if they didn't mind him hearing. The glass wall was not for their convenience, it was for his; with it, unless they chose to have it open, he couldn't hear them yammering and nattering, and unless they chose to have it open, they couldn't tell him the right way to go – as many of them did, for there are few accomplishments which people are so fond of airing as their knowledge of the route.

And how would he have got into his present plight which, in spite of his mad elation, one part of him knew to be deplorable – how would he have got himself into this jam, and been made to feel so many things he didn't want to feel, if he hadn't overheard – been forced to overhear – things which he wasn't meant to overhear – and behaved like a fool, an ass, a madman, as stupidly as a woman might have behaved?

The glass screen would be a protection against the possibility of this happening again, not a complete protection of course, and a very flimsy one if the customers had the means of working it under their sole control. But there was another type, such as taxis had, with two panels, one fixed, one sliding, the sliding one with metal handles on both sides of the glass, which he could use as well as they. What more natural, what more civil, what more considerate, than that he should close the panel from his side? – saying, in effect, 'I'm sure you would rather talk without me listening in,' but meaning for him, 'Thank goodness I shan't be able to hear the stream of imbecilities that you are pouring out.' And when they wanted to listen to the wireless they still could, even with the partition closed, for it was relayed by an amplifier to the back. So he would remain shut off from them – shut off from their voices, shut off from their feelings, shut off from any interference they might make in his life. Shut off from the outside world – shut off ... shut off.

The new car had these panels, which was one reason why he fell in love with it at sight.

When the bargaining was over, and Leadbitter had got the reduction that he wanted, he went out of the building, walking unsteadily. It wasn't drink, it wasn't the slight swagger which he occasionally allowed himself, it was pure fatigue. The exertions of the last few days, combined with lack of sleep, had drained his nervous energy; he felt light-headed. He would have been thankful to hold on to something. A sensation of triumph such as he had never known, not even on a battlefield, possessed him. It was the undiluted essence of experience, incommunicable, even if he had had anyone to share it with; a draught of ecstasy as ravishing to the senses as the fulfilment of physical desire. His tired flesh could hardly contain the pressure of his spirit, yet it too rejoiced, trying, faithful servant that it was, to let him feel his stature towering upwards.

Aware of each footstep and the need to keep his balance he struggled on and bought an evening paper; then looked round for a pub. A pub was facing him the other side of the street, but so tired was he that even while he was looking at it he could not take in what it was, and when he recognized it he still didn't know whether it would be open; his time sense had abandoned him.

But it was open, and thankfully he bought himself a whisky and sat down. Hardly had he swallowed the first mouthful when his head dropped forward and he fell asleep and dreamed, not of the car but of Lady Franklin. Even his subconscious was too tired to formulate its images; he only knew that she was there, and in her own surroundings, and the emotions he had been feeling about the car had somehow transferred themselves to her, and with a still more penetrating sweetness. The car was there too, though it was not quite like his car, and he was not showing it to her but giving it to her. 'Won't you accept it?' he begged anxiously. 'After all, it's more your car than mine.' At first she wouldn't and he was terribly upset: it seemed to him of the first importance that she should accept the car. 'Do take it,' he pleaded, 'it's my wedding-present to you.' At last she yielded. As she did so an extraordinary sensation of peace came over him, and at the same moment he drew out of his body a long nail, a foot long it must have been, and red and dripping with his blood. He was terrified and thought, 'Now I'm away', but to his astonishment he felt no pain at all, only an enormous relief and a still deeper peace; and when he looked at the place it had already healed up, and instead of torn flesh there was a tiny dry scar like a pearl.

He clung to the dream as long as he could, in spite of the noise of voices round him, but at last a particularly loud laugh awoke him, and he heard someone say, 'Dreaming of his old woman, I shouldn't wonder.' He jerked his head up and gave the speaker a straight look and said:

'Did you want anything?'

The man, a young fellow with a mop of red hair, tittered uncomfortably and said:

'Can you tell me the right time?'

Leadbitter, who had no idea what the time was, and didn't care, merely remarked:

'Next time you go out you'd better put your cap on.'

'Why?' asked the young man, unsuspectingly.

'You might get your block knocked off.'

Now the laugh was against the youth, who flushed and turned his back on Leadbitter. His companions muttered among themselves and screwing round their heads darted in Leadbitter's direction hostile glances which struck against the shiny visor of his cap and dropped off harmlessly. He would have liked to get up and go, and try to recapture his dream in more congenial surroundings. But the seed of hostility had sprung up in him, and he wasn't going to turn tail, although he felt too weak to fight, he couldn't have fought with the skin of a rice pudding. So he bought himself another whisky and sat down again, angry with the world, angry with himself, striving to recover the lost paradise whose soft, sweet airs still lingered in his mind, contending with the rising fumes of anger. After a third whisky he might feel able to take on the redhead and his gang. It wouldn't matter, he didn't have to drive, he couldn't; he had given in his old car, and wouldn't get the new one till tomorrow. But his swimming head and shaky hand warned him against starting anything. Impotent and frustrated and angrier than ever, he noticed the folded evening paper on his table, picked it up and began to turn the pages. The blurred print swam before his eyes, but he could see what the pictures were about, and of one he could even read the caption, so large was the type in which it had been splashed.

BEARDED PAINTER TO WED HEIRESS

it ran; and he didn't have to find out who the painter was, or who the heiress, for there was Hughie, very conscious of his beard, holding the lapels of his jacket and looking down with an unbearably smug and possessive expression at Lady Franklin, whose great eyes were turned up to his with as much awe and worship as if he had been not a man but a cathedral.

Leadbitter's heart contracted with disgust and loathing,

he felt physically sick and for a moment couldn't focus the picture. Then he took it to the window and screwing his eyes up read the paragraph below it. 'The bridegroom's present to the bride is her own portrait painted by himself,' it finished up. 'The wedding will take place at St Mark's, North Audley Street, on Saturday.'

On Saturday! And she hadn't let him know! She was too busy thinking of her Hughie. Another drop of bitterness. He couldn't remember what he had on for Saturday, but whatever it was it must be cancelled. If she had let him down, he wouldn't let her down.

Sitting at the table with his glass, and trying not to picture the scene, he saw it all too clearly. He had taken many a wedding party to that church and before driving off to stow himself away in some side-street, had watched the guests go in. They were going in now; and who was this among them, a tallish figure, not quite at her ease, judging by the restless movement of her eyes. Why it was Constance! She too had been invited, Hughie had seen to that. The cheek of it! Leadbitter saw her so plainly that he never doubted that she would be there. Rage flared up in him and reversed in one brief moment the decision it had taken days of arguing with himself to reach. And for once rage found an ally in love. How could he love her if he let this mockery of a marriage take place? How long would her fool's paradise last, before it crashed about her ears?

Today was Tuesday: there was no time to lose. Rising shakily he went to the bar, and with his speech a little slurred, said to the landlord:

'Could you oblige me with a sheet of notepaper?'

The landlord gave it to him, and an envelope and a stamp as well.

Leadbitter went back to his table and wrote a letter. Many versions of it had been in his head; he took the first that came. It would have been more prudent to use his clerk's typewriter, but the thing that mattered was to get the letter off, and indeed the whisky he had taken guided his pen so oddly that the sprawling capitals bore little semblance to his real hand. Licking the envelope he gave the landlord a nod of thanks for his help: and the landlord nodded back.

Out in the street he stopped to take his bearings. The mental revolution of those last few minutes had left Leadbitter stone sober. And it had done more – it had banished his fatigue and restored to him – not the elation he had felt over the car, but a clear tranquillity of spirit that he had not known since he was a child; never since those distant days when, on rare occasions, his mother used to tell him he had been a good boy, had he felt so utterly at one with himself. The recovery of lost innocence made him want to cry, and tears were standing in his eyes when he dropped the letter in the box.

When he got back to his flat he found an entry on his pad: 'Thursday 7 p.m. Mr Cantrip. To Richmond, wait and return.' His secretary had booked it for him. Well, it meant that he would see her again, and learn from her the arrangements for the wedding. He wouldn't use the car, he suddenly decided, until Thursday evening: its first trip should be with Lady Franklin.

Chapter 24

In Leadbitter's tired mind, the days ran into each other. Saturday, Saturday at two-thirty was the wedding; Thursday, Thursday at seven o'clock was the date of his engagement with Hughie. About half an hour before, he went round to the garage to fetch his car. It faced him, a nuzzle of shark-like, wind-cheating shapes, that even at rest suggested speed.

This was to be its maiden voyage, as Leadbitter had vowed it should be. But he had nearly broken his vow. The idea of keeping the car for a day and a half unused when he had plenty of orders booked which he would have to put out went against his business principles, while the notion of presenting a virgin car to Lady Franklin which had so attracted him at the outset now seemed too fanciful. It was the clash between an impulse and an instinct, and he had to laugh when he thought what a mug he was being. Yet he stuck to his resolve, and it turned out he was not the loser by it, for the limousine wasn't ready on the Wednesday, for which it had been promised, so he couldn't have worked in any case, unless he had gone to the expense of hiring another car.

Wednesday had been a car-less, but not a careless day: it had been a day of two-fold stock-taking – Leadbitter examined his accounts, and he also examined his emotional position.

The accounts were, in one sense, extremely satisfactory. He had extended his business beyond what he had thought possible; if it increased at this rate he might, in a year's time, be in a position to buy another car and hire a man to drive it. Then he would serve his best customers himself and leave the man the others – the first step to collecting what, in confident moments, he thought of, grandiosely, as a 'fleet' of cars. Then, at last, he would be seeing daylight.

On the debit side he had mortgaged his future by acquiring this expensive 'lim', on paper he was worse off than he had been even before Lady Franklin's gift enabled him to buy outright the old car. When he remembered this, and how everything depended on his health, he didn't feel too easy. He still refused to connect ill-health and tiredness; machinery, he knew, was liable to fatigue, but he regarded himself as a super-machine, capable of unlimited recovery. Yet though he wouldn't recognize his tiredness, his constitution did; it didn't welcome a whole day's driving with its old cheerfulness and after 'a long drag' it didn't get back to normal as quickly as it used to. With his physical ear alert for noises that shouldn't be there – a creak, a rattle, a knocking – his inner ear couldn't quite disregard those warning symptoms in himself, much as his conscious mind might discount them.

But, to be practical, the big car was after all an investment: it would bring him new customers, and good customers too, the snobbish type who preferred a large car when a small one would do just as well. And women's evening dresses were now so voluminous (perhaps to hide the shortness of their legs) that they couldn't easily get inside a small car. The new one would increase his prestige with himself and with the world.

With himself! There began the second examination. What of himself? Was he in as good shape as his accounts were?

A few weeks ago he would not have distinguished between them. Then he had no existence apart from the money he was making: the phrase 'I'm doing well' covered everything about him. But it wasn't so now. In those few weeks he had developed an emotional life in which, though it was based on money, Lady Franklin's gift, money didn't talk. He had been at times very happy, and at times very unhappy, for reasons quite unconnected with money. He didn't disguise that from himself. Was his emotional life to go on, and if so, what future had it?

Compared with his financial prospects, his emotional future was barren and bleak. Even his financial future was mortgaged. With the help of the H.P. he would pay that mortgage off. But there was no way of buying happiness on the H.P. – monthly instalments of unhappiness would not win happiness in the end: Leadbitter had learnt enough about the feelings to know they didn't work that way. Or did they? Could he, by an act of renunciation now, insure for himself happiness in the future, or since that seemed too much to ask, insure himself against unhappiness?

He thought of his dream in the pub, and the strange peace of mind that came from offering his new car to Lady Franklin, and the bliss when she accepted it, and he drew the long nail out of his body. It was only a dream, of course, but the sensation was still as vivid and as real as when he experienced it, and it was, he realized, an intensification of what his waking senses felt when he had the idea of presenting the car to Lady Franklin, dedicating it to her. The idea of actually giving it to her, handing over to her his only piece of capital, although she had half paid for it, made him smile – he must be balmy! Yet he toyed with it, and wondered if the car couldn't be the vehicle of a compromise, have something about it, something detachable which he could really give her, something within his means – the medallion of St Christopher, for instance, which he had transferred from his old car to this one. It had been a present to him from a customer, who had bought it, so the customer told him, in the South of France; it had an inscription printed round the edge, in French: the customer had told him what it meant, but Leadbitter had forgotten. But Leadbitter didn't want to part with it because he was superstitious about it: he might be parting with his luck. What else was there? Nothing – nothing that would do for a wedding-present – unless, yes there was one thing that might do, and it was a present that in the circumstances only he could give: a poor man's present, but an appropriate one, for it was something that with all her wealth she couldn't command. All the tea in China couldn't buy it! A free drive, that is what he would give her. He would explain to them both, to her and Hughie, when he took them out this evening for their pre-nuptial flight, that he would not charge them for his services at the wedding: he would bear the whole cost himself. If he only told Hughie, Hughie would almost certainly not tell her. He had no wish to spare Hughie's pocket, the wedding-present was not for him, but in sparing his he would be sparing hers, for it was from hers the money came. Leadbitter did not know the Latin proverb that money doesn't smell; but he would not have agreed with it, for to him it did smell, and quite strongly: it smelt of whoever paid it. Hughie had paid, but not with his own money; Leadbitter had never seen the colour of Hughie's money, much less smelt it.

Mentally he tried out on himself the effect – the releasing, liberating effect – of giving Lady Franklin a free drive. It gave him a reaction, certainly, and a pleasant one; but very faint compared with his dream reaction of giving her the car. Yet it was quite a sacrifice – four pounds or so was quite a sacrifice for a man in his position. Perhaps when he came to checking the accounts, and saw the item in red, the red of his own life-stream, that drop of bitterness would make the sweetness sweeter.

Even so, he confessed to a feeling of disappointment. Wasn't there something else that he could give her? He hadn't given many presents in his life but instinctively he knew that one was better than two: two presents robbed each other, made excuses for each other. Each hinted at the other's inadequacy; each seemed an afterthought. Better make a bold plunge with one. Supposing he did give her the St Christopher? At the thought, the clear call of renunciation roused his spirit like a bugle. He didn't want to part with it for it had befriended him; he owed his safety to it. Well, what matter? He would pass his safety on to her, that would be a gift indeed, and a gift that she might need, although he hoped she wouldn't. Besides, seeing the medallion in her car she would, she might, remember him; whereas she wouldn't, no one would, remember a free drive.

But he wouldn't give it to her under Hughie's eyes. He would post it to her, with a note enclosed, so that she got it on Friday, the day before her wedding.

For the wedding would take place: he had made up his mind to that. She would pay no attention to the anonymous letter. Why had he ever thought she would? As soon as he heard it drop in the letter-box he knew at once that it would have no effect: it was the responsibility and the decision – the responsibility for the decision – that had been weighing on him. He felt she ought to know. Now the responsibility had been taken from him, it had passed into other hands, and in those other hands (whose ever they were) it would be taken care of. And that meant – well, it meant that nothing unpleasant would happen to Lady Franklin. It couldn't happen, because he didn't want it to. He had written the letter expressly so that nothing unpleasant should happen. When she read it, if she did read it, she would have a good laugh and throw it on the fire: that was what people did with anonymous letters. She would not let it worry her; she would not believe it for a moment. If by any chance she mentioned it to Hughie, which she wouldn't, he would laugh too, and stifle her inquiries with a kiss. Was it likely that she would believe the letter, which she didn't want to believe, and not Hughie, whom she wanted to believe?

The knowledge that he, Leadbitter, was in the clear, put everybody else in the clear, too.

One thing he couldn't get out of his mind, though it was utterly irrational. He felt that this was the last time he would take Lady Franklin out. Why should it be? He had parted from her on the best of terms; why should she not continue to be his customer? Like several of his customers, she had a car of her own in the country but like them she never used it in London: she preferred to hire. So why not hire him? He had never made his dislike of Hughie clear to Hughie, Hughie could have no grudge against him.

Was it the feeling that until her marriage she was his, and afterwards she would belong to someone else, that gave such a sense of finality to this journey? Was his preoccupation with the wedding-present a way of getting her out of his system, of saying good-bye to her with the best grace he could – before beginning a life in which his imagination would be free of her? Was he assisting at the death of his romantic longings? For the first time since he had met her, she seemed to be outside his calculations; she was being wafted to another sphere where his imagination could not reach her. His presents were to help to usher her into happiness, they could follow her there, but he could not. He had been a foul-weather friend, blown to her by the ill-wind of her unhappiness. As a fair-weather friend she could have no use for him. This he realized and it might have saddened him but it didn't; he had the feeling of having accomplished a mission, he was happy in her happiness, of which he now almost believed himself the architect; and if no other mission lay before him, no other outlet for his emotions, no one for him to identify himself with, well, it was just too bad.

But he was not so friendless as he thought. While walking to the garage, holding in his hand the envelope that held St Christopher, a giant carrying a giant, he felt the tingling of expectancy. The car, the limousine, was exerting its magnetic pull; once with it, once alone with it, once part of it, self-contained and car-contained, he would be independent of the world. No more emotional experiments!

He wasn't quite happy with the gears: how could he be? – but the movement and feeling of the car delighted him. He drove it slowly – more slowly than the prescribed rate of thirty miles an hour – devouring his sensations. Seeing a pillar-box he stopped and slipped the slender envelope in; it weighed hardly more than a letter. 'To Lady Franklin, with best wishes, hoping it may bring you luck, my lady. From S. Leadbitter.'

What a different communication from the last one! And yet he got the same thrill from sending it – so great a thrill that he didn't notice that the box had been cleared and the medallion wouldn't go until tomorrow. But he still had something left to tell her, something he must tell her before their account was closed. He wouldn't be content unless he did. What was it? he wondered, driving slowly on, for the first time without St Christopher.

Chapter 25

WHEN one has made up one's mind that things are going well, and that one has helped to make them go well, it takes some time to realize that in fact the opposite is true, and that things are not going well.

Behind his rather stony mask Leadbitter was an acute observer of human nature, but his mind's eye was so firmly fixed on the ideal picture he had conjured up that he didn't suspect that it might differ from actuality. He did just notice that Hughie got into the car without saying 'good evening' to him, but put this down to natural preoccupation and the painter's casual manners.

Driving down the King's Road towards Belgrave Square he began to look forward to the moment of presenting the new car to Lady Franklin, the moment of the dedication, the first instalment of his wedding-present. He was glad that Hughie hadn't noticed that the car was new; it would be an anti-climax to announce the fact for the second time. Lady Franklin wouldn't notice it either, he felt sure, but she just might, and on that depended how he should word the introduction.

A muffled voice spoke somewhere but it sounded so far away that he could not locate it. But there followed a sharp tap on the glass behind which startled him. The partition – he had forgotten the partition! Pushing it back he turned and said:

'Yes, sir?'

'You're going the wrong way!' cried Hughie in an irritable, agitated voice. 'This is the second time you've missed the way! Don't you know your London better than that?'

'Aren't we going to South Halkin Street?' asked Leadbitter, stupidly.

'No, no, to Campden Hill.'

'You didn't tell me, sir,' said Leadbitter, sufficiently recovered to want to have the last word.

'I thought you knew.'

But as he turned northwards into Sloane Street he was so bewildered that he still hardly knew where he was going, and bungled a gear-change. What did it mean, this extraordinary development? Were they all three going out together? For his mind was still a one-way street, leading to Belgrave Square.

'No, not this way!'

'Sorry sir,' said Leadbitter, and turned once more to the left.

He wouldn't see Lady Franklin now, that was what smarted, but underneath another thought oppressed him, a tumour swollen with intense misgiving.

Constance, as usual, was on the doorstep, a tall slim figure, looking lonely in the half-empty street. Her eyes were turned towards them but her face was turned away and seemed to have grown smaller. Leadbitter got out and opened the door for Hughie, who hesitated a moment and then swung his long legs out and stood on the pavement beside Constance.

'Aren't you going to kiss me?' she said, lifting her head a little.

Then Hughie kissed her.

'I knew it wasn't going to be as easy as we thought,' said Constance, more to herself than him.

'Oh, *that* isn't so difficult,' said he, and followed her into the car.

'Why, it's a new car,' said Constance brightly. 'It's got a glass arrangement, that the other didn't have. We can be as indiscreet now as we like.'

Hughie didn't answer.

The glass partition was still open. Leadbitter had fully

meant to shut it, to keep out those alien voices which, if they did nothing worse, interrupted his feeling of communion with his car, the voiceless colloquy which served him better than conversation. But now he didn't want to miss what was being said, and seizing a pretext for keeping the window open, said through the aperture:

'Where to now, sir?'

'Oh, I dunno,' said Hughie. 'Richmond, I suppose. Does that suit you, Constance? – sweet lass of Richmond Hill?'

'Anywhere you say,' said Constance, chilled by his tone.

'Richmond then,' said Hughie. 'Usual place.'

Leadbitter made as though to close the partition, but he left a chink that might not show in the dark.

They drove on in a silence which neither of them seemed to want to break. At last Constance said:

'Perhaps it was a mistake for us to have come out this evening.'

'Perhaps it was,' said Hughie.

'Well, darling, it was your idea. I thought that in the circumstances –'

'Well?'

'Well, that it might be a little unwise.'

'I know, and I over-persuaded you.'

'Darling, you sound so sad,' said Constance. 'It was bound to be a sad occasion, wasn't it? Certainly sad for me, and sad I think, for you. It couldn't have been a celebration, anyway, but you wanted me to come, to show ... to show ...'

'Yes?' prompted Hughie.

'To show that nothing would be changed between us.'

'Yes,' said Hughie. 'But now it has been changed, at least I'm afraid so.'

'Why,' said Constance, and dread sounded in her voice, 'what has changed it?'

'Shut up, you fool,' said Hughie. 'He can hear us.'

'No, no, he can't, because he's closed the partition. ... Please, Hughie, tell me. If it's because you feel that we mustn't go on being ... what we have been to each other, well then I understand perfectly. I wasn't sure, you remember, that either of us would want to, after you were married.

'But you agreed to, didn't you?' said Hughie.

'Yes, I agreed to.'

'You agreed that my marriage to Ernestine shouldn't make any difference?'

'In that sense, yes.'

'Then,' said Hughie, 'what made you change your mind?'

There was a pause, after which Constance said in a hurt, bewildered voice:

'I'm afraid I don't understand you, Hughie. I haven't changed my mind. Have you changed yours?'

'Well, yes I have.'

'Please don't speak like that, Hughie. It isn't my fault. I guessed you might not like it when the time came.'

'What time?' said Hughie.

'When you were married, of course, darling.'

'I'm not going to be married, as it happens.'

'Not going to be married?' Through the consternation of Constance's voice sounded a faint note of relief and hope.

'No,' said Hughie. 'I'm not going to get married. Can't you guess why?'

'I haven't the least idea,' said Constance, defending herself against the accusation in his tone.

'Someone sent Ernestine an anonymous letter.'

'What, about us?'

'It named no names. It said I had a mistress, and that I meant to keep her, on Ernestine's money, after we were married.'

'Did she show it to you?'

'No, she read it.'

'And then what did she say?'

'What I just told you – that she couldn't marry me.'

'But didn't you deny it?' Constance asked.

'Of course I denied it. But she was too upset to take in anything I said.'

There was more bitterness than sorrow in his voice, and it silenced Constance for a moment; then she said:

'Oh Hughie, I am so sorry.'

'It is a bit of a mess, isn't it?'

'Oh dear, it is, it is an awful mess,' said Constance, the extent of the calamity growing on her. 'A horrible affair, horrible for you both. I can't quite take it in. I try to think of something to say but what can I say? – oh dear, oh dear, poor Hughie. I know you had grown fond of her – perhaps you were in love with her – I never asked you.'

'It doesn't much matter now whether I was or not,' said Hughie.

'No, I suppose it doesn't, in a way. I was only thinking of your feelings. ... But of course you must have built so much on what ... on what the marriage would bring you ... your whole future. Oh dear, it is too sad.'

'Yes, it is pretty grim,' Hughie agreed.

'It would have given you such marvellous opportunities for seeing people, and making contacts, and getting commissions ... and travelling ... and so on.'

'Yes, it would.'

'And social life and parties, endless parties. In the old days you said you didn't like smart parties, but I expect you were beginning to, who wouldn't? – and being lionized, and everyone appreciating you, and telling you what a good painter you were.'

'You needn't rub it in,' said Hughie.

'No, I was only thinking what it must mean to you to have lost all that.'

'All that and a damned sight more,' said Hughie.

'Yes, I suppose so. It's the finish of a lifetime's hopes. But, Hughie –'

'Well?'

'I don't know if it's any consolation, perhaps it isn't, but I never felt quite happy for you. When I said that Ernestine was corrupting, and you didn't like it, I meant that perhaps she scattered too many prizes – how can I say it without sounding priggish – governessy? – too much unearned increment – you don't mind my saying this?'

'Say anything you damned well like. I can't stop you, can I?'

'Please, Hughie, don't be offended – I was only looking for a silver lining. If you wanted to be a painter, and I think you did –'

'You never thought I was any good, though,' Hughie said.

'Ah well, don't bring that up now. I didn't want you to succeed too easily, and that's what might have happened, if you'd married Ernestine. Social life is death to the artist, so they say. Well, I don't know about that, but I know that Bohemian life is the artist's natural milieu.'

'You sound as if you hadn't wanted me to marry Ernestine,' said Hughie.

'My darling, do be reasonable. How could I want you to? Of course I wished you luck – because in a way it was a marvellous thing for you –'

'You sound as if you were glad I wasn't marrying her, said Hughie.

'Darling, please don't speak like that, of course I'm heartbroken. Don't I seem sorry? But you couldn't have expected me to like the marriage and ... and ... sharing you with Ernestine. And now ...'

'Yes, now?' said Hughie, challengingly.

'Do you want me to say it? Won't you say it for me?'

'I haven't the foggiest idea what you want me to say.'

'Haven't you, Hughie?'

'No.'

'Well, we still have each other.'

There was a long silence after this, which Leadbitter thought would never be broken. But at last Hughie said, in a detached speculative voice, and as if opening another subject:

'I wonder who sent that letter?'

Like one coming out of a deep reverie, Constance answered:

'Does it matter?'

'Well yes, I think it does. It must have been someone who didn't want me to marry Ernestine.'

'Well, that's self-evident.' A touch of the old sharpness, which concern for Hughie had blunted, returned to Constance's voice.

'Yes, it's self-evident,' repeated Hughie. 'And it must have been someone who knew about you and me.'

'A lot of people do, dear Hughie.' She was still hurt with him.

'I dare say, but they don't know one thing.'

'What is that?'

'Can't you think?'

'You haven't encouraged my thoughts very much, you know. You've been a bit short with me.'

'Perhaps I have. What I meant was, they couldn't know' – he spoke carefully – 'that our relationship – yours and mine – was to go on after the marriage.'

'Unless you told them, Hughie dear.'

'Now, Constance,' Hughie said, sitting up suddenly. 'Should I have been such a goddam fool?'

'No, I suppose not.'

'No, I shouldn't. And that narrows the field, doesn't it?'

'I don't see what you're driving at.'

'Well, it counts out everybody else, and leaves us two. Constance, I didn't write that letter.'

Leadbitter felt the tension tightening as if it was being wound up on a wheel.

'And so you think that I did?' Constance said quietly.

'Well, who else is there?'

Constance gave a despairing cry.

'Hughie, I swear to you –'

'But who else is there?'

'Hughie, I'll take every oath. You can't believe –'

'But who else is there?' Hughie repeated. 'And you said just now you didn't want me to marry her.'

Constance almost screamed:

'Oh, Hughie, Hughie, please don't say that! You'll kill me, if you say that. Surely you know me well enough, after all these years? Oh, Hughie, take it back, say that you didn't mean it, say –'

'Shut up, for God's sake,' Hughie said, 'or the man will hear you. Your voice is a bit loud, you know, it always was.'

They did not see Leadbitter slide the panel to. He had had his fill of listening. Now all that he could hear was a confused sound of sobs, reproaches, appeals, recriminations: a little world dissolving in inarticulate cries and torn-off shreds of speech. 'Well, that's that,' he thought. 'They've had it, both of them.'

Chapter 26

LEADBITTER drove on. They were getting near to Richmond. They would have been there already, but for running-in. To him it was a place like any other place; he did not think of it as pretty except on the rare occasions when he had taken Clarice there for an outing.

Darkness was falling; he couldn't see what was going on behind him, and the glass partition blocked the reflection, it was almost like a blind. They might be murdering each other, for all he knew. On Sunday at this hour it would still be daylight. Summer time came in on Sunday morning: he must remember to put his clock forward. He would remember all right; but would his customers? The change in the clock nearly always caught some of them napping; literally napping. The customer who sometimes went to early church had been in bed and asleep when Leadbitter came round at seven forty-five. Six forty-five she thought it was, and so she missed saving her soul, that Sunday anyway, and he had had the journey for nothing.

Still, it was all in the day's work, and so was this, this crying jag between Constance and her Hughie. Goodness knew how it would end. His mind recorded the fact that the whole situation had changed; but how the change was affecting him, he could not tell. Oh, for a little daylight! Put the clock on, put it on now, he thought: it was almost a grievance to his tired mind that the clock could not be put on until Sunday. Put it on now and everything would be different, new scenes, new faces, new thoughts – a new life beginning, if he could jump an hour. But he was tied to the present, and the past.

He tried to see his situation as a shape, or feel it as a weight, to have some idea of its extent and gravity. Was it growing larger or smaller, heavier or lighter? How important was it? Where did he come in? Physically, the partition cut him off from it; it was all going on behind the glass. But was it going on? The sounds seemed to have died away. Then all at once they flared up again, and there was a sharp tap on the glass. Leadbitter pulled it back.

'I'm sorry, Leadbitter,' said Hughie, 'but my friend isn't feeling very well, so would you drive us back to Campden Hill?'

'Very good, sir,' Leadbitter said and thought, That's the second time it's happened but this time they won't change their minds. And they won't come out with me again, either.

'Would madam like some brandy?' he asked. 'I keep some here, just in case a customer doesn't feel well. I don't drink myself,' he added.

'Would you like some, Constance?' Hughie asked.

'Yes, no, yes. How thoughtful of you, Mr Leadbitter,' Constance murmured. 'And have you a glass, too?'

Leadbitter produced it.

'How wonderful,' she said, 'the car's like a bar,' and laughed hysterically. The brandy caught her throat and made her cough. 'Thank you,' she spluttered. 'I feel much better now. Would you like some, Hughie, if Mr Leadbitter can spare it?'

'No, thank you,' Hughie said. 'You were quite right: it's not a celebration.'

There they are, thought Leadbitter, off again.

'It *is* a celebration, isn't it?' said Constance, almost giggling. 'Our last? Come on, Hughie; you don't like me, I know, you think I've double-crossed you, but just this once!'

'I don't suppose the driver has another glass,' said Hughie.

'I'm afraid not, sir.'

'Drink out of mine then,' Constance said, 'it wouldn't be the first time.'

'Thanks, but I'd rather not.'

'Why not?'

'I don't fancy it, somehow.'

'Oh, Mr Leadbitter,' Constance said, 'please give me some more brandy. If it isn't too much to ask, please fill my glass again.'

Leadbitter leaned through the opening and filled up the glass. It was a small-sized tumbler, but it held quite a lot.

'Oh, I'm spilling it,' she said, 'please stop, and turn the light on.'

Leadbitter did so. The light revealed with cruel distinctness his two customers crouched in their respective corners, having put all the space between them that they could. Anger had hardened Hughie's face, misery had aged Constance's: they were like caricatures of a couple who had quarrelled.

Constance gulped down half a glassful, choking over it, and then burst out:

'Dear Mr Leadbitter, you seem a kind man, at any rate you have a kind face' (no one had ever said this to him before), 'please tell me how I can convince this cruel, obstinate man that I haven't done something that he says I did. He says that no one else but me could have done it, but how does he know? I'm not a saint, I've never pretended that I was, and I suppose I'm not over-truthful: which of us is? But I shouldn't lie about a thing like that, should I? I'm not that kind of woman, and he knows it. When a person is very much in love with another person, Mr Leadbitter, they do all sorts of things, and I've done many things that I'm ashamed of; but I shouldn't send anyone an anonymous letter, it simply isn't *me*, and I should have thought he would have known it, being quite an intelligent man, although not really a good painter. Dear Mr Leadbitter, won't you drink some of your own brandy?'

With a hand shaking from alcohol-released hysteria she held the glass out to him, but Leadbitter shook his head.

'I'm afraid I don't drink, madam.'

'Oh, but you should,' said Constance. 'It makes life much

more pleasant. It isn't very pleasant now, is it? He says I've wrecked his life because I wrote this letter, and now he can't marry a rich woman who would have kept him in luxury and idleness. And he's wrecked mine by thinking I could do it – no, not by that. Let me be quite honest. If I had done it I should only have done it out of love for him and because I didn't want to lose him. He might have forgiven me for that, mightn't he? – and then I wouldn't have minded that he thought me capable of a mean action. But he doesn't love me – he won't even drink out of the same glass with me – that's what I really mind! It won't do him any good, will it, to be so hard, and it won't do his art any good, either. You can't get any paint out of a dry heart. Art and heart, you could make a joke out of that, couldn't you? Who will care, when all this is over, that someone sent an anonymous letter? Why, it may not even get into the papers. But I shall care, all my life. Dear Mr Leadbitter, I'm sure you know all about people, you must have known so many. Please tell him I didn't do it!'

Leadbitter didn't answer, but pressed the self-starter with his thumb. When the car was under way he said:

'No, you didn't do it.'

A silence followed which was broken by Constance saying with a nervous giggle:

'You heard, Hughie? He says I didn't do it.'

'How does he know?' asked Hughie with a sneer.

'Because I know who did,' said Leadbitter.

The silence was much longer this time and of a different quality.

'You know: who was it?' Hughie demanded.

Leadbitter didn't answer.

'Oh, Hughie,' broke in Constance, 'please don't bother him. He says I didn't do it. Isn't that enough?' She might have been another person speaking, there was so much happiness in her voice.

'No, it isn't enough,' said Hughie truculently. 'I want to know who –'

'But darling, does it *matter* who sent it? What matters is that *I* didn't. Does anything else matter? Now we can be like we were before. Oh darling, I am so happy. Please kiss me, Hughie.'

Hughie kissed her. It was a long embrace. When it was over, Constance said:

'Darling, I feel so sleepy. I think I shall go to sleep.'

'Oh, do you?' Hughie said. His voice sounded smoother, but there were angry glints in it, like foam on a sea that is still rough after the wind has dropped. '*I* feel rather hungry.'

'Well, couldn't we go and eat somewhere?' said Constance.

'Yes, but where?'

'Why not Richmond?'

'It's not a bad idea,' said Hughie.

'Then we can have a real celebration.'

'Darling, I don't think you ought to celebrate any more. You're drunk already.'

'Well, perhaps I am a little. Wouldn't you like to be? You are so very sober, darling.'

'It might be an improvement,' Hughie said.

'I'll ask Mr Leadbitter if he can spare us some more brandy,' Constance said.

Without answering, Leadbitter handed her the brandy and the glass.

'You don't mind drinking from the same glass with me now, do you?' said Constance, pouring out the brandy with a shaking hand.

'Thy drinks be forgiven thee,' hiccupped Hughie, 'no levity intended. But you mustn't have any more,'

'Well, just a mouthful, so that we can drink to each other.'

Their eyes met across the single glass.

'Hughie,' said Constance, 'Constance,' said Hughie in the same breath. 'Restored to each other,' Constance added. 'For keeps,' said Hughie. In two gulps he drained the glass.

'Oh, you brute,' said Constance. 'I wanted to drink to

someone else. Perhaps Mr Leadbitter could spare us some more brandy.'

'Certainly, madam,' said Leadbitter, 'if there is any.'

'Oh, surely there must be. It wouldn't give out, would it? It's like the widow's cruse.' She poured out another glassful.

'Whom did you want to drink to?' Hughie asked.

'Can't you think of anyone?'

'Well, perhaps I could,' said Hughie.

'So could I, and I think it would be nice. What do you think?'

'I'd rather not,' said Hughie decisively. 'It wouldn't go down very easily. She has all she wants, hasn't she? What good would our good wishes do her? I think I'll drink it myself.' He suited the action to the word. 'Now there's no more brandy.'

'You greedy hog,' said Constance. 'Let's think of her and then turn down an empty glass.'

She did so, and then looked up. The sliding panel was shut.

'I don't think he can have heard what we said, do you, Hughie?' she asked.

'No, but he's an eavesdropper all right,' said Hughie. 'I mean to tax him with it later on.'

'Oh no, don't bother him. We needn't see him again.'

'Yes, but I want to *know*. ...' He opened the partition. 'Leadbitter, we've changed our minds. We're going back to Richmond.'

'Very good, sir,' said Leadbitter and drove straight ahead. This time he didn't close the panel.

Constance and Hughie sat in silence for a little while, a vague doubt creeping mist-like through their minds.

'I suppose he *is* going to Richmond?' Constance said. 'He didn't turn round, did he?'

'I can't remember,' Hughie said. 'Anything may have happened, while you were creating.'

He spoke affectionately.

Presently Constance said, 'Perhaps you'd better ask him if we're on the right road.'

Hughie cleared his throat and said:

'I say, is this the road for Richmond?'

'It's the Richmond road.'

'But are we going the right way?'

'I shouldn't know if you're going the right way,' Leadbitter said, 'you're the best judge of that.'

'Now look here –'

'I'm looking, sir,' said Leadbitter. 'I have to look, to drive the car.'

Hughie leaned back against the cushions, to consider the next step.

'Is everything all right?' whispered Constance.

'I think so. His manner's a bit queer.'

'Well, I suppose he might have said the same of ours, not long ago,' giggled Constance, happily.

All at once the car turned left up an incline. They were crossing a bridge over the Thames; on both sides they could see the lights reflected in the water.

'I don't think this is right,' said Hughie.

'Oh darling, does it matter? Right or wrong, it's all such fun.'

'Yes, but . . . Leadbitter, where are we now?'

'Just crossing the river, sir.'

'But do we have to cross the river to go to Richmond?'

'We have to cross it some time.'

The road was clear ahead and Leadbitter accelerated.

'Aren't we going a bit fast?' asked Constance. 'Not that I mind.'

Leadbitter didn't answer. They were going fast, too fast for the engine of the car, which might be irreparably damaged, too fast for their own safety. But did it matter? So few things seemed to matter.

'There's one thing you haven't told us,' said Hughie suddenly, 'and that is how you know that my friend didn't send that letter.'

'Oh, don't bother him,' put in Constance. 'We don't want a post-mortem on it, do we? What matters is that I didn't send it – I'm in the clear. That affair is closed, isn't it? Unless you still think –'

'No, I don't,' said Hughie. 'But I still want to know – please don't drive so fast, Leadbitter – who did send it. Who could have known about us? I certainly told no one.

'Nor did I,' said Constance.

'Oh, didn't you?' said Leadbitter in his harshest voice. 'Are you sure you didn't? Think again.'

There was a pause.

'My mind has become a blank,' said Constance. 'But I don't talk in my sleep, and there's no one to hear me if I did.'

'It's an absolute mystery,' said Hughie. 'We didn't tell anybody, and yet someone knew.'

'You didn't tell anybody and yet someone knew,' sneered Leadbitter. 'Odd, wasn't it? But you *did* tell someone.'

'Who?' asked Hughie, still incredulous.

'You told *me*,' shouted Leadbitter. 'Do you think I'm deaf? What do you think I am? Do you think I'm just a bit of the car, or one of these damned bloody automatons? Do you think I can sit here without hearing all the poppycock you talk?'

'Now listen –' Hughie began.

'Listen? I should just think I was listening – I can't help listening, worse luck.'

'Don't take that tone with me,' said Hughie, attempting dignity, 'and don't drive so fast. You realize you've done me a great injury, don't you? Or are you in the habit of sending people anonymous letters?'

'I'm not in the habit of driving spivs who earn their daily bread by night like any common prostitute,' retorted Leadbitter.

'Perhaps not, but what is it to do with you how I behave? I haven't done you any harm, have I? I've always paid you –'

'*You've* paid me?' Leadbitter said. 'You make me laugh. I know where the money came from.'

'Oh please don't worry him, Hughie,' Constance said. 'He's upset, you can see that. After all, he told us that he sent the letter, and he needn't have told us. He could have left you thinking it was me, and then how wretched I should have been, and I don't think you would have been happy either. Now we're both happy, at least I am, and what else counts?'

'You're not selfish, are you?' Leadbitter said. 'You always think of other people, don't you? Here I've been sitting in this car an hour and more, and heard you talking, and what's it all been about? First Hughie moans because he can't get married, and then you moan because he puts the blame on you; talk about people being sorry for themselves! And then I say you didn't send the letter, and all at once everything in the garden's lovely. "Nothing else matters if I'm happy!" ' – and Leadbitter mimicked Constance's voice. 'You couldn't spare a thought for anyone else, could you? All this time I've been waiting to hear a name and I haven't heard it and I should like to hear you say it, one of you –'

His voice became more threatening.

'Whose name, Hughie?' Constance whispered. 'Whose name does he want us to say?'

Hughie didn't answer: they both searched their minds.

'I'm not going to wait much longer,' Leadbitter said. 'It's an uncommon name and you both know it. If you don't tell me I've got a plan for you, and it will jog your memories all right –'

'Does he mean Ernestine?' said Constance, wondering and frightened.

Leadbitter hesitated a moment.

'Oh no, I don't mean her,' he said. 'She doesn't come into it, does she? She doesn't matter, does she, she doesn't count. She's not worth mentioning. She was only your stooge, your sugar-mummy, whose money was to keep the two of you on heat! It doesn't matter how she feels, does it, when she's lost her fiancé – though he was a heel and she's well rid of him. It doesn't matter how she feels – she may be dead for all you care! Is she dead?' he demanded suddenly.

'No, of course not,' Hughie said. 'She isn't dead. Lady Franklin isn't dead. Why should she be?'

'How is she, then? You never told us. You told us all about yourself and how *you* felt – you didn't say how she was when you left her – if she was ill or crying, or standing or sitting or lying down – How *was* she, or didn't you notice?'

'She cried a little,' Hughie said.

'She cried a little! Did she ask for anything, or did you help her?'

'I left her to herself,' said Hughie. 'What else could I do? She wouldn't say any more.'

'You left her crying? You didn't stop to ask if there was anything you could do? You just left her? Or did you say, "Sorry, but I'm off to see my Constance now"?'

Hughie didn't answer, but Constance, who was crying herself, said:

'He's quite right, Hughie. We should have thought more of Ernestine, of course. I don't know why we didn't ... I ... I hope she isn't too unhappy.'

'Oh no, she's not unhappy,' Leadbitter said. 'She's gone out to a party – she's having a whale of a time, singing and dancing, just like we are. We're all happy, aren't we? But I know someone who isn't, though you'd never guess who.'

He was talking to the air in front of him, and crouching over the wheel.

'Don't tell us of anyone else who is unhappy, please, Mr Leadbitter,' Constance said. 'I don't think I could bear it.'

'Oh yes, you could,' said Leadbitter. 'It isn't anyone who matters, nobody who counts. But if she knew – shall you tell her it was I who sent the letter?'

'Why no, of course not,' Constance said. 'What good would it do? Besides, we shan't be seeing her again.'

'I shan't be seeing her,' said Hughie, finding his tongue, 'but *you* will, Constance. There's no reason why *you* shouldn't see her – she doesn't know it was you who – And I think you ought to tell her.'

'Why?' said Constance.

'So that she shan't suspect the wrong person. So that she shall suspect the right person, if you like,' he added vindictively.

'*I* shan't tell her,' Constance said.

'Then I shall. If I can't see her, I can write to her, I shall have to write to her about . . . about a lot of things, and then I'll tell her.'

'You'll tell her?' Leadbitter said.

'Yes, why not? She'll know then she has an enemy, and be on her guard.'

'An enemy?' said Leadbitter. 'Me, her enemy?'

'Only an enemy would have sent that letter.'

'I'm not her enemy,' said Leadbitter contemptuously.

'You acted like one. If you're not, why did you send the letter?'

'Because,' said Leadbitter, 'because . . .' he stopped. 'You won't believe me if I tell you.'

'We'll try to, won't we?' Hughie said.

'I'd like someone to know,' said Leadbitter, reflectively. 'I'd like someone to know, but not you, you — And come to think of it, there's only one person, one person in the world, I want to tell it to. The rest, well, they can think what they like. You can think what you like. But I'd like her to know, I'd like her to know I didn't mean to hurt her, for if she doesn't, what's the use of going on? I shouldn't want to.'

'Look here,' said Hughie. 'Can't we talk about this after dinner? I don't know where we've got to – we seem to be going up a mountain. Do you know where we are?'

'I haven't been noticing,' said Leadbitter. 'She said to me

once, "If you have anything to tell anyone, tell them, or it may spoil your life, as it has mine." I thought it funny at the time, that you should want to tell anybody anything, except where they get off, but now I don't, I want to tell her, and I can't tell her, you see. But if you tell her that I sent the letter, without telling her why –'

'We don't know why,' said Hughie. 'You haven't told us.'

'It was because,' said Leadbitter, 'because ... No, I can't say it. ... It wouldn't make sense to her. She'd ... she'd feel insulted. But promise me one thing.'

'Well, what is it?' Hughie asked.

'Promise you won't tell her that I sent the letter.'

'I won't promise anything of the kind,' shouted Hughie. 'You got us all into this mess, and you must stand the racket. What does it matter what she thinks of you – you're only a hireling!'

'Oh, so I'm only a hireling, am I?' answered Leadbitter. 'Well, I shan't be much longer.' A wave of revulsion for everything his life had meant to him swept over him irresistibly. He pressed his foot on the accelerator. The car sprang forward. The street was dark; towering buildings on the right shut out what light there was. The darkness was in Leadbitter's mind too; he couldn't see to think, and when a tree suddenly loomed up half-way across the road, with a warning white blaze on it, he was never to know whether he drove into it on purpose or not. But when he saw the crash coming he turned round and shouted, 'Tell Lady Franklin that I –'

For a few minutes the car stood by itself, in the empty, ill-lit street, as motionless as the tree-trunk from which it had rebounded. Untouched at the back, still gleaming with newness, in front it was a wreck of torn and twisted metal, like the idea of a death agony by a modern sculptor. Then a passer-by stopped and peered at it, and was soon joined by another and another, and when a little group had formed, curiosity overcame their dread and they went nearer. The chauffeur was sitting with his head resting on the driving wheel.

'Why, he's asleep!' said someone.

But he wasn't. Later it was found that a strut broken off the driving wheel had run into his chest, a chromium-plated spike of metal, so thin that when they pulled it out the wound was scarcely visible.

Chapter 27

HUGHIE died in hospital but Constance gradually recovered. She had had concussion and shock and for some days her mind was in confusion. When it began to settle down her first thought was of Hughie.

She would have to adjust herself to life without him. She had done that once before, in a sense, when he told her he was going to marry Ernestine; but the misery of those moments was soon over and it was entirely an emotional response. Besides, there was a great difference between not having him in her life and knowing he was dead. Now she tried to think about him, not just feel about him. How much would she miss him? She had to find an attitude towards him, and it would be no help to blind herself to his faults.

During their last ride together those faults had been very much in evidence. She knew his faults, of course, and thought she knew the answers to them – the answers to his critics, of whom she herself was chief. You couldn't trust him, she admitted that, and by admitting it, by making it a kind of postulate, she had drawn its sting. 'Oh, we all know you can't trust Hughie!' His unreliability had become a proverb, and as impersonal as a proverb, but when she saw it in action, and smarted under it and blushed for it, it didn't seem impersonal, it seemed the essence of him. She blushed for herself too, remembering the lash of Leadbitter's tongue; he had flayed them jointly for their selfishness. Some of his strictures came back to her; she deserved them every bit as much as Hughie had. A spasm of self-dislike went through her, and disliking herself she couldn't help, almost for the first time, disliking Hughie. Her vision of their relationship was changed. No longer could she see herself as his protector, the stronger of the two; she realized that he had been the stronger and made her act out of her character.

For this she couldn't forgive him, but not to forgive him made her miserable; it poisoned the past and would poison the future. She simply must forgive him, but how? – how find a thought that would reconcile her to him? It came, the same thought that had alienated her, but turned the other way round. For in life she and Hughie, though they had been lovers, had not been quite together; always there had been the feeling that she was too good for him. Everybody told her so, and though she denied it, in her heart she believed it, and when she was with him was possessed by it, feeling a governess even in his arms.

She could not look down on him now; *vis-à-vis* Ernestine they were equally at fault.

But to a humanist like Constance it was no help to admit that they had both acted badly. She did not subscribe to Christian ethics; self-abasement, she felt, would get her nowhere. She believed in giving herself her due. If in the crisis she had let Hughie rule her, it was a momentary lapse and an exception; she had always thought of him as depending on her, and if she ever thought of death in relation to the two of them, it was her death that she dreaded, for his sake, because without her he would have no one to keep him afloat. For that reason, and because he was younger than she, it never occurred to her that he might die first – or die at all. In fairness to herself she realized that her surrender to his proposal that she should remain his mistress after he was married was not so abject as it seemed: with Ernestine he would be lost, but with Constance to keep an eye on him he might still be saved. He was her charge, her trust; and it was a steady consolation to her that she had never failed him and now could never fail him. She had been through a great deal with Hughie; many times she had asked herself if she could go on loving him, and always in the end the answer had been yes; each time it had been easier to say yes; and now that he was dead she still said yes. The old pattern of their relationship had reasserted itself, and she could still think of him with love – another consolation, and the greatest, which for a fleeting moment she feared that she had lost.

When the news of the accident came out, Constance was too ill to read the papers. Afterwards she was shown two or three accounts. Under the splashed headlines they were factual and objective; they said that Hughie's head had gone through the inner wind-screen, but they did not suggest that there had been special friendship between him and Constance. Their three names were there, of course; but within twenty-four hours the first wave of public interest had spent itself. The accident was just another case of death on the roads.

Constance herself could not remember it or what happened just before it. In front of the place where it should be a black mist hung, not solid like a curtain, but as impenetrable. Within the darkness something moved, something that struggled to come to life, to be born out of the womb of her memory. Throughout her convalescence it nagged her with a sense of incompleteness, like an untied shoe-lace – though she had far more serious things to occupy her, interviews with the police, for instance, trying to get facts out of her about the accident. An empty brandy bottle and a used tumbler, both intact, had been discovered in the car: was the inference that the driver had been drunk? No, said Constance; she had been unwell and drunk some of the brandy that the driver kept for emergencies, and Hughie had joined her, but to the best of her recollection the driver had taken nothing, and this was confirmed by the post-mortem. (Leadbitter had been carved up as well as killed.) Hughie had asked her to dine with him at Richmond; she had felt ill and they were coming back. Then how was it that the accident occurred in Hampstead, when she lived on Campden Hill? And why was the car heading northwards when it struck the tree? Constance said she had no idea, and pleaded loss of memory.

This black-out was, from one point of view, very convenient for her; as long as she did not contradict herself, she could choose what to remember. No one could check up on her loss of memory. As the days passed the black mist receded, leaving visible to her conscious mind many things she had genuinely forgotten, like rocks uncovered by the ebbing tide. But the thing she wanted most to know did not declare itself.

The accident had been a face-saving business all round. It had saved her face, Hughie's, Leadbitter's, and Ernestine's.

Had it saved Ernestine's? Did anyone besides herself know that for Ernestine the blow had been a double blow? Did Ernestine suspect Constance of knowing?

How delicate was it, her own situation? Her friends had come to see her, they had written; only a very few had failed to make some sign. They had condoled with her on her misfortune and congratulated her on her escape – emphasizing the one or the other according to their temperaments and their several estimates of where she stood. Perhaps the absentees had stayed away, and the silent had refrained from writing, because they could not make their minds up, or had made them up in a way unfavourable to her. She would want them now, her friends, and she must look them up and atone for her neglect of them – for how easy it is, when one is in love, to neglect one's friends! Beside the voice which is so much nearer and more urgent, their voices sound like a distant murmur, hardly intelligible. She would need all her friends for a life that from now on must be based on friendship, not on love.

Ernestine was not a real friend; should she go and see her? Yes, her conscience said, but Constance had always kept her conscience in its place; she didn't believe in encouraging it; she liked it, as she liked her wine, to be dry. She thought a soggy, suppurating conscience did more harm than good and had trained herself to be suspicious of its promptings, unless some obvious good would come of them.

What good would come of seeing Ernestine?

But was a drama of human feeling into which she had, for many years, put everything she had to give, unselfishly as well as selfishly – was it to be dismissed as unmentionable, because of one slip at the end? Was human understanding so bankrupt that she could not even approach the other woman, could not even press her hand and go away without speaking? It seemed it was; it seemed as though the maximum effort of two hearts, expended on the self-same object, could never coalesce, could never touch, could never be so much as made known to each other; for every consideration that reconciled her to Hughie's death to Ernestine would be an added insult, a new cause for suffering. Another woman's experience! Far from telling Ernestine about it, she must keep it from her with every lie at her command. This should not be difficult, for Ernestine was utterly unsuspecting; her mind was in the clouds when not turned inwards on itself. Her egoism and her idealism, which were complementary, repelled objective fact. Yet might not a spark somehow fly between them – a thought that common humanity had kindled, even if it had no bearing on their joint experience?

It was Constance's good fortune that her thoughts controlled her feelings. But she knew that with Ernestine it was the other way about; if any thought was going to help her, it would have to be presented in an emotional form.

No such thought occurred to Constance, but the sense of mission was inherent in her, and now that Hughie was gone instinctively it sought another object. She did not connect Ernestine (why should she?) with the unidentified memory at large in the mist, yet separately they were always in her thoughts. 'What can I say to Lady Franklin?' and on the last morning of her stay in hospital the answer, or a part of it, came to her. She was awakened by the voice of a man shouting, shouting with so much urgency and such a clamour of sound, that it might have been someone in the street below her, crying for help. At first the words were indistinguishable; then they were borne to her on a kind of echo: 'Tell Lady Franklin that I –' After the 'I', which had a frenzy of appeal in it, like the last affirmation of an identity on the threshold of dissolution, she heard no more; but even while she recognized the voice as Leadbitter's, two things happened in the depth of her consciousness; she knew that the lost memory had been recovered, and knew what she must say to Ernestine.

But afterwards she doubted, doubted first if the message was complete. Clearly it was not complete; the vital part was missing. Had it eluded her, was it still adrift in the limbo of concussion? She didn't think so; the sense of wholeness had come back to her, the nagging shoe-lace had been tied up; all that Leadbitter had said, she had remembered. But the second doubt was harder to dispose of. How could she go to Ernestine with half a message? How could she convey its urgency without its meaning? To Leadbitter it had meant, she was convinced, all that he had it in him to mean: it was the final utterance of his spirit. If only she could have had a record of it, with every intonation and vibration sounding! Then it would have told its own tale, unfinished though it was. But spoken in her woman's voice, emasculated, across the tea-cups, how could it fail to be an anti-climax? 'Really, Miss Copthorne, if *that* is all you have to tell me!' – for even Ernestine could be alarming in her regal moods.

And how should she present herself? Not wearing a white sheet for Hughie – that she would never do. Bluffing her way through the interview with a jaunty boldness? 'It wasn't so bad, you know, just the usual kind of head-on crash. We hadn't time to be frightened. I couldn't go to Hughie's funeral, I was out of action, but no doubt you were there? They are rather sad occasions, aren't they, though they can be funny. I expect that all Leadbitter's relations turned up at his. I should have liked to send a wreath – the working class make such a thing of funerals – but I didn't know where to send it. . . . Oh yes, I could have, because it must have happened after the post-mortem – I suppose he had to be buried somewhere? – by which time I was *compos mentis*, more or less. He had a message for you, by the way.'

That wouldn't do, either. She simply couldn't imagine herself in the other woman's presence. Supposing Ernestine refused to see her? Would she then feel absolved from further effort, either on her own behalf, or Leadbitter's?

What – she kept asking herself – had Leadbitter wanted them to tell Ernestine, that he couldn't say himself? For it was they who were to tell her, and not he. Why? Had he foreseen his own death? Had he perhaps decided on it?

Thinking of Leadbitter's last moments, and the words that had been almost forced out of him, Constance grew more and more confused. Did he want them to say he hadn't sent the letter? (Hughie's threat to tell on him was one of the things she had found hardest to forgive.) But then he would have said, 'Don't tell Lady Franklin that I – sent the letter,' because she wouldn't suspect him, presumably, unless they told her. Did he want them to say that the letter was a lie? 'Tell Lady Franklin that I – made it up?' He might have meant to say that. The letter was her only clue; whatever the message was, it must have been to do with the letter. Yet she couldn't mention the letter to Ernestine: it was the very last thing she could mention.

What did he want to say to Ernestine so urgently that he died trying to say it?

She couldn't think, but she must take the message, meaningless though it was, or Leadbitter's ghost, with its harsh, desperate voice, would haunt her, unappeased.

Chapter 28

A SECRETARY replied to Constance's letter saying that on her doctor's advice Lady Franklin was not seeing visitors, but that she very much wanted to see Miss Copthorne, and suggested tea on such and such a day. But (the secretary added this on her own account) would Miss Copthorne not stay too long, as Lady Franklin got very quickly tired.

On a sunny afternoon Constance arrived at the house in South Halkin Street, noticed the net curtains drawn across the window and rang the bell. She felt more nervous than she had felt for years; any curiosity she had had evaporated, the things she had prepared to say fled from her, she only wanted the interview to be over. She hardly took in her surroundings, though she noticed that the sofa on which Lady Franklin had reclined for her portrait had been pushed against the wall and was so covered with cushions that there was no room even to sit on it: it had the air of being roped off.

Lady Franklin came in a moment later, looking smaller than Constance remembered her, but dressed in the old blend of blue and white. She brought so little personality with her that she scarcely seemed to disturb the air; the room itself did not recognize its mistress, it felt no different after she had entered, and when she said in her fluttering way: 'Oh, Miss Copthorne, I am so pleased to see you,' it was almost as if she had not spoken.

'I mustn't stay long,' said Constance, sinking into a chair beside the low tea-table, and feeling she had already stayed a long time, 'for I know how quickly you get tired.'

The words were no sooner out of her mouth than they seemed altogether too positive a statement to make about Lady Franklin.

'They tell me I get tired,' said Lady Franklin, rather vaguely, 'and I suppose I do: it is so easy to feel what you are told that you feel, isn't it? And less trouble, too,' she added with the ghost of a smile.

A woman who can take her state of health on trust from someone else can't be very ill, thought Constance, but she said as sympathetically as she could: 'I know just what you mean. I have been ill, too, and when the doctor asked me how I was, I sometimes used to answer, "That's for you to say." '

'Of course you have been ill,' said Lady Franklin, sliding into self-reproach, 'much worse than I have. How are you feeling now?'

'Oh, much better,' Constance said. 'I start work again on Monday.' She paused, overwhelmed by self-consciousness; and an absurd idea came to her that she ought to explain to Lady Franklin what the word 'work' meant.

'I sometimes wish I had to work,' said Lady Franklin. 'The pressure of outside circumstances is something one can't invent for oneself, can one? And when outside pressure stops, inside pressure begins. Or does that sound affected?'

'No, of course not,' Constance said. 'I don't know what I should do if I hadn't to work.'

'Do you find it an answer to everything?' asked Lady Franklin.

'I hope I shall,' said Constance, thinking, I shall never be able to shift the weight of unspoken words that lie between us; I might as well go now.

'I have found another answer,' said Lady Franklin, looking away from Constance, 'at least it has found me. ... I could tell you ... But why should I bother you with my affairs?'

Constance grasped at this.

'I hoped,' she said with difficulty, 'that you would tell me something, so that I could also tell you ...'

'Will you begin?' said Lady Franklin.

'No, I'd rather you did.'

'Well, Nature is merciful in a way, I feel. She doesn't really mean us to suffer.'

'You think not?' said Constance. 'I confess I've sometimes wondered.'

'I think not. You see, I suffered a good deal over the accident . . . and everything.'

'I'm sure you did.'

'But I don't suffer now, or not as much.'

'I'm glad to hear that,' Constance said.

'You knew Hughie well, didn't you?' said Lady Franklin, and her out-thrust underlip began to tremble.

'Yes, very well.'

'Did you think him very talented?'

'No, not really,' Constance said.

'I did, but perhaps I was wrong. Perhaps I was wrong about him altogether. If he had lived –' Lady Franklin stopped.

'Yes?' said Constance cautiously.

'He might have made some woman happy. . . . You, perhaps.'

'Me?' said Constance. 'But he would have been married to you.'

Lady Franklin clasped and unclasped her hands.

'No . . . No . . . We had broken it off. I thought you would have known.'

'I did know, as a matter of fact,' said Constance, reddening.

'I thought you must have. It was kind of you to say you didn't. Now I sometimes think I could have married him – that I ought to have – but I didn't think so then. . . . I was so bewildered . . . and hurt, too. It wasn't so much his loving another woman that I minded, as his not loving me.'

'I don't quite understand,' said Constance. 'Won't you explain?'

'It was the letter . . . the letter someone sent to say he had a mistress, and meant to go on seeing her after we were married. I believed it at once . . . I always believe what people tell me. But now I'm not sure I do. Supposing an enemy of his had sent it, out of spite? Or an enemy of mine? I didn't know I had one, but perhaps we all have. I hadn't time to think, I was so stunned. And just because I didn't want to believe it, I thought it must be true.'

'Did he deny it?' Constance asked.

'Oh yes, but then he had to. Oh, I hated not being able to believe him, but what could I do? I couldn't *make* myself believe. It wasn't till afterwards – long afterwards – that I began to wonder if ... if I hadn't done him the most cruel injustice, and missed my own happiness, too. Anonymous letters are often untrue, aren't they? People I've asked have told me so.'

'Did you tell anyone about the letter?' Constance asked.

'Oh no, indeed not, that was a thing I have to be so grateful for – I didn't tell anybody, I couldn't. I did nothing at all. I didn't take any steps – you know, to cancel the arrangements – until I heard about the accident. And then of course, I had to. It was much easier than I thought it would be – the mechanical part, I mean – just a matter of writing and paying – and everybody was so sweet to me. ... I haven't finished answering the letters yet. It helped me a great deal at first to know that people were sorry for me, but after a time I couldn't bear it – everyone taking it for granted we were still in love with each other, and then I stopped reading the letters and put a notice in the paper to say I would answer later. In a way it was the letters all saying the same thing that made me wonder if I had been mistaken about Hughie. And that was the worst part – wondering if I had misjudged him.'

'Would you rather think that he had loved you, or that he hadn't?' Constance heard herself asking.

'Oh, I don't know. Sometimes I would rather think he hadn't, because less seems lost like that, and sometimes I would rather think he had, because then I could remember him with love, instead of with those horrible mixed feelings, not knowing what to think. The uncertainty was the most tormenting part. It split me into two countries, which were always at war. And then a most wonderful thing happened.'

Lady Franklin stopped and the two women looked at each other questioningly.

'I hardly like to tell you,' Lady Franklin said, 'because it must sound rather silly and as if I was taking myself so seriously. But it's what I meant when I said that Nature doesn't mean us to suffer, and is always planning a way out, however much we may oppose her. Because there's always something in us that wants to suffer, isn't there?'

'I should have to think about that,' Constance said.

'Well, if it hadn't happened I couldn't be talking to you as I am, it would have been too painful, and I was half dizzy with drugs, too. The stuff they poured into me! But now you see how calm I am.'

'I shouldn't have said that you were very calm,' said Constance, and was sorry she had spoken when she saw the cloud that gathered between Lady Franklin's brows.

'Oh, but compared with what I was! I was dreaming, I think – I couldn't always tell the difference – when suddenly all this that we've been through, both of us, seemed to dissolve and float away like a mist, and I was back again.'

'Back again?'

Lady Franklin smiled apologetically.

'How could I expect you to understand my private language? I used to call it "back again", you know, after my husband's death, when I slipped back into that sort of obsession I had. The doctors tried to help me out of it, but I kept slipping back. Well, I was cured, I needn't tell you how, and afterwards all this happened. Quite unbearable, it seemed – and then suddenly, without warning, something slipped and I was back again, back with my grief for Philip. Oh the relief of it!'

'Relief?'

'But yes. You know how a bright light can hurt one's eyes – in some countries they use it as a torture. And it's still there if you shut them. Well, all at once it dimmed, as if my soul had fainted, and now it's a kind of twilight, in which everything looks very much the same, and my feelings are the same, too – they don't vary. I don't really suffer, I don't know why I ever thought I did! It's like being in church, where nothing ever happens, or can happen, except to the spirit. I believe you can cure an illness by an illness – well, that's what's happened to me: only I don't count this an illness, it's a deliverance.'

When Constance said nothing, Lady Franklin went on, but more tentatively and apologetically:

'You see, where I am now, though I can't get out, nothing can come in – none of this could have come in, if I'd stayed where I was, as Nature meant me to. I shall always feel sorry about something – the doctors told me so; it's no good my trying to get angry and blame others. Even if they are to blame, I don't get any satisfaction from thinking I am in the right. I do get some from knowing I was in the wrong, as I was about Philip. I couldn't sleep before, but now I can sleep, I can sleep for hours – I was asleep just now, when you came.'

'I'm sorry if I woke you,' Constance said, 'and yet, in another way, I'm not. I don't like to hear you talk like this. I don't believe it's natural, even if you say so, to live in a padded cell. Why it's like madness –'

'What if it is?' cried Lady Franklin, jumping up and pacing the floor in front of her visitor. 'Isn't madness preferable to sanity, the kind of sanity I've had for these last weeks? Madness is my friend. Life, Life, they used to say, you must get back to Life; they tempted me out of my retreat, talking of Life. But what has Life done for me? Life's my enemy, the only one I ever had, unless it was whoever sent that letter. If I went back to Life, as they call it, what should I go back to? Wondering about the letter, was it true or not, whether I killed him by breaking off the engagement – as I believe I did, though not directly of course. And there are scores of others "if's". What is there for me in Life, but to flounder for ever in these cruel uncertainties, not even knowing what I want to believe? Far better not to think and not to feel but to pass the time in a kind of drowse, as I do now, making amends to Philip for my neglect, for not being there when he died, and wishing I had told him that I loved him. If that be madness, well, I welcome it! At any rate the past can't change or spring surprises on me.'

'But is that true?' asked Constance. 'I mean about the past not springing surprises? Supposing, for instance, I were to tell you something about the recent past that changed your view of it – would you want to hear?'

Immediately Lady Franklin became extremely agitated.

'Yes ... no ... I should have to think and you would have to remind me, so much of it is gone. No, I think I'd better not know.'

'But I think that you should know,' Constance said, raising her voice.

'No, please, I've quite decided. I'm a misfit. I bring unhappiness to everyone. Shut up in myself, I can limit the harm I do. I've made all the arrangements' – Lady Franklin's voice became brisk and business-like – 'my secretary will acknowledge the remaining letters with a printed form. I hate doing that – it seems so ungrateful, but I want to be impersonal – I want to fade out. The presents have been sent back, all except ... all except ...' A look of distaste that deepened into nausea crossed Lady Franklin's face. 'All except a very few that came after the accident. I've only to open them, see what they are, thank for them, and send them back, yet somehow I can't do it.'

Constance seized on this admission to intervene.

'But couldn't you?' she said. 'Couldn't you? Forgive me if it seems like meddling, but do try to. Mightn't it be easier for you, while I'm here. I won't look, of course, while you are opening the parcels; I won't say anything; I'll go into another room if you like.'

'Perhaps I could,' said Lady Franklin, 'perhaps I could. ... I know I ought to; I ought to thank my friends for their kind thought. I put them away somewhere, I don't know where, but I could find them if you would excuse me a moment.'

She went out.

I must rouse her, Constance told herself; I must make her see that there was more in all this than a plausible excuse for skulking, and cherishing her grief which she finds the sole object of existence. If only I could ruin her financially, or in any way! – then she would have to bestir herself. If I could make her realize that she can't impose her feelings on events! But she can – that's just her trouble. Perhaps we all can, if it comes to that – but it's easier for her, with all her money. And as though to confirm her thought the door opened to let in Lady Franklin, followed by the butler, his arms full of parcels. At her request he laid them on the sofa, in the crevices between the cushions, for there was no room on the knick-knack laden tables.

'Shall I go now, my lady?' Simmonds asked, and Lady Franklin said, 'Yes, please go now, and if I want you I'll ring.' The butler went away. 'You see,' she explained, 'I've had them out before, and told him to take them away, for I don't like being in the room with them. But perhaps when you are here –'

She got up and looked down at the parcels, and Constance, forgetting her promise, did the same. From much handling the parcels had a limp, tired, crumpled look, as if they knew that nobody had wanted to open them. Even to Constance they gave out so much discouragement that she turned her eyes away; and the knowledge that she had been partly the cause of all this, but couldn't say so, or couldn't usefully say so, seemed to frustrate her being at its source. She wished she could go; she wished she hadn't come. Her mind spun round like an electric needle that has lost its bearings. The pointlessness of feeling anything! If I believed in punishment, she thought, this might be it, to have the meaning drained out of experience, because there's no longer any moral value in it.

Why had she come? She remembered and on an impulse said to Lady Franklin:

'I quite forgot. I had a message for you.'

'A message?' said Lady Franklin, wonderingly. 'Who would want to send me a message?'

All at once Constance had an idea, and it so excited her that it drove all other thoughts out of her mind. Who cared if it was true? But yes, it must be true; it explained everything, and why had she not thought of it before? But the words to express it wouldn't come; she had stage-fright, she had forgotten her lines.

'It will seem very strange to you,' she said. 'But *he* ... he asked me to tell you.'

'He asked you to?' said Lady Franklin, and began to tremble.

'Yes,' said Constance, too intent on what she was going to say, and how to say it, to make it clear who 'he' was. 'He thought you had had a raw deal and he was sorry for you. He blamed us, he called us every name under the sun. He was quite right, of course.'

'He blamed you?' said Lady Franklin. 'I'm afraid I don't understand. How were you to blame?'

'It was something he had overheard,' said Constance, blundering on. 'We were talking and he couldn't help hearing what we said. He had known all along, it seems, and it upset him terribly that you ... should have been deceived.'

'It upset Hughie?' Lady Franklin cried. 'You mean it upset him about the letter? Oh, don't let's speak of it. ... I know he was upset, almost as much upset as I was. And he said it wasn't true. He said it over and over again. Perhaps it wasn't.'

'No, no, not Hughie,' Constance said, appalled at the turn the conversation had taken. 'I wasn't talking about Hughie. It was the chauffeur, Leadbitter, who was driving us.'

'But what did Leadbitter know?'

'He knew ... he knew ... Don't ask me, Lady Franklin.'

'But you must tell me, for this is most important. Leadbitter knew that you and Hughie –'

'He knew nothing about us, Lady Franklin, nothing whatsoever.'

'But a moment ago you said he did, and that it upset him. You must tell me – I insist on knowing.'

'No, no, Lady Franklin. There isn't anything to tell – there isn't really. Leadbitter –'

'You needn't say any more,' said Lady Franklin. 'You have told me. I wish you hadn't, because it was one of the things I didn't have to know. I could have kept it at arm's length, as I did other things. You have forced me out of my shelter into a world where every fact is painful to me.'

'Not every fact,' said Constance. 'Leadbitter –'

Lady Franklin coloured slightly.

'Well, what of him?'

'He loved you, Lady Franklin. The last thing he said was, "Tell Lady Franklin that I love her" – he died saying it.'

So Leadbitter got his message delivered after all.

Lady Franklin walked away from the sofa and sat down, leaving Constance still looking idly at the presents.

'Does it make any difference?' Constance asked.

Lady Franklin took a long time to answer.

'I think it does,' she said at last. 'I think it does. So it was Leadbitter who sent the letter?'

'Yes.'

'And what he said was true?'

'Yes.'

'Why did he send it, do you think?'

How dense she is, thought Constance, and said, almost impatiently, 'Because he loved you.'

'Thank you,' said Lady Franklin, 'thank you. It was kind of you to come, but you must go now.'

When she looked up she was alone. She glanced uncertainly about her and her eyes fell on the unopened parcels. The familiar inhibition came on her with a crushing force that negatived all effort. Take them away – put them out of sight! But half-way to the bell she stopped, and looked back, ashamed, ashamed for the first time of her unhappiness, and mistrustful of it. She stole back to the sofa. One parcel was much smaller than the others, a slip of a thing, only an envelope. It was a little dingy, as all the parcels were, and she hated handling dirty things. Tearing it open she felt she was tearing open the sheath that covered her. She held her hand under the envelope and shook it gently; there was a flash of blue and silver, like a glimpse of the sky, and in her palm, covering it, lay a round medallion. She saw at once what it represented: St Christopher carrying the Christ child. Something was written round the rim, but in the half-lit room she couldn't read it. She put the medallion down on a table and felt inside the envelope, and not finding anything thought, 'Oh dear, I shan't know whom to thank, or whom to return it to.' Then her fingers closed on a sheet of paper and drew it out. She could not see to read the writing either, and was going to turn the light on, but changed her mind and picking up the medallion took it with the letter to the window and drew the curtains back.

'To Lady Franklin,' she read, 'with best wishes, hoping it may bring you luck, my lady. From S. Leadbitter.'

Tears came into her eyes and blinded them, for this was a present that couldn't be returned: there was no one to return it to. Brushing the tears away she studied the medallion, and now, in the sunshine that was pouring into the room, she read the legend printed round the margin:

Regarde Saint Christophe et va-t-en rassuré.

Tears filled her eyes again and dimmed the stalwart, naked figure of the giant. One hand grasped his staff, the other, too strong for its purpose, held the child, who smiled down from his shoulder. Onward he strode into the flood. She couldn't help identifying him with the giver, who had escorted her through waters deep as these and who had parted with his luck to make it hers. 'Behold St Christopher, and fearless go thy way.' She felt the reassurance of his presence, a promise like the dawning of another day; he had awakened her once, though into other arms than his, and had he not awakened her again?

She pressed her lips to the cold metal, lips which the living Leadbitter had pressed to his. She could not bear the keepsake out of her sight and sat holding it, as if the warmth of her hand could give it life. Strength for what lay before her seemed to come from it; gently she put it down where she could still see it, and, going over to the sofa, began to untie the parcels.

THE GO-BETWEEN

(*now a major film starring Julie Christie and Alan Bates*)

'Of all the novels L. P. Hartley has written I think *The Go-Between* is the best . . . It is in what is to me the best tradition of fiction' – John Betjeman in the *Daily Telegraph*

In one of the first and finest of the post-war studies of early adolescence, an old man looks back on his boyhood and recalls a summer visit to a Norfolk country house at the beginning of the century.

Not yet equipped to understand the behaviour of adults, he is guiltily involved in a tragic drama between three grown-up people. The author forcefully conveys the intensity of an emotional experience which breeds a lasting mistrust of life.